Eloise Jarvis McGraw

The Golden Goblet

Mariposa School of Global Education
6050 N. Calmfield Avenue
Agoura Hills, CA 91301
818-707-7144

US $6.99 / CAN $9.99
ISBN 0-14-030335-9

The price of thievery…

Confused and jostled, Ranofer was swept along by the crowd. He was trying to force his way around a stubbornly motionless donkey when a hand caught his arm. Turning, Ranofer saw that it was the old man he had met in the papyrus marsh.

"It's an execution, young one. *Ai!* Turn back. You'll see enough killing before you're as old as I."

Ranofer squinted toward the palace walls, partially visible beyond the palm-fringed garden of a nobleman's villa. The drums were pounding louder, as if to drown out a faint but spine-chilling screaming. The small, struggling figure of a man was being hoisted by one roped foot up the palace wall, to be fastened halfway to the top and left dangling, head downward. Another followed.

"Who are they, Ancient?" Ranofer asked. "What have they done?"

"They are tomb robbers, young one. They broke into the Places of Silence, they stole away the dead pharaoh's treasures and sold them in the market place. Aye, they deserve what they get, but you don't need to watch it."

"Tomb robbers!"

Shivering, Ranofer stared at the distant copper-brown figures writhing against the white wall….

OTHER BOOKS YOU MAY ENJOY

The Golden Goblet

Eloise Jarvis McGraw

PUFFIN BOOKS

PUFFIN BOOKS

Published by the Penguin Group

Penguin Young Readers Group, 345 Hudson Street, New York, New York 10014, U.S.A.
Penguin Group (Canada), 90 Eglinton Avenue East, Suite 700, Toronto,
Ontario, Canada M4P 2Y3 (a division of Pearson Penguin Canada Inc.)
Penguin Books Ltd, 80 Strand, London WC2R 0RL, England
Penguin Ireland, 25 St Stephen's Green, Dublin 2, Ireland
(a division of Penguin Books Ltd)
Penguin Group (Australia), 250 Camberwell Road, Camberwell, Victoria 3124, Australia
(a division of Pearson Australia Group Pty Ltd)
Penguin Books India Pvt Ltd, 11 Community Centre, Panchsheel Park,
New Delhi - 110 017, India
Penguin Group (NZ), Cnr Airborne and Rosedale Roads, Albany, Auckland 1310,
New Zealand (a division of Pearson New Zealand Ltd)
Penguin Books (South Africa) (Pty) Ltd, 24 Sturdee Avenue, Rosebank,
Johannesburg 2196, South Africa

Registered Offices: Penguin Books Ltd, 80 Strand, London WC2R 0RL, England

First published in the United States of America by Coward-McCann, Inc., 1961
First published by Puffin Books, 1986
This edition published by Puffin Books,
a division of Penguin Young Readers Group, 2006

47   49   50   48   46

THE LIBRARY OF CONGRESS HAS CATALOGED THE PREVIOUS PUFFIN EDITION AS FOLLOWS:
McGraw, Eloise Jarvis.
The golden goblet.
Summary: A young Egyptian boy struggles to reveal
a hideous crime and reshape his own destiny.
[1. Mystery and detective stories.] I. Title.
PZ7.M1696Go 1986 [Fic] 85-43415
ISBN: 0-14-030335-9

Printed in the United States of America

The Golden Goblet

Chapter I

THE stream of molten gold flowed smoothly from the crucible, reflecting in its surface the cloudless blue of the Egyptian sky. The boy Ranofer slowly tightened his grip on the two stones between which he held the crucible as he tilted it farther and farther, devotion in every careful movement of his hands and bare brown shoulders. Presently the last drop of flame-colored liquid had run without splash or bubble into the hollowed stone.

With a sigh of satisfaction the boy set stones and crucible aside, and wiped the sweat from his hands upon his cotton kilt. It was a good ingot; the goldsmith would be able to find no fault with it. Already the metal was setting, the brilliant red-yellow fading to scarlet, then to cherry. In half a minute it could be turned out and the mold oiled for the next pouring.

Dreamily Ranofer watched the colors dull. Splendid images drifted through his mind, golden forms and shapes, any one of which might be the destiny of this very small ingot that he, Ranofer the son of Thutra, had poured. It might become part of a wide and glittering collar, or the inlay on a fine dagger for some nobleman's tomb—or

7

better, a cup fit for Pharaoh himself, shaped like a flower and hammered to fragile thinness.

Well, perhaps not the cup, Ranofer admitted to himself after a little reflection.

It was only a small ingot, after all. Besides, such a cup as he had pictured could never come from this particular goldhouse. No one here had the skill to fashion it, not even Rekh the goldsmith himself. Only Zau, the greatest gold-worker in all Thebes, could make such a cup. Zau the Master could make anything. From his artist's fingers sprang objects of such wonderful beauty—cups, bowls, boxes, necklaces, daggers, great golden collars, bracelets, exquisite amulets—that Pharaoh himself would be served by no other smith.

To think I might have been his pupil someday, if my father had lived, Ranofer thought. He all but said he would accept me. *Ai!* If my father had not died! If I had never had to go and live with Gebu! If I had never even heard of Gebu!

The unwelcome picture of Gebu's face broke through Ranofer's preoccupation, scattering his daydreams and rousing him to present reality, in which Zau the Master had no place. He was aware again of voices, of the clang of tools around him in the mud-walled courtyard, and the sharp, hot odor of metal mingling with the soft afternoon breeze off the Nile. It was the month of Hathor in the Season of Growing, and the air was cool despite the heat from the hooded furnaces that lined the courtyard. Even Lord Ra, the sun, did not scorch and burn in this pleasant wintertime, but shed his radiant light beneficently upon the brown backs of the men bent to their work, striking blue gleams from their ink-black hair and snowy kilts, glancing with blinding intensity off gold ingots and gold wire coils and the scraps and bits of gold that littered the low worktables. Instead of an answering sense of peace Ranofer felt only the sore and familiar longing for other days, when he could have rejoiced in a gentle sun and work he loved—when both his father Thutra and Zau the Master were a part of his life, a large part, and his half brother Gebu the stonecutter no part at all.

Do not ruin the day by thinking of Gebu! the boy told himself. Do you not see enough of him and his heavy hand at home? That ingot has set, and here you stand idle.

He turned the ingot out and tried to lose himself again in his tasks; but the thought of Gebu, like the ache of a tooth, was hard to lose. Besides, his tasks were those of a hireling; no matter how expertly he did them, he could not hope to progress to anything better, as even the most stupid apprentice did. No matter what illustrious futures he imagined for the ingots he poured, his own future remained the same—pouring more ingots, making charcoal, sweeping off the jewelers' benches—while others engraved the daggers and hammered the cups. All because of Gebu.

Why can *I* not be apprenticed? Ranofer asked himself for the hundredth time. Because Gebu does not wish it! But why does he not wish it, the pig, the son of Set the Devil? Why must he place me here in the goldhouse if I am never to learn anything?

No matter—it was useless to try to fathom the ways of that Accursed One. His reasons were his own, and to protest brought only beatings, as Ranofer had found out long ago. Here he was and here he would stay until Gebu ordered otherwise.

Ranofer picked up the ingot, which was now cool

enough to handle, and carried it to the nearby workbench on which the drawplate stood. It was a circular slab of stone, held upright in a vise and pierced with a ring of holes of diminishing sizes. One of the apprentices stood there drawing wire, his shoulder muscles bunched with the effort of pulling a greased, reed-slim ingot through a hole just too small for it. It would be slimmer yet when it had passed through the hole. Then it would be passed through the one just smaller, and so through every hole in turn, growing longer and slimmer all the time, until it changed from an ingot into wire. On the bench beside the apprentice lay a coil of wire, finished and ready for its last annealing. Beside the coil lay a row of three thin ingots waiting to be drawn. Ranofer added his own, the thinnest of all. Perhaps by evening it would be wire, rounded and tempered, ready to fashion into a linked collar for some lovely lady's neck. Somewhat comforted by the thought, he returned to oil his empty mold.

Too late he saw a familiar hunched figure emerging from the rear door of the shop, directly next the pouring table. It was Ibni the Babylonian porter, already bobbing and grinning at sight of Ranofer. Wishing Rekh the goldsmith would suddenly send him on an errand to the other side of Thebes, Ranofer turned his back on the man and reached for the oil jar. Ibni only edged closer, ducked his head even farther between his shoulders, and scrubbed his hands together ingratiatingly.

"Ah, greeting! And how is little Ranofer today?" he asked. His voice was like the sound of a badly made flute, and sibilant with his Babylonian accent.

"I am well enough," Ranofer mumbled.

"Indeed! This worthless one rejoices that it is so. And

what of my revered friend, your half brother and protector, Gebu the stonecutter? Is he also well?"

"Aye." Ranofer smeared oil into the mold, keeping his frowning gaze directly on his work. He could not have said why his dislike of Ibni was so intense. The man's servility disgusted him, and so did his cheese-white hands with their dirty nails, and the stained teeth he revealed in his constant grin. But it was more than that; there was something slimily questionable about the Babylonian that always sent prickles up Ranofer's spine. Why Gebu permitted his occasional visits to their house was a mystery Ranofer had never cared to probe into. Gebu and Ibni were certainly not friends. They were more like master and dog.

"And the honored Gebu, did he enjoy my little gift of date wine last week? Did he find it as tasty as ever, young Ranofer?"

"He did not say otherwise."

"What did he say, little one? Did he speak not at all when you handed the wineskin to him? For indeed you *did* hand it to him, did you not, in his own hand, as you have done before?"

"Aye, in his own hand, exactly as I have always done!" Ranofer threw an impatient glance at Ibni and encountered the sharp glint he had often surprised in the other's usually vacant eyes. It vanished instantly, and the Babylonian's smile spread wider than ever. Ranofer's distrust deepened accordingly. What does he want, the sneaking serpent? thought the boy. Aloud he said, "How can I remember what he said, now, nine days later?"

"Ah, well, it is of no matter. Doubtless my poor gift is not worthy of comment, though he honored me by en-

11

joying it. It is a humble wine, but of a good flavor. My wife makes it herself, from our own dates."

"I know!" snapped Ranofer, exasperated at hearing it for the fiftieth time. He knew, also, that Gebu never drank the wine, though he always seemed eager to get it. Invariably he waited until Ranofer was asleep, then in the night secretly poured it out on the pavement of the courtyard. Many times the boy had seen the brown stains next morning, still damp and faintly reeking of fermentation. There was something about the whole thing that was not what it seemed, something from which Ranofer uneasily turned his mind whenever he thought of it. It was not healthy, he had long since learned, to pry into Gebu's affairs.

Meanwhile, Ibni was finally coming to what Ranofer recognized at once as the point of the conversation.

"... aye, a very good wine, though humble. Now if you would grant me the smallest of favor, young Ranofer, pray tell your brother that I shall send him another little wineskin on the morrow, which I beg he will accept with my highest regard. Tarry a bit outside the shop tomorrow at sunset, and I shall put it in your hand."

Ibni took himself off at last. Stoppering the oil jug with nervous fingers, Ranofer watched him sidle past the wiremaker's bench to the big water jar, get himself a drink too brief to indicate real thirst, then go back through the rear door to his job of washing the raw gold. Ranofer was reminded of an adder slithering back into its hole.

He did not want that water, thought the boy. He had no errand in the courtyard at all, but merely invented one that he might find out whether I put his precious wineskin into Gebu's hand and tell me to wait for another tomorrow. But why? What is so important about a little skin of wine? Why can he not simply hand it to me sometime during the day, instead of making a great secret of it outside the shop?

"Ranofer!"

The boy jumped guiltily. It was Sata, the First Craftsman, calling to him from inside the shop. Hastily he spread a scrap of clean linen over the mold and hurried across the courtyard.

The light dimmed and cooled as he moved under the overhanging thatch of palm fronds and into the long, three-sided shed. In a corner glowed two of the boxlike furnaces. On a low stool before one of them sat Rekh the goldsmith, using a pointed blowpipe to direct the heat onto a golden ornament he held carefully in copper tongs. Three apprentices leaned over him watching, unmindful of the chatter of the porters washing raw gold in the big vats at the back of the room, of the weigher calling out numbers to the scribe standing beside the balance scales, of the loud *ping, ping,* of the Second Craftsman's hammer upon a half-finished bowl. Ranofer lingered a moment. He too would have liked to watch Rekh work, to note his way with a blowpipe and how the flame must heat the bosses of the ornament, thereby adding a precious detail or two to his scant knowledge of the craft he had loved since babyhood. But Sata called again.

"Ranofer! Come here, boy! By Amon, I'll wager the snails would pass you by! Here, brush my table, and mind you lose not a grain of gold. I want the sweepings refined and poured again before the sun sets."

"Aye, *neb* Sata."

As the First Craftsman moved away, scowling as usual,

13

to set a finished collar upon the shelf, Ranofer hurried to the low worktable. A woven grass mat was spread on the ground before it. No one but Rekh used a stool. Dropping to one knee and sinking back on his heel in the habitual pose of the goldworker, the boy took up the hare's foot and began to sweep gold dust, scraps, clippings and bits of wire from the table top into the sheepskin that hung beneath its scooped-out front edge. There was more gold to be recovered from these leavings than one would suspect. He had poured that slim little ingot, now lying yonder in the courtyard beside the drawplate, from just such sweepings as this. Presently he would be pouring another.

"I have finished, *neb* Sata," murmured the boy. He scrambled to his feet, and unhooking the sheep hide from the table, emptied its contents into an earthen bowl. He had returned the hide to its place and was starting for the courtyard with the bowl when the deep, gentle voice of Rekh the goldsmith stopped him.

"Wait, Ranofer. You have forgotten to weigh your gold."

"Weigh it? I have nothing but the sweep here, *neb* Goldsmith."

"Nonetheless, it must be weighed. Did you not hear my orders this morning when—nay, I remember, I had sent you into the Street of the Potters to fetch those crucibles." Rekh sighed, arose from his stool and limped across to Ranofer, still holding the golden ornament in his tongs. His heavy face was worn but kindly as he looked down at the boy. "Know then," he said, "that our weights do not tally properly at the end of each week, nor have they for some months. Gold has been missing, in such small quantities that for long we blamed the scales. But it is not the scales."

Deeply shocked, Ranofer stood with the bowl forgotten in his hands. "Gold missing?" he repeated. "A thief in the night, *neb* Goldsmith?"

"Nay, the guard's eyelids never close, and the storeroom seals are unbroken. It is someone in this shop who is robbing me."

"In the shop? But how? How could he—"

"There are many ways to conceal a lump or two of gold, Innocent One," put in the Second Craftsman gloomily.

"Aye," agreed one of the apprentices. "I have heard of men hiding small ingots in their mouths."

"Or under their sandal straps," said another.

"Or in a loaf of bread."

"There are as many methods as there are thieves," Rekh said wearily, "and we must discover the one which is plaguing us. The first step is to keep daily account of every grain, even the sweep. We shall catch him before long."

Ranofer was standing like an image, a sharp suspicion in his mind. Who in this shop would steal gold—who was treacherous enough, low enough—save Ibni the Babylonian? It was only too easy to picture his white, moist hand with its filthy fingernails reaching out stealthily, but there was no way to prove such a suspicion.

The goldsmith's hand grasped Ranofer's shoulder and shook it gently. "What ails you, boy? Are you asleep, or struck dumb?"

"I—I—neither, *neb* Goldsmith." Ranofer hesitated, his troubled eyes on the man before him. Rekh was an unimpressive figure, similar in build and feature to a hundred other men, with a suggestion of paunch and a foot maimed

15

long ago by spilled molten metal. The falcon ornament held in his tongs was no better than half the goldsmiths in Thebes could fashion. He was no genius like Zau, no artist like Thutra the father of Ranofer. He was only an honest and kindly artisan, just now saddened by treachery.

"Nothing ails me, honored Master," murmured the boy. "I only wonder what evil one could find it in his heart to rob so good a man."

Rekh's homely face relaxed with pleasure. He was not accustomed to being called "honored master" by even his lowliest hireling. "Do not trouble your head about it, Ranofer. But make certain to weigh your sweep, that we may make this robber's task too difficult to continue. Now—" Rekh frowned suddenly, explored the boy's bare shoulder with his fingers, then turned him about. "What is this? Another stripe on your young back? Nay, two of them! Who is it beats you, boy? Only last week—"

"It is nothing, no one!" Ranofer shrank hastily out of his grasp. "Your pardon, *neb* Rekh, I will weigh the sweep now."

Scarlet with shame, he dodged around the Second Craftsman's workbench and hurried to the scales. With eyes on the floor, he waited while the weigher sang out the measure to the scribe, then took his bowl and hurried out, leaving Rekh still frowning after him. His shoulder had begun to throb and smart from the goldsmith's touch, like a sleeping devil roused to angry wakefulness, but the greatest pain was in his mind. It was humiliating beyond measure to have attention called to those welts, lying there across his back like the mark of the slave. Might the crocodiles eat that Gebu! Now they had all seen—everyone in the shop—and no doubt were scorning him for a poor

16

sort of creature, cringing and puny, unable to defend himself.

Then there was Ibni. Heavy as a yoke, responsibility settled over Ranofer's mind. He was convinced Ibni was the thief, though he could not say why. Ladling water into his bowl of sweepings from the big water jar, he wondered how he could prove it. The slimy creature might carry gold anywhere—in his mouth, under his sandal strap, in a loaf of bread. Imagine, gold in a loaf of bread!

Or in a wineskin?

Ranofer stood motionless, feeling all his flesh crawl. In a wineskin. Perhaps in the very ones he had been carrying home to Gebu each week? The ones whose contents were always emptied onto the pavement in the dead of night, as if the wine itself were of no value?

Osiris the Merciful forbid it! thought the boy. If it is so, then I too have been a thief, though I did not know it. Nay, it cannot be so! It must not be so!

Yet that slim little ingot, the one he had poured but a short time ago, how easily it would slip into a wineskin!

He let the dipper crash back into the water jar and started for the small washing trays at the front of the courtyard, darting a glance toward the wiremaker's bench as he passed. What he saw made him stop in his tracks. Only one ingot lay beside the drawplate. When the Babylonian passed this way for the drink he had not wanted, four ingots had been there. Another coil of wire lay ready for annealing. That accounted for one of them. The apprentice held another, greasing it for the drawplate. But where were the others? Where was that smallest one, which would slip so easily into a skin of wine?

Ranofer's feet took him across the stretch of sun-warmed pavement to the wiremaker's bench without his ordering them to move. "Your work goes swiftly, Hapia'o," he said nervously.

"Swiftly? Thoth's mercy! The snail has wings compared to the hours of this day. I vow I've been pulling wire since the First Hill rose out of the waters of time, and still I've not done."

"But—but have you not? Only a short time ago there were four fresh-poured ingots on this bench, and behold, where are they now?"

Hapia'o's hands stopped their work. "Where would they be?" he demanded. "On this bench and that, being drawn, or hammered, or—" His eyes narrowed with anger as he seized the boy's arm. "What is this you say? Do you accuse me of this thieving the master spoke of?"

"Accuse you?" gasped Ranofer, aghast at the hornet's nest he had stirred up. "As Maat is my witness, I had no thought of it! Have the *khefts* taken your senses, friend Hapia'o?"

The apprentice loosed his arm, looking somewhat sheepish. "Aye, perhaps they have. I see you meant no harm. But when there's theft about, every man grows thin-skinned. By Amon, I'll not be sorry to see this thief caught and the shop rid of him!"

"Nor will I!" Ranofer said. He tried to smile carelessly, but the bowl he held was trembling. He had still not found out what he wanted to know. "Theft is a wicked thing," he went on, careful to avoid the hornets. "I've no doubt you have watched your ingots today as the falcon watches the lark."

Hapia'o laughed as he threaded the tapered end of the greased golden rod through a hole in the drawplate.

18

Grasping the point with his copper pincers, he began to tug it toward him, his muscles knotting. "That I have!" he agreed jerkily. "Abhi took two—for bracelets—Zoser the little one for—thread. And I myself have—used the others. I'll not—weigh short at the end of the day, you may—stake your life on that!"

"I believe it, friend," murmured Ranofer. Zoser, he thought. Zoser has the little one. As he hurried on to the washing trays, he glanced toward Zoser's bench. There he was, pounding rhythmically upon two sheep hides, between which the smallest ingot would be stretching flatter and flatter into a sheet thin enough to be cut into thread and woven like linen into beautiful shining cloth. Relief swept through Ranofer like a fresh breeze off the river. Ibni had not stolen the little ingot, perhaps he had stolen nothing at all.

I am imagining the whole thing, Ranofer told himself. The wineskin has some other explanation. It must have. Someone else is the thief.

"Welcome, friend Eyes-on-the-Ground," said a voice half-amused, half-diffident.

Ranofer looked up to find the new apprentice, Heqet, smiling at him uncertainly over the washing trays. He was a boy of twelve or thirteen, no older than Ranofer himself, though he was bigger. Both boys still wore the youth-lock, a thick strand of hair left to grow from one side of their shaven heads and fall in an ebony curl to the shoulder. Both also wore amulets dangling from one wrist, to protect them from *khefts*. Neither could boast more than a single short garment, held at the waist by a rag of a sash. There the resemblance ended, however, for Heqet was rich in

19

prospects. He was safely apprenticed and destined to become as fine a goldsmith as teaching could make him.

For a moment pure envy filled Ranofer, as it had when Heqet first appeared in the shop, three days ago. Heqet's smile wavered and Ranofer controlled his feelings quickly, realizing they must show in his face. With as civil a nod as he could muster, he stepped to the new boy's side at the bench and drew a washing tray toward him.

"May your *ka* be joyful," he murmured. "Does the work go well?"

"Aye, well enough, though I do not know my head from my tail in this place, as the cat said when she tumbled into the fowler's net."

After a moment's astonishment—jokes were few in his life—Ranofer's rare smile spread slowly over his face. Heqet brightened.

"By Amon!" he said. "I thought you a surly type at first, but I see you're not. Listen, then. I know no more of what I'm doing than a hound knows of kittens. Do you understand this gold washing?"

"Aye, of course I do."

"Then instruct me, for the sake of Ptah the Bearded! That scowling one, the First Craftsman, said nothing but 'Wash these sweepings, young one!' with never a word as to how or why. Are they clean yet?"

"Aye, but there's trash still with them in the water," said Ranofer, peering into Heqet's bowl. "Have you not poured it through a cloth?"

"Cloth?" echoed the other blankly.

Ranofer pointed to the coarse linen straining cloths hanging below the bench. "Come, do as I do."

Together they stretched cloths over the shallow washing trays, poured in water and gold together. As the cloth sank to the bottom of the tray, the particles of gold clung to it in a glittering residue, allowing the trash to be poured off along with the water.

"Now again, with fresh water," directed Ranofer.

"Ah," Heqet remarked presently. "I begin to find reason in this, as the priest said when he discovered the dead rat under the altar. How is it your hand is so practiced, friend? Someone has taught you well."

"My father taught me," said Ranofer before he thought.

"Your father? He is a goldsmith? The gods smile on you. What else does he teach you?"

Ranofer was biting his tongue for mentioning it. "He teaches me nothing now," he answered curtly.

"But why?"

"Because he went to his tomb ten months ago, to join my mother, who has been with the gods these many years."

Heqet glanced at him, then returned quickly to his work. "May their *bas* have food and drink forever," he murmured. There was a moment's awkward silence, during which Ranofer struggled without much success against the familiar frightened loneliness that had swept in again as through an opened door.

Heqet said presently, "No one told me your name."

"Ranofer the son of Thutra."

"*Aii!* I have heard of Thutra the goldsmith."

"Many heard of him. He was a friend of Zau the Master. Zau himself praised his work."

"Many will hear of you too, perhaps, when you have finished your apprenticeship here and become a—"

"I am not apprenticed here."

The other turned in surprise. "You are not apprenticed to Rekh the goldsmith? Then what—"

"What am I doing here?" Ranofer's own thought flashed back into his mind: *Why does he place me here in the goldhouse if I am never to learn anything?* Hard on that thought followed the image of the wineskin, like a dismaying answer. He turned to Heqet more brusquely than he intended. "I am a porter. I pour ingots and wash sweepings and run errands." Ibni's errands? he thought with sinking heart. "For five *deben* a month. It is work you will not long be troubled with. After your first month the hirelings will do it for you. *I* will do it for you. It is all I am allowed to do. Yet I understand annealing and wiremaking as well as the First Craftsman. I have even graven arm bands and hammered out cups." He sloshed gold and water into his tray. "Perhaps not very good cups," he added more humbly. "But they were cups."

And gone now, he added to himself. Gone like everything else, like my father's house, and the garden with the acacia trees, and old Marya who used to make me date cakes; and the workshop with the shelves all around the walls, and golden collars and daggers hanging from them. Gone like my father.

The workshop came clear into his mind, until it seemed as if he were there again, this minute, smelling the acacia blossoms just outside the door. Hour upon hour in the old days, he had leaned upon his father's workbench watching the long, strong hands of the artist shape a bowl or a massive ornament, fashion chains and necklaces of such delicate grace that the eye delighted in them. He could remember the very feel of the smooth-worn wood under his elbows, the heat of the lamp on his cheek as he learned with his eyes, with his memory, asking countless questions. Even through the last two years, the ailing years, of Thutra's life the artist had lain on a couch in the workroom, watching his son's first efforts at raising and engraving, teaching him to improve his designs. Besides the goldwork there was Yetti, the old greyhound, to romp with, and the tales his father read him from the leather scrolls, and every morning, lessons at the scribes' school, so that Ranofer too had begun to read a little. Now there was nothing, less than nothing. Now there were hunger and beatings and this new, hideous suspicion about the wineskins.

Heqet cleared his throat uncertainly. "It is an evil thing that you cannot go on learning," he said. "Where do you live then, if not in the Apprentices' Quarters or with your parents?"

It was a moment before Ranofer answered. He kept his eyes on his hands, which were raking the gold scraps aimlessly about on the cloth. At last he said, "I live with my half brother, Gebu the stonecutter."

"Oh! You did not say you had a brother."

"*Half* brother!" Ranofer repeated. He grudged admitting even that relationship. Until the confused and griefstricken morning of his father's death ten months ago, he had been only vaguely aware that there was another son of Thutra, somewhere in Thebes—a first-born, child of an early marriage, whose name was never mentioned in Thutra's presence.

Twisting the wet cloth around the mass of sweepings, Ranofer cast about for some way to change the subject. He did not want to talk of these things, or even think of them. He must speak of something else, quickly, before this boy could ask more questions.

Heqet was already talking. "Half brother, then. But I do not understand this half brother of yours, my friend. Why does he not apprentice you to Rekh, that you may learn to make beautiful things like your father?"

"Because—because I must earn the *deben*." Five a month, when he could be learning the skill that would bring him dozens! The answer sounded foolish even to himself, and in the light of what he now suspected it was absurd. Nervously avoiding Heqet's puzzled gaze, he added, "Gebu cares nothing for goldworking. He sees no value in apprenticing me to Rekh."

"Then it is strange he does not apprentice you to himself, at the stonecutting shop. It seems to me he would think your labor there of far more value than—"

"I know not what he thinks! He prefers me to work here."

"Then why, since you are here, will he not—"

"Let me be!" Ranofer gasped, whirling on him. "Can you not let me be? I am tired of your questions!"

Abruptly he left the bench, twisting and wringing the bag of gold scraps. Scarcely knowing where he stepped, he blundered his way to the far end of the courtyard and spread his sweepings on a sun-warmed sheep hide to dry. Already he was miserably regretting his rudeness to the young apprentice, who he knew had meant no harm. Now Heqet would again decide that he was a surly type, and would no longer care to be friends. Too often it happened so. If only they would not ask me questions, thought Ranofer. Why must they make me talk of these things that I wish to forget?

Meanwhile, there was this gold to be dried and melted, and in haste, too, for the Great God Ra was sinking lower and lower in the sky. Soon the god's shining boat would touch the tops of the western cliffs, and the working day would be done. Before that an ingot must be poured from these sweepings, as the First Craftsman had ordered.

Ranofer spread a fresh cloth over the glittering debris on the sheepskin, pressing it down with his palms to hasten the drying process. He found himself thinking how easy it would be to drop a few of these scraps into a wineskin when no one was watching. True, the Babylonian seldom handled the sweep, nor had he stolen the little ingot as Ranofer had at first suspected. But he did have access to the storeroom, he did work all day washing the raw gold, fresh from the mines, in the big vats at the rear of the shop.

That was the answer! That was where Ibni got the gold, from the leather sacks, heavy with trash and gravel, brought in each week from the mines in the southern desert. What could be easier than to drop a pinch of gold dust, a few nuggets, into a wineskin instead of into the washing vats? The difference in weight would be written off as trash, which defied precise weighing, or laid to a fault in the scales. In fact it had taken Rekh and his weigher all these months to decide that it was not the scales.

Sick at heart, Ranofer transferred his sweepings to a crucible and set it on the coals. He must tell Rekh at once, of course. But—

Watching the flames glow scarlet around the crucible, Ranofer thought about that "but." To inform on Ibni would be nothing. Ranofer would be heartily glad to see

25

the last of him, and for the shop it would be good rid-dance. But to do that he must inform on himself, as well. He must confess that it was he who had carried the gold away, time after time, every ten or fifteen days of all the months he had worked at the shop. And—Ranofer went cold with panic—it would mean informing on Gebu, as well.

Great Amon, he would kill me! thought the boy. He would kill me and throw me to the crocodiles, or sell me for a slave as he is always threatening, or . . .

In the crucible the gold collapsed suddenly into molten scarlet. Ranofer snatched the stones that protected his hands and began pouring the metal into the mold he had oiled to receive it. It was difficult. His hands were shaking so that he could scarcely control the flow.

I am not really sure of all this, he thought. I have no proof. That's it, one must have proof. Perhaps it is all my own imagining. I will not tell Rekh yet.

When the day was done he hurried from the shop, un-able to meet the goldsmith's kindly eye.

Chapter II

THE light was beginning to fade as Ranofer left Rekh's courtyard and hurried down the Street of the Goldsmiths toward the Nile. Behind him the sky flamed over the mummy-shaped outline of the Libyan cliffs, gateway to the awesome Valley of the Tombs of the Kings. Directly ahead of him, across the river with its vivid, square sails, rose the high east bank and the other half of the ancient city of Thebes. Massive gateways, temples, roofs and whitewashed walls rising thick along its crowded streets traced a long, angular pattern against the sky.

To Ranofer it was a different world, that city across the river. Here on the western bank was the Thebes he knew, a vast jumble of workshops and laboratories known as the City of the Dead. Its low, mud-brick buildings formed a broad belt between the green fields at the riverside and the strip of desert at the foot of the western cliffs, spreading north almost to the cliffs' curve, giving way in the south to high-walled gardens and the villas of rich noblemen, which clustered around the dazzling white pile of Pharaoh's palace.

Turning from the Street of the Goldsmiths, Ranofer en-

27

tered a sun-baked thoroughfare thronged with workers from every part of the City of the Dead—artisans, laborers, apprentices—whose guttural speech and varied odors filled the air around him. They were clean-shaven, with skin the color of tarnished copper. Their eyelids were rimmed and elongated almost to their temples with black eye paint, best protection against Egypt's glaring sun. Their shoulders were broad and bare, their hips narrow and wrapped in cotton *shentis* of purest white. Their hands, those strong and supple hands now gesturing or fingering their amulets or swinging idly at their sides, were the cleverest in the world, for these were the glassmakers and papermakers, the weavers, carpenters and potters, the sculptors, painters, embalmers, masons and coffin builders of Hundred-Gated Thebes, and Thebes, as all men knew, was the center of the universe.

Because of these artisans, full of laughter and vigorous life though they were, the western half of Thebes was called the City of the Dead, for most of the objects they fashioned with such skill vanished into Egypt's tombs to become the possessions of the dead. Even the lowliest fisherman went to his eternal rest accompanied by a little food and furniture, a length of new linen, a string of beads, his weapons or tools—whatever comforts the living could provide for the *ba* of a loved one beginning his Three Thousand Years in the Land of the West. As for the wealthy, their tombs were underground mansions crammed with gold and treasure. Death provided a constant market for the wares of the City of the Dead, and the living bought much for themselves as well. Therefore the shops hummed with industry day after day, and the craftsmen were many.

Now this day was done and the artisans were homeward bound. A few turned in the direction of the Nile, where high-prowed ferry boats waited to take them across to Eastern Thebes, but the majority scattered to homes near their shops in the City of the Dead.

Ranofer was among the latter but he lacked their eagerness. On the contrary, the nearer he drew to his own street, the more slowly he walked. At the best of times he would rather go anywhere than home. This evening he dreaded it with all his soul. Gebu had two aspects, one noisily jocular, one ferociously quiet. There was no knowing which to expect on any given day, and indeed there was little to choose between them, as Ranofer had long ago learned. It was a matter of whether one preferred to be kicked aside like a bit of debris or subjected to a concentrated and abusive notice. Whichever it was to be tonight, Ranofer did not see how he could face Gebu and conceal the thing he knew, and he did not know what he was going to do about it.

As the last corner appeared ahead, his reluctant feet slowed still more and finally stopped altogether. He stood a moment, took an irresolute step backward, then swerved suddenly and ran down a lane between two of the flower fields near the river. He must think this out. He would go home presently; later he would go, because he must, but first he must think.

Once past the flower fields the lane narrowed to a path that meandered through the thickets edging the river. The ground turned marshy here; patches of sedge and papyrus marked pools of shallow water, and the farther Ranofer went the more the bushes of the thicket gave way to clumps of slender, rustling reeds higher than his head.

He was soon wading oftener than he was walking, but the thick, soft mud felt good to his feet, and he wandered aimlessly on, trying to make himself believe that his suspicions were unfounded. Perhaps one of the apprentices had been hiding gold dust in his sandal. Perhaps the other porter—

It was no use. The missing gold, the wine Gebu wanted but never drank, the grinning Babylonian with his sharp glance and his soft, insistent questions, all fitted into a picture too clear to doubt. What was he to do about it? To tell Rekh would mean accusing Gebu, and to accuse Gebu . . .

Ranofer stood nibbling his thumbnail. The very idea of accusing Gebu made him shiver. Yet the thieving must be stopped, and there was only himself to stop it. Perhaps if he only threatened to tell what he knew . . .

He had reached the true marsh now, where thicket gave way entirely to the dense fringe of papyrus growing in the shallow margins of the Nile. As he turned back toward dryer land the reeds behind him rattled, and he whirled.

"Good evening to you, young one!" said a surprised voice. An old man had appeared through the papyrus stalks, wading up to his calves in the brown water. He was stooped and leather-skinned, with one blind eye and hair like coarse white linen thread. There were smears of river mud on his bare knees and his *shenti,* and on the gnarled hand with which he held the reeds aside as he gazed with mild astonishment at the boy. Behind him was a small, elderly donkey loaded high with papyrus stalks. Ranofer had seen the pair often hobbling about the streets of the City of the Dead, but their sudden appearance here sent his wits scattering like startled birds.

"G-good evening to you, Ancient," he stammered at last.

"So you've a tongue after all," remarked the old one. "I wondered if Exalted Lord Crocodile had stolen it."

"Exalted? Do you speak of the crocodile-god, Lord Sobk, or only of the muddy beast in the—"

"Hst! Softly, boy!" The old man darted a glance, half-humorous, half-anxious, toward the Nile. "Perhaps his lordship is muddy, yes, but what is a little mud? Speak politely of the noble beast, as one learns to, who must work each day within reach of his jaws."

Ranofer smiled uncertainly and the old man's face seamed into a thousand wrinkles of pleasure.

"There now! He can smile, too, eh, my Lotus, my little donkey? Perhaps he is not so burdened with trouble as we thought when first we saw his face. Is this not a strange hour to come fishing, young one? Ra sailed through the Gates of the West half an hour ago."

"I—I did not come here to fish," muttered the boy, immediately nervous again. Did his thoughts show so plainly? If so, there was small chance of hiding them from Gebu. He must come out with it somehow.

He snatched one of the stiff blooms from a nearby clump of sedge and showed it to the old man in explanation. "I came only to seek a flower for my—my friend. I must go now, Ancient. May your *ka* be joyful."

Abruptly he turned and ran back the way he had come, leaving the old man to make what he might of it. I will threaten to tell what I know, he resolved as he hurried between the darkening fields. I will make Gebu promise to stop. It is the only way.

The dusk had filled the streets now, and this time Ranofer did not pause when he came in sight of the last corner, but set his mouth tight and hastened into the Street of the Crooked Dog. It was a narrow and dirty lane, its houses joined one to another to form a continuous wall on either hand, like the sides of a canyon. Ranofer pushed open the third door on the left and slipped into the courtyard, his bare feet silent on the rough pavement. Closing the gate behind him, he stopped and looked about warily.

The dim light was kind to the skimpy walled court, glossing over some of the rubbish that littered it, concealing the smaller cracks and the peeling whitewash of the narrow, mud-brick house that occupied the west half of the enclosure. The storerooms forming the ground floor of the house were dark and empty, with their doors ajar. From the rear of the court a stair sloped above them to a single high room overlooking the street. From the open strip under the roof of this room yellow torchlight glowed, and Ranofer's eyes fixed on it. Gebu was at home.

Moistening his lips, the boy drew a long breath and padded across the courtyard toward the storerooms. Perhaps he could find something to eat before—

The storeroom door squeaked, betraying his presence. "Who's there?" growled the stonecutter's voice from the upper room. "Is it you, Useless One? Get you here to the stairway."

Silently Ranofer turned from the storeroom door and walked to the foot of the stair. His half brother stood at the top, a torch in his hand. Obviously there was to be no jocularity tonight.

I must tell him now, Ranofer thought. I must threaten him.

"You are late in coming," the harsh voice grated. "Very late. Where have you been?"

"At—at the shop."

"Until this hour?"

"I was delayed. There was a last ingot . . ." Ranofer's voice trailed away as Gebu started down the stairs, thrusting his torch into a bracket on his way. There was no expression on Gebu's face. He was like a figure hewn out of one of his own blocks of stone. His legs were massive columns, his face a crag, with a granite-hard jaw and eyes black as chunks of obsidian beneath their painted lids. One of the eyes winked spasmodically at intervals, lending an eerie liveliness to an otherwise motionless countenance. He reached the foot of the stairs and stood there winking, his bulk dwarfing the boy, who was thin as a reed.

Again Ranofer moistened his lips. I must tell him! he thought. Instead he said, "It is true I walked down to the river on my way home, in order to cool my feet in the mud. You can see, I plucked a bloom while I was there." With fumbling hands he extricated the wilting blossom from the folds of his sash. The stonecutter looked at it, then at Ranofer. Suddenly a fist like a boulder crashed against the side of the boy's head, sending him sprawling.

"Scum! You have been some other place. Where did you go? Who did you talk to?"

"No one, I swear it!" Ranofer cried. "Only an old papyrus cutter I chanced upon in the reeds, with his donkey."

"You lie."

"Nay, I speak truth, as Maat is my witness!" Ranofer dodged a kick and scrambled to his feet, shrinking back against the wall. If he had needed further evidence for

33

his suspicions, here it was, in this accursed one's distrust. Rubbing his cheek, he blurted angrily, "You need not fear. I have told no one about the wineskins—and what is in them—yet!"

Instantly he was aghast at his own temerity. Gebu had gone menacingly still.

"Indeed," he said softly. "And what is in the wineskins, save wine?"

"You know that already, and Ibni knows. But I did not know until today."

Gebu moved closer, thrusting his face into the boy's. "*What* do you know?"

Ranofer swallowed, pressing back against the wall in a vain effort to retreat. He *knew* nothing at all, nothing he could prove. "I know gold has been missing from the shop," he insisted. "I know they are weighing even the sweep."

"Indeed," said Gebu again, but in a different tone. He straightened slowly and his great shoulders relaxed. His speculative eyes went over the boy, so deliberately and in such pitiless detail that Ranofer became vividly aware of every defect in his unprepossessing small person—the ribs that showed, the undernourished arms and knobby knees, the dusty rag of a *shenti* that always hung askew on his hips. By the time Gebu turned his eyes away, Ranofer felt more insignificant than the lowliest beetle in the roadway.

"And what has all that to do with me?" Gebu said.

"I—it—I tell you the goldsmith is suspicious! I dare not carry the wineskins home any more, or they will—"

"Worthless One!" The heavy hand slapped back and forth across Ranofer's face, almost negligently, yet with a

34

force that twisted a crick into his neck and set his ears ringing. "I know nothing of this gold, and if you do, you had best pretend otherwise. As for the wineskins, they contain date wine and you will bring them to me as before."

"Nay, I will not do it!" Ranofer cried miserably. He knew he had failed. Everything had gone wrong somehow. Gebu was no longer worried, he was only contemptuous. "I will not bring them," he repeated.

"Aye, you'll bring them." Gebu half smiled and his eyelid jerked. "Are you so stupid that you do not understand? I know nothing of your stolen gold. No man can prove otherwise. If you would put your own head in a noose, you have only to go babbling to Rekh."

"*My* head?" Ranofer stared at him, bewildered. Then he felt his scalp prickle as he realized what Gebu meant, why he had suddenly ceased to worry—and why it was utterly useless to say a word to Rekh. Gebu would merely deny that he had ever seen the gold. He would deny any knowledge of the Babylonian, of the wineskins, of any part of it. He would shrug and shake his head over the wickedness of boys, and point to Ranofer as the thief. Gebu could be very convincing when he chose. And who would defend Ranofer? Not Ibni, certainly. He would only add his accusations to Gebu's. Not Rekh, who would be scornful and hurt. There would be no one, except himself, to speak the truth, and who would believe his tale?

Bitterly conscious of defeat, Ranofer turned away and started for the storeroom. Instantly Gebu jerked him back.

"Where are you going, pig's son? Did I say I was finished?"

"I—I want my bread. I am hungry."

"*Your* bread! When did it come to be yours? By Amon, you have grown too toplofty of late, behaving like Pharaoh instead of the gutter waif you are. Aye, a waif, and remember it! Where would you be this moment, had I not offered you food and lodging out of the goodness of my heart? Sleeping in the dust of the streets, aye, and fighting the dogs for their leavings. Instead, you live comfortably on *my* bread."

"It is mine too. I earn five *deben* a month and give you all of it."

Gebu's heavy lip curled. "Five *deben*. A fortune!"

"It is all they will pay for porters' work!" Ranofer was struggling against tears. Without hope, he offered the old plea. "I could earn more, much more, if I could learn, become a pupil, a craftsman—"

"Listen to the princeling! What do pupils earn? Nothing. *They* must pay, instead, for their instruction. Who would pay for yours, Fatherless One, Homeless One?"

The last words cut like strokes of a lash. Ranofer bent his head under them. "An apprentice, then. If you would apprentice me to Rekh!"

"Take care I do not apprentice you to some fishmonger. Ingrate! I could have you bound over to myself, at the stonecutting shop. But did I? Nay, I found you work to your liking. Come, is it not so? Was it not I, Gebu, who placed you in Rekh the goldsmith's shop?"

"Only to help you steal," Ranofer whispered.

"Watch your tongue." Gebu raised one fist. With the other he shoved Ranofer against the wall and pinned him there. The boy sucked in his breath, squinting in expectation of the blow, his back pressing against the rough bricks

36

until their edges dug into his flesh. The fist knotted tighter, tighter. Ranofer, with every nerve and muscle taut, felt a wave of fear that was almost nausea.

With a scornful laugh Gebu lowered his fist to his side, leaving the boy limp and covered with cold sweat.

"Look at you!" the stonecutter jeered. "Cowering there like a cringing puppy. Can you not stand on your feet when I talk to you?"

Ranofer straightened, sick with humiliation. Accursed One! he thought. I hate him, I hate him! He makes of me not only a thief but a coward. "It is only that I am hungry," he mumbled.

"Hungry. Always you are hungry. Why did you not dig yourself a few lotus roots while you dawdled by the river? Many such brats as you get nothing else and think themselves well off."

The lecture might have gone on for some time, but Gebu had evidently grown bored with baiting him. Still muttering irritably, he plucked the torch from its bracket and strode down the court. Ranofer followed in silence. The invariable reaction to a scene with Gebu had begun to set in, a fatigue so deep it penetrated mind and body alike.

Gebu went into the second storeroom, emerging presently with one of the small, flat loaves of Egyptian bread; but when Ranofer reached for it, he drew it back. "Did the Babylonian say anything today for you to tell me?"

Wearily Ranofer prodded his memory. "Aye. He said he would send wine tomorrow."

"Good." Gebu's eyelid fluttered as he stared fixedly at the boy. "You will bring it. Do you understand?"

He broke the bread, giving half to the boy and thrusting the rest into his own mouth. "I'm expecting friends," he mumbled through it. "Open the gate when they come."

Winking vindictively, he made for the stairs and vanished up them, taking the torch with him.

Ranofer stood alone in the dark courtyard, holding his piece of bread. Half a loaf. It barely covered his palm, and the emptiness in his stomach felt as big as the whole temple of Amon. The emptiness in his heart matched it. Gebu's last warning had needed no underscoring. On dragging feet he padded into the storeroom, felt his way to the big water jar and drank thirstily. Afterward he searched, though without hope, for another bite of something—a forgotten onion, a mouthful of stewed lentils left from Gebu's meal. The storeroom yielded nothing more except the tantalizing fragrance from boxes and kegs all sealed and forbidden him.

He left it and crossed the courtyard to the farthest corner where his sleeping mat was spread under a straggling acacia tree. Flinging himself upon the rough fibers, he held the bread to his nose, and its yeasty fragrance brought the saliva rushing into his mouth. He began to eat slowly, carefully, making each mouthful last as long as he could.

All too soon it was gone, leaving him only the craving for more. He lay back, pillowing his head on his hands. He could have given me the whole loaf, he thought. They are small enough at best—I could eat twenty of them. Thirty! The pig was punishing me for trying to defy him. *Aii!* If only I were free of him! If only I could climb aboard a boat and sail far, far away, and never see this courtyard or the Street of the Crooked Dog again in all my life. What if I tried it? What if I ran away tomorrow?

The thought filled him with the old panic. Ah, but what would I do then? he thought. How would I live?

It was impossible. He would not think of it. He would think of a day to come, when he was a man, and would have gold of his own, and could buy all the bread he wanted. But how would he get this gold, if he grew up ignorant, fit only to be a porter? No matter, he would get it somehow. Perhaps he would find it. People did find gold sometimes, hidden away in the crevices of the hills, or under an old house, buried there by someone long dead and forgotten.

Aye, that was it, he would find it. Ranofer closed his eyes, smiling to himself. He could almost see the little gold ingots, row on row, lining the walls of some secret cave that only he would know about. He would take one home each week to Gebu, and there would be no more beatings. Nay, there would be no Gebu! He would have a house of his own, he, Ranofer the son of Thutra. He would buy fresh-salted fish, and milk and lentils, and a honey cake—many honey cakes! The gods would smile on him, and Osiris himself, Osiris the Merciful, would speak out of the wind to him and direct all his affairs. Aye, and better than all, he would use the ingots for gold-working! He would make a broad, fine bowl with a pattern of reed flowers inlaid in silver wire, and he would make a little eye-paint pot with a hinged lid, and a brace-let. Perhaps two bracelets. How would he fashion them? In the form of snakes, perhaps, with garnet eyes. Or should he shape them like lilies, with long stems twining about the arm? Aye, like lilies. And they would be more beautiful than the moon, and all Thebes would stand in wonder before them. Zau the Master would see them and would carry them to Pharaoh, who would buy them immediately for many coppers, and the fame of Ranofer the goldsmith would spread through all the Black Land. He would take a few pupils, only the talented ones as Zau did, and become—

A knocking sounded at the gate. Ranofer jerked up his head and stared about dazedly. The stars had come out over the silent courtyard, revealing the rubbish-strewn pavement and peeling walls in all their ugly reality. He sighed, dragged himself to his feet and walked across the court.

The moment he unlatched the gate it was shoved open with a violence that all but knocked him down. Massaging his bruised ribs, he squinted resentfully into the glare of a torch.

"Where is the stonecutter?" grunted a thick voice.

It was Setma, the Nile-boat captain. One needed only one's nose to recognize his characteristic aura of river stink and barley-beer fumes. Ranofer jerked his head in the direction of the stairway. "Up there."

The man brushed past, almost dropping his torch in his unsteady progress along the courtyard. In his wake came another man, a tall, stooped figure with a dark cloak folded about him like drooping wings. He was not drunk like the riverman, but Ranofer drew back from him instinctively. Wenamon, he was called; he was a mason. He paused, gazed at the boy a moment with glittering bright eyes, then followed the riverman to the stair on feet that made no more sound than a *kheft's*.

Shivering, Ranofer latched the gate and went back to his mat. Gebu was bad enough, but his friends were worse. Ranofer had long been sure that Wenamon possessed the

Evil Eye. He fingered his amulet nervously, hoping it had protected him, but he knew it had no power over the Evil Eye. That required a different amulet, the *ouzait*, shaped like the sacred eye of the god Horus. His was only the life sign, *ankh*, a green-glazed cross with a looped top, tied to his wrist with seven knots to bind his spirit to his body. He could remember the old magician his father had bought it from, and how safe he had felt when it was made fast over the exposed pulse through which his *ka* might try to escape. Safe! Aye, it had kept his *ka* in his body, but it had saved him from little else. Not from Gebu, not from beatings and hunger, not from Ibni and his hateful wineskins.

Ranofer rolled onto his back, trying to switch his thoughts again to the secret cave full of ingots, but the little golden bars kept turning into wineskins in his mind, or into loaves of bread that vanished when he tried to touch them. His stomach knotted with hunger, and his mind with worry. He could not bring that accursed wineskin on the morrow, knowing what it contained. Yet, what would Gebu do if he appeared without it? Fear dried his mouth at the very thought. He was afraid of Gebu and his heavy fist, afraid of his own hunger, most of all afraid of the void that yawned always on his right hand, waiting for Gebu to turn him out. Sleeping in the dust of the streets, fighting the dogs for their leavings . . .

I am a coward, he thought. A cringing puppy, as Gebu said. And tomorrow I shall become a thief, because I am afraid.

Saying it, even to himself without a sound, somehow cleared his mind. He, Ranofer the son of Thutra, a thief? Staring up through the ragged branches of the acacia to the stars spangling the dark sky, he could see only the kindly face of Rekh the goldsmith rising before him in reproach. He turned over and flung an arm over his eyes.

I'll not do it, he told himself fiercely. Never, never! Not a grain of gold, not a scrap will I bring that Evil One, let him beat me all he likes. Let him have his bread. I'll find my own somehow, or do without, but I'll be no thief.

The reproachful face faded from his mind, and his tension vanished, driven out by the exalted sense of heroism with which his own words had filled him. He began to picture himself, a larger, more muscular self, nearly Gebu's size, standing with proudly upflung head before the stone-cutter, defying him, smiling coolly at his raging, easily side-stepping his poorly aimed blows, and walking at last from the hateful courtyard without deigning to glance back. Then he would go to the goldhouse of Zau the Master and beg to be accepted as a pupil. Had not Zau *almost* said he would accept him, a month before his father died, when Zau had come to inquire after his old friend's health? He had looked at the little cups and arm bands Ranofer had hammered out, and he had said to Thutra, "Your son shows skill. Perhaps, when he is older . . ." Then the evil day of death had come, and old Marya had told Ranofer, weeping, that there would be scarcely enough coppers left for bread after his father's tomb was furnished, and the embalmers paid, and the offerings made to the priests of the Necropolis. He could not even go back to the scribe's school where he had been learning to read, much less think of Zau, who charged a pupil's fee. Even though Zau was there among the mourners at his father's house that morning, Ranofer had not dared to speak to him, but had stood watching him from a corner, thinking, *Later, maybe later, when I am older.* All the world was grief and confusion that day.

Then Gebu had come, a solid form blocking out the sunlight in the doorway so that everyone turned to look. In the silence he had stepped into the room as if he owned it, as indeed, it seemed, he did. He had a scribe's paper that proved his claims as first-born. Before this stranger with his scrap of paper Zau and Thutra's other old friends had stepped aside, departing one by one to their houses and out of Ranofer's life. Soon old Marya vanished too. Gebu sold her at the common slave market to pay for funerary arrangements. He sold the last of Thutra's goldwork and his tools and his worktable. Then he took everything left in the house, including Ranofer, and moved them to the Street of the Crooked Dog, and that was the settlement of Thutra's estate.

Ranofer found himself sitting up on his mat in the courtyard, staring blindly into the dark. Frowning, he threw himself down again, pulling an edge of the matting over his bare legs.

No need to think about all that again, he told himself. All will be different now. I shall defy Gebu, I shall leave the Street of the Crooked Dog forever. Ah, then anything will be possible! The golden ingots, those ingots in that hidden cave I shall discover, I can use those to pay my pupil's fee. Then Pharaoh will buy my necklaces for Queen Tiy, who is beautiful and kind, and she will smile on me, Ranofer the son of Thutra—and I will not be a thief!

Curled into as tight a ball as possible against the chill of the night, Ranofer slept at last.

Chapter III

RANOFER woke with the feeling that something important and fine had happened. He sat up, peering around him sleepily. Then he remembered his decision of the night before.

Wide awake at once, he scrambled to his feet, and his eyes went automatically to the upper room. Was Gebu still sleeping or had he gone to his work? No matter, I am not afraid of him, thought Ranofer. It seemed unnecessary, however, to court trouble by investigating the matter. He stole across the courtyard, which was dingier than ever in the cool morning light. There was nothing at all on the storeroom shelves except empty crocks and baskets, and a dish containing the crumbs of last night's loaf. Gebu had not yet breakfasted and Ranofer decided not to wait for him. Hunger was a better companion. Drinking deep from the water jar, he yanked his sash tight around his hollow middle and let himself out the gate.

Running on fleet, silent feet down the Street of the Crooked Dog, he felt frightened but jubilant. Today he would begin a new life. No longer would he be a cringing puppy, ashamed of the welts on his back, avoiding Rekh's

eye. He would weigh the gold, every grain, and pour the
ingots and wash the sweep, and he would *not* carry home
the wineskin when the day was done. "Gebu does not
want it," he would say to the Babylonian. "He bids me
tell you he does not like your wine."

Great Lord Ra burst over the eastern horizon just as
Ranofer turned into the broad road that edged the fields
of the flower growers. Beyond the emerald fields he could
glimpse the surface of the river, jeweled with sunlight.
A flock of pintail ducks planed down over the papyrus
marsh and vanished among the reeds.

"*Sah,*" murmured Ranofer automatically, reminded of
his lessons with the scribe. He halted and dropped to one
knee, scratching the hieroglyph of the pintail duck in the
dust with his finger. By adding a vertical stroke beside it,
and the picture of a man kneeling, one could write the
word *sah,* "son." Ranofer admired his handiwork a moment, then changed the kneeling man to a sitting woman,
obliterated the stroke and replaced it with a bread loaf.
Behold! *Saht,* "daughter."

Ranofer smiled. It gave one a sense of power to be able
to write words. He wished, though, that he had not added
the bread-loaf "t." It reminded him of his empty stomach.

He got up and hurried on. There were many people in
the street now, calling greetings to one another as they
set out for their work. Everywhere, once he had thought
of it, Ranofer saw hieroglyphs. There on a doorstep was
a wickerwork basket, "k"; yonder, "n," the ripples on the
water. The vulture wheeling above the slow-moving boats
was the guttural sound, "ah." Even the boats themselves
and the rising sun, the amulet on his wrist and the beetle

45

crawling in the dust were the same as the careful signs he had learned to draw on his clay tablet.

He had not forgotten them. Perhaps if he urged his memory further, practiced each night as he lay on his mat... Nothing seemed impossible today.

Buoyant with hope, he turned into the Street of the Goldsmiths. Ahead of him, just emerging from the Apprentices' Quarters and finishing his breakfast as he ran, was the new boy, Heqet. The two exchanged tentative glances, then Heqet's snub-nosed face broke into a smile.

"May Ra shine upon you, comrade."

"And upon you," Ranofer returned eagerly. It was clear his rudeness was forgiven. "Did you pour your ingot without splashing yesterday?" he asked as they started on together.

"Aye, in a manner of speaking," the other said with a grin. "Which is to say, I watched the Second Craftsman pour it."

"He will let you do it yourself today," Ranofer said. In spite of himself his eyes strayed to the food Heqet was eating as he walked. "What have you there?" he added, trying to sound unconcerned.

"Only a fig," Heqet replied. He glanced at Ranofer, then looked again more closely. "I have another. Will you eat it?"

"I? Oh, no, no. I merely asked. I do not care for figs. They—" Ranofer's hasty protests were cut short by a dismal growling from his empty belly, which felt even vaster than the temple of Amon this morning. Heqet, still watching him, dug a second fig from his sash and held it out.

"Come, take it, Ranofer. It will quiet your rumblings, as the man said when he tossed his right leg to the crocodile."

46

Ranofer found himself grinning broadly as he imagined the crocodile's surprise. This Heqet must be the drollest fellow in Egypt.

"You look quite different when you smile," said Heqet, studying him curiously. "Why do you not do it more often?"

"I—I do not know."

"There! Now I have made you solemn again. I should put a curb on my tongue. Here, take the fig. That should cheer you."

Ranofer took the fig. The temptation was stronger than his pride. Thanking Heqet awkwardly, he set his teeth into the crisp golden skin. Pure honey dripped into his mouth with every bite. He thought he had never tasted anything so good.

The sun was pouring into the broad courtyard of the goldsmith's shop, flooding ovens, benches, crucibles, with a radiance that made even the washing vats seem things of beauty. Parting from Heqet inside the gate, Ranofer hurried into the shop to begin his first task, that of helping the weigher and the scribe issue each man's portion of gold. Rekh and the craftsmen had not yet arrived, but the storeroom door was open and the older apprentices were lining up in front of the scales. The weigher emerged from the storeroom with a basket of ingots just as Ranofer took his place beside the waiting scribe.

"Rejoice, friends," puffed the weigher, bobbing his head to the room in general. "We will begin. Name the master's wishes, Hotepek."

"Four measures to the apprentice Hapia'o, for beating into a sheet," droned the scribe, reading from his tablet and at the same time keeping a sharp eye on the scales as his companion weighed out ingots to equal four measures.

"Done," the weigher grunted as the scales balanced.

"Four measures to Hapia'o," echoed Ranofer. He dug the ingots out of the leather weighing bag and handed them to the apprentice.

The scribe made a mark on his tablet and read the next instruction. "One-half measure to Geryt, together with one-twentieth measure of copper and of silver, for preparing solder."

The morning ritual went on, each worker accepting his portion from Ranofer and carrying it to the courtyard to begin his task, while the scribe kept strict account of every grain.

Rekh the goldsmith arrived as the last measure was doled out. He greeted the men in his deep, gentle voice, smiled at Ranofer and bade him make ready the big furnace. As the boy started for the charcoal bin, Rekh limped past him and spoke to the scribe.

"Well, Hotepek?"

"Master, the figures remain the same, though I checked them thrice over. The weights do not tally. Again we are lacking. It is not a large amount, but still it is gone."

Rekh was silent, and the boy dared not turn from the bin of charcoal to look at his face. He did not need to. Too well he could imagine the kindly eyes clouding, the smile fading into discouragement.

Rekh sighed. "I do not understand it," he murmured. "Eh, well, we shall have to take other steps, though I do not know what. Weigh all sweepings again today."

"Aye, Master."

Ranofer bent over the bin, outwardly intent on scooping

charcoal into the furnace pan, inwardly cursing the Babylonian and Gebu alike. Rekh's limping footsteps stopped behind him.

"Anubis save us, that is enough charcoal, boy," the goldsmith said in a tone of mild surprise. "It is only a small box I wish to solder, not Pharaoh's throne."

"I crave pardon, *neb* Goldsmith," the boy mumbled, hastily returning a scoop or two of the black lumps into the bin.

"It is of no moment." Rekh hesitated, then added, "Your shoulder is better today. I am glad, *shari*."

There was affection in his voice, and his use of the term "small one" brought sudden tears to Ranofer's eyes, so vividly did he recall his father's voice using that very endearment. He scowled fiercely to cover his emotion and, not knowing what to say to Rekh, made no answer at all. In a fluster of self-consciousness he turned his back, dropped a hot coal into the nest of charcoal in the furnace and began to blow on it vigorously.

"Gently, gently!" exclaimed Rekh. "Blow only a little at first or the flame will not come. Sometime before midday you had best make more charcoal. The bin is nearly empty."

He limped on to his bench to resume work on the jewel box he was making for the tomb of a wealthy Theban. Ranofer, flushing hot as he coaxed the flame, could only fume at his own bungling. Again he had behaved rudely to one whose friendship he most desired. Could he not at least have thanked Rekh for his concern about the shoulder? Could he not have smiled? And why, oh why had he puffed away at that coal like an ignorant novice, when he had known for years exactly how to coax

49

a flame into being? Rekh would think him a dullard, unfit to learn the goldsmith's trade.

Well, he would prove otherwise somehow. Ranofer's brow cleared and his heart lightened again. He could not stay gloomy today, knowing the trouble would soon be gone from Rekh's gentle eyes. There would be no gold missing this week, nor the next, nor the next, forever. Giving a last puff to the fire, which was now blazing merrily, he hurried to answer the First Craftsman's call.

It was the middle of the morning before he had a moment to spare for the depleted charcoal bin. Glancing into it guiltily, he snatched up a basket and plunged out into the sunny courtyard before anyone else could cry, "Ranofer! Come hither!" He was filling his basket at the wood-box when Heqet came up beside him.

"I was looking for you, friend. The ever-scowling First Craftsman bids me ask if you will be making charcoal today."

"Aye, this very minute."

"Good, then. I'm to watch you and learn how it's done. Will you teach me?"

"Gladly." Feeling a pleased importance, Ranofer led the way across the sun-warmed pavement to an idle furnace. "If you do it yourself, you will remember better. See that copper box? Fill it with these little logs from the basket."

"Aye, *neb* Ranofer." With a grin and a mock obeisance, Heqet began to arrange logs in the firing box, and Ranofer used his moment of leisure to watch the work going on around him. Eagerly his eyes moved from bench to bench, sliding over Hapia'o, who was still beating ingots into sheets, lingering on the older apprentice next him, who

50

was winding gold wire about a rod, preparatory to clipping it into links for a necklace. Ranofer waited until he thrust it into the fire for annealing, and made careful note of the exact dull red it reached before it was pulled out again. Across the way young Meryra knelt before one of the shaping stakes, hammering his first bowl. Meryra's brow was furrowed, and Ranofer's ear told him why. The metal was not ringing true. The sound set Ranofer's teeth on edge. Meryra would have a sorry and crooked bowl, he reflected, if he did not hold his elbow higher, and he must stiffen his wrist or that sharp-edged hammer would leave marks all over the gold. The craftsman should have given him one of those round-faced horn hammers weighted with lead, for his first attempt. Thutra would have done so.

"Is it enough, Master Ranofer?" came Heqet's voice. "It may be I could crowd in one or two more logs, but—"

"Nay, that's enough," said Ranofer, hastily returning to the business at hand. "Now the lid must go on. But do not fasten it too tightly or there will be no place for the gases to escape. We will do it thus—do you see?—leaving a little space there."

He helped Heqet wire the box shut, then turned to stir up the fire. "Now take the other handle, friend. We'll set the box in the furnace. So. There is nothing else to it."

"But when the gases have all escaped?"

"Then the wood will be charcoal, and one may take it off the fire to cool. Is it not simple?"

"Simple if you know the trick of it, remarked the vulture as she laid a falcon egg." Heqet chuckled at his own joke, then waved Ranofer away. "Go on to your next task, friend, I'll see this done. Many thanks for the lesson."

Today he does not ask me questions about myself, thought Ranofer as he moved away. Perhaps he understands that I do not wish to answer them. We shall be friends after all.

Pang, pong, pang! Once more the sour notes of the hammer offended Ranofer's practiced ear. He paused behind Meryra's bench, squirming inwardly as he watched the work being done all wrong. Finally, with some misgivings, he touched the apprentice's elbow.

"Eh? What is it? Can't you see I'm busy?" Meryra scowled over his shoulder. He was a youth of about seventeen, with the blunt hands of a farmer. Goldworking did not come easy to him, and it was obvious his poor results with the bowl had ruined his usual even disposition.

"I crave pardon, friend," Ranofer said. "I know why your bowl is not shaping properly. Will you allow me to tell you?"

Mollified by the courteous tone, Meryra shrugged his big shoulders. "Well, what, then, if you think you know? It's certain I don't."

"You are not striking the metal true. Hold your elbow higher and bring the hammer down smartly. Then it will shape as you wish."

Meryra frowned suspiciously from Ranofer to the hammer. "Perhaps it will, perhaps not. If I strike it sharply will it not mar the surface even more? See the hammer marks there already."

"You should have a different hammer, one with a round face. But this one will not mark if you keep your wrist very stiff and firm, to control your aim. Would—would you let me show you?"

"*Ast!* I won't, then. You might ruin it."

"Aye, I might," Ranofer agreed humbly. "I have little skill and less experience. But I have watched my father raise a hundred such bowls and I know what should be done."

"Perhaps you do, perhaps you don't," the other grumbled, but he looked thoughtful. Once more he placed his half-formed bowl upon the shaping stake and, raising his elbow high, gave a sharp, firm tap. The stake rang like music. Meryra's face brightened. He turned the bowl upon the stake and struck again, then again, then again. Each time the ring was true, and already the curve of the metal was beginning to assume the proper angle.

"By Amon, you're right!" he exclaimed.

"Aye, quite right," put in an amused, quiet voice. Both turned to find the goldsmith leaning on the next bench. He straightened, limped over to Meryra and, taking the hammer from his hand, dropped it into its slot in the tool rack. "Try the cow's-horn mallet, my son," he advised. "It will not play tricks on you. As for you, Ranofer," he turned interested eyes on the younger boy, "come with me. I have a task for you."

Flushing with pleasure and confusion, Ranofer followed him to one of the smaller furnaces. Upon the low table beside it lay a stone hammering block and a coil of gold wire. Rekh motioned for him to kneel on the mat and, extracting a mallet from the tool rack attached to the table, handed it to him.

"Now, Small One. You know something, it seems, of the goldworker's art. Do you know the manner of making the little leaves we use to ornament ladies' jewelry?"

"Aye, Master."

"Good. Make one now, while I watch."

53

Ranofer dared not believe his ears. "*I* make one, *neb* Rekh? Out of real gold?"

Rekh only nodded toward the coil of wire and waited.

Trembling with excitement, Ranofer could scarcely make his fingers loosen a strand of the wire and straighten it. He, Ranofer, was to be allowed to work in gold, to learn a bit, to practice, to fashion a leaf. *Aii!* Might the gods smile on Rekh the goldsmith. Might they make him rich and honored, might Pharaoh himself shower gold upon him!

Ranofer's mind, fluttering as uselessly as his fingers, focused suddenly upon the fire. Was it hot enough? He stirred it, then glanced anxiously at Rekh. "May I use the blowpipe, Master?"

"Use whatever you need."

Once clasping the familiar shape of the blowpipe, Ranofer's hands steadied and so did his nerves. He could do this. He had done it many times, with Thutra watching from his cot. There was nothing new. Just snip a length of wire, grasp it firmly in the little tongs and—careful now.

With infinite caution Ranofer held the tip of the wire in the flame, blowing a light, steady stream of air through the pipe. The flame blued to intense heat. Presently the wire tip melted and ran up into a bead. At once Ranofer removed it to the stone block, dropped the blowpipe and seized the mallet instead. One sharp tap and the bead flattened to a tiny leaf shape, with the remainder of the wire its stem.

He studied it anxiously, running his tongue over his lips. Was it good enough? Was perhaps the stem too long, the edge too thick? He raised his eyes slowly to the gold-

54

smith's face. Rekh was smiling, he was nodding approval at the leaf.

"It is a good leaf, Ranofer. But then, it was the first, and I was here behind you, watching every move. One is always diligent with the first. I wonder, would you use such care in making a fifteenth? Or a fiftieth?"

"To be sure, Master," Ranofer said in surprise. "How could I do otherwise? Without care, the leaf is ruined and must be done over."

"Aye, so it must." Rekh picked up the leaf and examined it once more, then put it aside on the bench. "Very well. This day the Lady Irenma'at has ordered a necklace of many strands, ornamented with greenstones and golden leaves. Fashion me those leaves, fifty of them, each one the twin of the last. When you have made them, bring them to me in the shop."

He turned and limped away, leaving Ranofer staring after him in a ferment of joy. Fifty leaves! He, *he* was to make the ornaments for a grand lady's necklace! Perhaps she would wear it to a dinner party at the villa of some great lord or count, perhaps to the palace itself. Aye, to the palace. And Queen Tiy, Beloved of the Two Lands, would notice it, and ask whence it came, and who, *who* had fashioned those delicate leaves, each one a work of art, and Pharaoh himself would lean from his throne to see the necklace better, and . . .

To work, stupid one, Ranofer chided himself. Dreaming will fashion no works of art. Cease gawking at the gold, and use it.

The day passed in a blissful haze which not even the gnawing of Ranofer's empty stomach could penetrate.

Even after the leaves were finished, the fiftieth the twin of the first, and all made with supreme and loving care, his spirits continued to soar. Perhaps Rekh would now let him make leaves every day, perhaps allow him to anneal wire, spread solder just so on the boxes, and learn and become skillful. Even back at his old chores of washing the sweep and pouring molds, Ranofer's rapt face and hurrying small body radiated such joyful hope that a contagion of laughter and joking swept over the whole courtyard. Even the First Craftsman ceased to scowl, though he could not have told why.

At last the day was done, a good day, a fine fortunate day, favored by all the gods. It lacked but one thing to place the seal of total success upon it, and that would take place very soon.

Ranofer timed his leaving to coincide with Heqet's. With his friend beside him he stepped confidently out the courtyard gate, into the long shadows striping the Street of the Goldsmiths. At once he spotted the Babylonian waiting for him in a doorway ahead. He walked on, a little nervous now but trying not to show it. Surely, with Heqet beside him, Ibni would not even dare approach him. Ibni was not so easily put off. As the two boys drew even with his doorway, he stepped out, grinning and bobbing his head, holding out the wineskin.

"A little gift for your honored brother, young Ranofer. I pray you, carry it home to him. True, it is a poor gift and unworthy of him, but the wine is made by my wife from our own dates, and though humble—"

Ranofer drew a long breath and faced him. "Gebu does not want it," he said. "He bids me tell you he does not like your wine."

Without waiting to see the effect of his words, he hurried on. Heqet followed, glancing back over his shoulder.

"A queer fellow, that porter," he remarked. "I think you offended him, friend Ranofer. He has an ugly glint in his eye."

"Let him! I'll not fetch and carry for such a one. I think he's half crocodile, with his grin and his stinking breath."

Ranofer swelled with satisfaction. He had bested his enemy with exactly the scornful phrases he had imagined this morning, and the seal of success was on the day. He dismissed Ibni from his mind, sniffing the air luxuriously. The shop's hot odor of molten gold had given way to the fragrance of lotus and marsh weed, mingled with the familiar reek of the Nile and the pungent smell of natron and spices from the Street of the Embalmers, which they were passing at the moment. To Ranofer, lightheaded with hunger and triumph, all the world seemed tinged with remarkable beauty. The western cliffs burned amber in the last of the sunshine. To the north a falcon wheeled slowly over the shining walls of Pharaoh's palace, as if to proclaim the presence within of the royal god-king he symbolized. Yonder from the fields, like flute notes, sounded the creaking of the water wheels.

"The gods smile on Egypt," murmured Ranofer.

"And on you too today, is it not so? I saw you making leaves there like some elder craftsman. And by the Hidden One, the master himself could have done no better."

Ranofer drank in the praise and the respectful glance which accompanied it. "My father taught me how to make them." In a burst of confiding he added, "Perhaps Rekh will teach me more now. Perhaps someday I shall be a master goldsmith and make necklaces for the queen."

"May Amon grant it," Heqet replied warmly. "Then perhaps you will smile more often." They walked on in sudden silence, each a little abashed by his own sincerity. As the familiar palm-thatched outlines of the Apprentices' Quarters loomed ahead, Heqet resumed his usual flippant tone. "Behold, the Great Palace of the Downtrodden approaches. Is it not a monument fit for the gods themselves? *Aii*, what a life we lead there! Dancing, parties, mad frivolity. Well, friend, I fear I must leave you now, as the hare remarked to the hunter. Farewell, and may Nuit guard your sleep."

Ranofer grinned and waved, reflecting that anyone would smile more often when Heqet was around. He went on alone, trying to ignore the aroma of frying fish that drifted from the Apprentices' Quarters and, it seemed, from every other house he passed. In spite of himself there rose in his mind the image of a golden-brown *bulti* fish, crisp without and succulent within, served on a platter and giving off fragrances sweeter than the lotus.

Do not think of it, he ordered himself.

To forget it he began to run, almost colliding with a group of glassmakers as he turned into the main thoroughfare that paralleled the Nile. He dodged in and out among the homebound workers, shouting greetings to Kai the baker's boy and a few other urchins he knew. He was turning his whole attention to physical activity so that he might not notice the nagging uneasiness beginning to force its way into the conscious part of his mind. It grew stronger the nearer he drew to the Street of the Crooked Dog, but the stronger it grew the faster he ran, refusing to let it in, shoring up the bulwarks of his mind against it.

Only when he drew up, breathless, at his own doorway,

flung it open and stepped inside, did his defenses crumble like faulty dikes. Faced with the dingy, familiar courtyard, all the eager hopes of the day vanished beneath a torrent of blackest fear.

He had come home empty-handed. He had defied Gebu.

In vain he tried to summon the proud resolve, the brave words he had planned last night. Behind him the gate swung shut with a click like the jaws of a crocodile closing. And yonder, across the court, Gebu rose slowly from the bottom stair.

Half an hour later, Ranofer sat hunched on the rough pavement of the courtyard, trying to stop the bleeding of his nose. Gebu still stood over him. His face was rock-hard, save for the convulsively winking eye. His fists were like stones. He spoke in a voice that was hoarse with fury.

"Has understanding now entered your head, Slow-Witted One?"

Ranofer managed to nod. He could not speak. His body was raw with pain, his mind was like a disordered room still ringing with panic.

"I am ready to instruct you further, if need be. You will bring the wineskin tomorrow, to atone for your empty hands tonight. You'll bring it next time also, and the next, and the next. Do you hear? Do you understand?"

Again Ranofer nodded, and the fresh welts on his back throbbed like a fist opening and closing. Gebu continued to glare at him a moment. Then he thoughtfully fished a particle of food from between his teeth.

"By Amon, I'll wager you'd hop fast enough if you were under my eye all day. You've grown lazy and insolent, playing about with gold, doing as you pleased. How would

59

you like it, Spawn of Crocodiles, if you were never to walk through Rekh's doorway again?"

Ranofer raised startled eyes and Gebu's lips twisted.

"Aye! You had best dance to my tune. You are a goldsmith's helper. Is it not what you want? Fail me once more, only once, and you'll find yourself a stonecutter's apprentice instead. I must have some use of you."

He moved on up the stair, leaving Ranofer aghast. Stonecutter's apprentice? Apprentice to Gebu! Within reach of his fists all day, pounding chisel against stone with great heavy mallets instead of fashioning leaves or watching the gold turn crimson in the crucible? Seven years of bondage, all the while learning a craft he hated, with never a chance for the one he loved?

Dismay changed quickly to despair. It's no use, he thought. No use, no use.

Dazed with pain and hunger, he crept to his mat and buried his head in his arms.

Chapter IV

RANOFER awoke with the plan fully formed in his mind. He sat up, blinking and confused. Was he still dreaming? Surely when he closed his eyes last night he had felt no hope, seen no way out. Yet this morning a solution was here before him.

Carefully, afraid to believe in it yet, he examined his plan. Except for one small risk, he found it flawless. Obviously the gods had brought it to him while he slept.

Doubtless it was one god only, he thought more humbly as he rolled up his mat and started for the storeroom. A minor god, one of no importance, who perhaps helped me for my father's sake. Or perhaps it was no god at all, but my father himself!

He stood still beside the water jar, feeling the tears come into his eyes and sting the lids. If that were true! If he could think his father's *ba* sometimes fluttered out of the tomb by night on its little bird wings and came to see if all was well with him . . .

His eyes narrowed suddenly in an effort to call back a memory of the night or perhaps a dream. No, it was not a dream. Something had happened, deep in the middle of the night. A step? A sound? That was it, a sound. It had half wakened him and he had been afraid for a moment, because he had thought it was the squeak of the leather hinges on Gebu's bedroom door. He knew now it had not been the hinges. It was the soft fluttering of his father's *ba*.

Finding the earthen mug in his hand, he dipped it into the water jar and drank. As he did so an idea came to him. He turned quickly to the shelf. On it was a plate containing two bread loaves, half an onion, and the scanty remnants of a salted fish, the leavings from Gebu's breakfast. It seemed a banquet, and never had Ranofer been so glad to see plenty, instead of not enough. Scrupulously he divided the food in half, taking pains even with the crumbs. One half he ate, the other he knotted into his ragged sash as he hurried out of the courtyard. In the street he cast an anxious glance at the sun. If he hurried, there would be just time enough to thank his father properly.

A few minutes later he was scrambling breathlessly along a path northwest of the City of the Dead, where the cliffs curved far inward toward the river. In the sandy wasteland around him were the graves of the city's poor, each with an earthen jug or plate beside it holding the sun-dried remnants of a funerary offering. Behind this common burial ground the rough face of the cliff was honeycombed with the better tombs of artisans and scribes and merchants, carved into the rock itself. One of these was Thutra the goldsmith's. Arriving at the place, Ranofer stopped a moment to catch his breath. Then respectfully he entered the tiny chapel of his father's tomb.

It was no more than a shallow alcove hewn into the face of the cliff, with an offering table against one wall and a small stone statue of Thutra opposite. Facing the entrance was a false door, built against the bricked-in side of the shaft that dropped straight downward to the burial chamber itself. Ranofer looked with large eyes at this door. It could not open. It was not made so. Yet through it his father's *ba* had magically emerged last night and fluttered on silent wings to the Street of the Crooked Dog to help his son.

Ranofer turned to the little statue. It was not a good likeness. Gebu had hired an indifferent sculptor whose price was cheap, and the result looked nothing like the Thutra Ranofer remembered; but it was all he had.

"Father," he said softly.

His voice seemed to set up a curious rustling in that silent place. He darted a wary glance at the false door, not knowing whether to feel hopeful or afraid. However, no wraithlike, human-headed bird appeared.

Untying his sash, he arranged the bits of food upon the plate on the offering table. It looked a poor enough meal to set before one's father. Perhaps he should not have eaten the other half.

Father will understand how hungry I was, he thought. Turning to the statue again he whispered rapidly, "Father, thank you. I am sorry I could not bring a better gift. Please, please come again."

With a little bow and a last awed look at the false door, he backed out of the chapel and set off hurriedly for Rekh's shop and his work.

By the time he arrived at the Street of the Goldsmiths he had thought over the plan once more. It was a good plan except for that one risk: he must confide in Heqet. Dared he trust so much to another's ears and tongue?

63

Especially to a boy he had known only two short days? The more he thought of it the larger the risk seemed.

No matter, I must take it, he thought. There is no other way. If I can find him alone somehow . . .

Heqet was nowhere in sight as Ranofer hurried toward the familiar gate. Indeed the street was almost deserted. Guiltily Ranofer broke into a run, but he entered the courtyard to find the morning weighing already over, and everyone scattering to the first tasks. Red-faced and breathless, Ranofer presented himself to Rekh.

"I crave pardon, *neb* Goldsmith, for coming late. I could not help it. I—I carried an offering to my father's tomb."

"May his Three Thousand Years be full of joy," Rekh said gravely. "You are excused, Son Who Honors His Father. Go now to the First Craftsman and find out your task."

Sata was at the far end of the courtyard, with Heqet beside him. The craftsman turned as Ranofer came toward them, and his roar could be heard all over the shop.

"There he is at last! Where have you been for half the morning, Tardy One, idler? No excuses! Here, show this Ignorant One how to make hard solder. I want four days' supply ready by the time Ra's chariot is *there*."

Pointing irascibly straight up, Sata stalked away.

Heqet put a finger in his ear and wiggled it rapidly. "I thought I heard a voice, the cow remarked as she stood on the leopard's tail."

"Sata is not so bad as he sounds," Ranofer said with the laugh Heqet always drew out of him. "Still, we've none too much time to make four days' supply of solder. Come along."

What luck! he was thinking as he led the way to the scales. We can talk as we work, with no one suspecting. I wish I knew for a certainty that Heqet can guard a secret. I must try to find out more about him. I'll ask him questions, personal ones such as *he* is always asking. He has discovered enough about me in the past two days!

While they waited for their supply of metals to be weighed out, Ranofer tried in vain to devise such questions. He could not think of a one. It did not help that he had constantly to answer the dozens that flowed from Heqet as usual without the slightest effort.

"Oh, do we mix copper in the solder?"

"Of course. You cannot solder gold with gold."

"Why not?"

"Because your work would melt at the same moment as your solder, donkeyhead! The solder must melt first."

"Oh. Then what's the silver for?"

"We use it too."

"In the solder?"

"Aye. I'll explain everything presently. Go fetch the molds."

"Of course. Which ones?"

"Well, one is flat, and—"

"Like you were using for the ingots?"

"Nay, never mind, I'll fetch them myself," Ranofer said distractedly. "Here, take the metals to that far oven yonder and wait for me."

A few moments later he spread everything upon a workbench beside the designated oven, which he had chosen because no one chanced to be working near it today. Before Heqet could start talking again he said in a low voice, "I have something to ask of you. It is important."

Heqet looked at him, then glanced around the court-yard. "Ask away, friend. There is no one listening."

Ranofer's lips parted, then closed again as his courage failed him. "Aye, but first I—first we had best begin the work." Avoiding Heqet's curious eye, he reached for a pair of snippers, motioning the other to do the same. "We cut these scraps and lengths of wire into small pieces. About this size, you see. Copper in this bowl, silver in this, and gold here." As they began to snip, he searched his mind frantically for those clever probing questions. "Where do you live?" he blurted finally, then flushed because of all questions he might have selected this was the least clever. Also the least useful, he told himself exasperatedly.

"Why, you know," Heqet said with mild surprise. "At the Apprentices' Quarters."

"Nay, I mean at home, where your parents live."

"Oh, they live upriver, at Hermonthis. Did you wonder why I do not sleep at home?"

"Nay, I merely—it does not matter to me where you live, of course."

"It matters exceedingly to my parents," remarked Heqet with a laugh. "Our house is small, and I have six brothers and a sister, all younger than I. Things got a little crowded, as the mole explained when he crawled out of the anthill."

Ranofer flashed him an uneasy smile but pressed on with his questions. "Your father, he is an artisan, perhaps?"

There was a short silence. Ranofer looked around to find Heqet studying him, sharp intelligence written over every feature of his homely, good-natured face.

"Nay, my father is Overseer of Storehouses on Lord

66

Mahotep's estate. It is a position of trust and I was brought up to know that word. Many times I have helped my father tally the mistress's cupboard, with all her fine trinkets, the golden boxes, the necklaces, the goblets with silver stems. It was handling them that first made me want to make such things, I think. Many times, too, Father bade me take delicacies to the master's table, to see if I would tuck a honey cake into my own sash, or eat just one grape. Often he whispered me a trumped-up secret, to test if I would blab it to another." Heqet paused again, smiling. "You need not worry, Ranofer. I know how to keep my lips sealed."

Ranofer's face felt as if fires were burning beneath the skin. "I ask your pardon," he mumbled.

"No need of it, friend. I am not offended."

In a somewhat awkward silence both boys turned back to their snipping. Presently Heqet remarked cheerfully, "Solder making is the easiest of tasks, if this is all there is to it."

Ranofer returned with a start to the business at hand. "We have only begun. I fear my mind is not on my work, as the—the donkey said when the—the—"

"As the worm said when the lark bit its head off," Heqet supplied glibly.

Both boys giggled and the atmosphere was easy again. "I do not know how you think of all those jokes," Ranofer said as he dragged the mold forward.

"Nor I," Heqet said airily. "Are we to snip no more? There is metal left over."

"We'll do that later. Poke up the fire a bit. Now, do you see this block of charcoal, with the hollow in it? And this funny-looking mold?"

Rapidly Ranofer explained the hearthstone mold, a stone ground flat, with a bar-shaped depression in the center and little grooves scraped from it to let the air out. As he talked he wired the block of charcoal firmly to one end of the stone, then began measuring snippets of metal into the hollow in the charcoal.

"Gold first, then the copper. Not too much, you see. It makes the solder a good rich color, but if we used copper alone the solder would not flow easily. Therefore we add silver too. Now put it to the fire. Nay, not the *stone*, great Amon! Turn the whole thing about. It is the block of charcoal we want to heat."

"It is true, I am a donkeyhead," Heqet said meekly.

Ranofer laughed, then grew serious. "Nay, you are not. You saw at once why I was asking you those questions."

"I did not blame you, friend. Only a fool pours beer into a vessel without making sure it will not leak. Look, the charcoal is glowing."

Both boys leaned over the oven.

"There!" Ranofer said as the metal snippings collapsed into liquid. "Now tilt it. Gently!"

Together they watched the molten puddle run from the hollowed charcoal into the stone mold to which it was wired. Half a minute later they were knocking a thin, flat bar of solder out onto the workbench. Ranofer picked it up and showed it to Heqet.

"There it is. Do the next one yourself, and I will go on snipping. While we work I—I will tell you this thing."

Ranofer glanced around the courtyard. Everyone was busy. Ibni was nowhere in sight. He took up the snippers, Heqet the tiny measuring scoop. Their heads bent close together. Ranofer drew a long breath, hesitated one more anxious moment, then plunged straight into the middle of his story.

"Heqet, I know who is stealing gold from the shop."

"Great Ptah's whiskers!" Heqet's head snapped up, his jaw dropped.

"Shhh! I know who is stealing and I know how he is doing it."

"But—are you certain?"

"I am certain."

"Then you must tell Rekh. Why, it is wonderful, he—"

"Hssttt! Keep your voice down! I *want* to tell Rekh. But I cannot, I—"

"Why can you not?"

"Because I have been helping the thief."

Heqet became very still. Without daring to look at him, Ranofer whispered, "I did not know I was helping. I swear it! I did not even know gold was missing until Rekh told me two days ago. Then I started thinking." He turned to Heqet miserably. "It is those wineskins."

"Wineskins?"

"You saw Ibni try to give me one yesterday. I carry them home. I have been doing it for months, never knowing. Do you see? Ibni is nothing but a tool in the hands of my half brother. And so am I."

Heqet's eyes looked into his, wide and comprehending. Suddenly the First Craftsman's bellow rang across the courtyard.

"Well, dreamers? Do you mean to stand all day and gawk at one another? Get on with your solder making."

Both boys jumped to their work. For a few moments, until Sata turned back into the shop, their hands flew and their tongues were still. Then Heqet, straightening from

69

the oven, murmured, "You can tell Rekh. He would not believe you meant to steal from him."

"Perhaps not. It makes no difference. It is not Rekh I fear. It is Gebu!"

"Gebu? What would he do if you told?"

"What would anyone do with a tool that turned on him? Look out, your mixture is melting." As Heqet bent hastily to the mold, Ranofer went on snipping and whispering with equal urgency. "What would *you* do, with a hammer that would not balance or a knife that would not cut? You would break it in anger, then get another."

"But if Gebu is seized for the thefts—"

"Gebu will never be seized. Only Ibni, or I."

Heqet thought a moment. "You refused to take that wineskin yesterday."

"Aye." Ranofer gave an involuntary shiver. "I'll not refuse the next one, you may be sure of it. Gebu is a devil, I tell you. I do not want to go on thieving for him, yet I must until Rekh is told."

"Then Rekh must be told."

"Aye, but I cannot do it. I cannot, Heqet! Therefore—"

"Therefore what?"

"Therefore I want *you* to tell him."

"I?" Heqet faced him, startled.

"Why not? He will believe *you*. Oh, you must, I beg it of you!"

"But I know nothing about it, how it is done, or—"

"I will tell you all that. There is only one way it could be done, I am sure of it." Rapidly Ranofer explained what he suspected about Ibni and the big washing vats.

Heqet nodded slowly. "I had not thought of those vats, nor has Rekh, I'll wager."

"For proof, Rekh need only find where Ibni hides that wineskin. Some cranny in the storeroom, very likely. He must drop the gold in bit by bit, a grain at a time, because ten days or more go by between the times I am called on to take home Gebu's 'little gift.' " Ranofer spat angrily, then with a glance toward the shop, picked up his snippers again.

"It is clever, so hard to trace," Heqet said. "Yet I see quite well how it could be done."

"You have not yet said that you will tell Rekh."

"I will tell him, friend."

Ranofer drew in his breath with painful relief. "Thank you. I thought you would help me, but I— And you will not whisper to anyone that it came from me? Because Gebu would learn of it."

"I'll not mention your name. Leave everything to me. Perhaps I had best not go to Rekh at all until tomorrow, since you and I have been seen talking together today."

"Aye, that would be best. I'll not come near you for a few days."

"Hsst! Here comes Sata."

The boys sealed their agreement with a glance and fell busily to work. There was no chance to say more, not even another "Thank you," for Sata stayed near the rest of the morning. After the midday break the boys separated to different tasks; but Ranofer's head rang with the words all day: "Thank you, thank you, *thank you!*"

Then, that evening as he was leaving the shop, he saw Ibni waiting, with the wineskin in his hand. Ranofer stopped, aghast. He had forgotten that this was bound to happen. He would have turned back into the shop, dodged down an alley, vanished into thin air if he could, but there was no avoiding the Babylonian this time. His voice was as wheedling as ever, but there was an open threat in his eyes as he stepped in front of Ranofer and blocked his way.

"Ah, greetings to you, little one, I feared I had missed you with my little gift. You were mistaken yesterday, were you not, when you told me the message from your honored half brother? Did you not find out you had misunderstood him? Surely he would like a little wine, made from our own grapes."

"Give it to me and be gone," Ranofer said through set teeth. He snatched the wineskin and stalked by the Babylonian, taking pleasure in treading on his toe as he passed.

Half blinded by angry tears, he almost walked straight into Heqet, who was lurking in a doorway farther down the street, waiting for him. Ranofer motioned in silence toward the wineskin.

"Aye," Heqet said. "This will spoil our plan for tomorrow, won't it?"

"It spoils everything, everything! Here is the proof we need, in my hand, before we even had time to make use of it. Now we will have to wait and wait and wait, until he has collected more, in another wineskin."

"We will wait, then. Four or five days will make little difference, after all."

"How do we know? I do not want to wait."

"If we must, we must." Heqet touched Ranofer's shoulder awkwardly. "Never fear. We'll catch him, as the tortoise said to the snail."

Ranofer tried to smile, but he could not help feeling that Heqet's simile had for once been unfortunately

72

chosen. He started homeward, the hated wineskin under his arm.

When he arrived at the Street of the Crooked Dog he found Gebu in such roaring good humor that he knew the beatings, at least, were over for a while. Wenamon, Gebu's friend of the noiseless feet and drooping cloak, had been paying a call. The two were on their way down the stair as Ranofer entered the courtyard.

"*Hai!* It is the little messenger!" bellowed Gebu, as his eyes went to the wineskin. To Wenamon he added in an undertone, "Though it is of small importance now, eh?" and burst into a roar of laughter. Before Ranofer had time to wonder what he meant he beckoned peremptorily. "Well, well, come here, messenger, make your delivery, and receive your reward."

Ranofer approached cautiously, handed the wineskin to him and jumped back out of range. He did not trust Gebu's rewards. This time, however, Gebu paid no attention to him. He was showing the wineskin to Wenamon, with a grin.

"A gift from a friend, grown on his own vines, and made by his wife's hand. Is that not touching? A pity we cannot drink it."

Ranofer did not think so. It was obvious Gebu had drunk a great deal of wine already. He started for the storeroom to see if there were anything to eat.

"Stay! Do you not want the reward I promised?" Gebu shouted.

"I had that yesterday," Ranofer muttered.

"So you did, but you'll like this one better, I daresay." There was a metallic clink on the pavement behind Ranofer. He whirled in astonishment and saw a copper ring-

73

coin lying there. "Well? Pick it up, pick it up. Do you think it is a scorpion? Now go buy food and eat it. I can count every rib in your back. First take this wineskin up to my—" Gebu stopped abruptly, then grinned at Wenamon and finished, "Nay, I will take it."

He staggered noisily up the stairs. While he was gone Ranofer stood clutching his copper and enduring Wenamon's steady, bright-eyed gaze. It made every hair on his head prickle and it seemed to go on forever. At last Gebu reappeared, however, singing at the top of his voice. Without taking further notice of Ranofer the two left the courtyard and started down the street in the direction of the docks.

Ranofer wasted no time in taking advantage of Gebu's sudden generosity. The moment the sound of raucous singing had faded around the corner, he slipped out of the gate and ran in the opposite direction. With luck, Kai the baker's boy would have a few loaves left, and he could eat his fill for once.

Chapter V

GEBU'S joviality lasted for several days, and as was usual during these periods, Ranofer fared better as to food. His stomach ceased gnawing, but his anxieties did not. He was able to show fair patience for the first day or so of waiting for the grains of gold to accumulate in Ibni's next wineskin. But after that, though he told himself it was still too early, he could not help expecting every moment to see Heqet's signal that Rekh had been told, and all was well. At last, on the fourth morning, close to midday, he noticed Heqet standing close beside Rekh's worktable, ostensibly watching the goldsmith raise a bowl, but actually whispering to him under cover of the hammer taps. Ranofer turned away quickly, terrified that someone else would notice. He need not have worried. Anxiety caused him to make so many blunders the rest of the day that the whole shop's attention was irritably focused on himself.

When he reached the goldhouse next morning, he glanced instantly toward the big washing vats. Ibni was there the same as every other day, unconcernedly dumping a sack of raw gold into the vat.

For a moment Ranofer could not believe it. Surely, once

Rekh knew, he would turn Ibni out of the shop forever. Surely it *was* Ibni who was doing the thieving? Perhaps Rekh did not know yet; perhaps Heqet had been telling him something else yesterday. Or, horrid thought, perhaps Rekh had not believed him.

All day Ranofer went about his duties mechanically, forcing himself to abide by his own decision that he and Heqet should not be seen in conversation. At last, in the late afternoon, he could bear it no longer. He watched his chance and stooped close beside Heqet on the pretext of helping him stoke an oven.

"Have you told him yet?"

"Aye! Yesterday."

"I thought so. Why does he not do something, then?"

"I do not know. Perhaps he cannot find the wineskin."

"Did he believe you?"

"I am sure he did."

"You—did not mention my name?"

"You know I would not."

There was nothing to do but go on waiting, that day, and the next, and the next.

Eight days gone already, Ranofer thought as he walked homeward one evening. Yet nothing is changed at all. There must be much gold in that wineskin by now. In another day or two Ibni will be waiting for me again, handing me the filthy thing, and I shall have to take away that proof, too, and then we must start all over and wait and wait and wait some more! I cannot do it. I cannot! I'll run away first. I'll slip away to the docks at night, that's what I'll do, and hide on a Nile boat and go wherever it takes me. *Ai!* But then what would I do and how would I live?

Suppose the boat was sailing south, straight into Kush, where men are barbarians, and the gods are not true gods, and people speak gibberish instead of talking sensibly as Egyptians do? Suppose—

A sharp collision with a puffing fat man brought Ranofer up short. Next instant he was knocked off balance again by a group of urchins scrambling past him, to be shoved aside in their turn by workers dashing off the ferry-boats they had just boarded, and into the road. Blinking, Ranofer stared about him. Something was happening. People were shouting, gesturing to each other, beginning to run all in the same direction, southward, toward the palace.

Confused and jostled, Ranofer was swept along by the crowd, trying in vain to catch a glimpse of the palace walls over a sea of bobbing heads. At the sound of drums up ahead, and the squeal of trumpets, his curiosity drove even his anxieties from his mind. He was trying to force his way around a stubbornly motionless donkey when a hand caught his arm.

"Don't hurry, young one. You don't want to see it."

"See what? What is it?" As the crowd streamed past, Ranofer tried impatiently to free his arm, but the donkey's owner held it fast. Turning, Ranofer saw that it was the old man he had met in the papyrus marsh.

"It's an execution, young one. *Ai!* Turn back. You'll see enough killing before you're as old as I."

Ranofer squinted again toward the palace walls, partially visible beyond the palm-fringed garden of a noble-man's villa. The drums were pounding louder, as if to drown out a faint but spine-chilling screaming. The small,

77

struggling figure of a man was being hoisted by one roped foot up the palace wall, to be fastened halfway to the top and left dangling, head downward. Another followed.

"Who are they, Ancient?" Ranofer asked. "What have they done?"

"They are tomb robbers, young one. They broke into the Places of Silence, they stole away the dead pharaoh's treasures and sold them in the market place. Aye, they deserve what they get, but you don't need to watch it."

"Tomb robbers!"

Shivering, Ranofer stared at the distant copper-brown figures writhing against the white wall. Because of these wicked ones and their thievery, the *ba* of some long-dead pharaoh was now starving and destitute in the Land of the West, stripped of the magical protection of his jeweled amulets, robbed of the food and gold and furniture and weapons placed in his tomb to sustain him in luxury for his Three Thousand Years of paradise. If the wicked ones had harmed his mummy, then even his *ba* was dead, for a man's soul could not live if his former body were destroyed. Murder of the soul was a terrible, unnatural crime, hideous to think about.

His flesh crawling, Ranofer hastily turned his back, pulling away from the Ancient. "You are right, I don't want to see it. Let me go, Old One."

"You have wisdom as well as youth. A most unusual combination."

The old man released him, chuckling, and Ranofer started back along the street. Such cheerfulness grated on him today. The Ancient followed, however, giving a tug on his donkey's lead rope.

"Come along, my little Lotus, quicken your hoofbeats.

It is not every day we may walk with one so young and wise. Though indeed, I believe he is trying to run away from us."

"Nay, I am not." Ranofer slowed his pace, ashamed of his surliness. To make amends, he patted the donkey's coarse-haired, fuzzy head. "I see you have sold your papyrus," he added, nodding toward the empty pack baskets.

"Aye, at the sailmaker's. They pay little, but it is enough for Lotus and me. Today was a good day. My baskets near burst under the load." The old man cackled happily, digging six copper ring-coins out of his skimpy sash and exhibiting them to Ranofer. "I shall have cakes with my lentils tonight, and sleep sound on my mat." He whirled the rings on his finger tip, then tucked them away, patting his sash complacently.

"Where do you live?" Ranofer asked.

"Yonder, where the fields of the flower growers end and the desert begins." The Ancient pointed a thin finger westward. "The land there is waterless, but free to anyone. I built me a little house, out of bricks I made with my own hands. Aye, every brick," he repeated, as Ranofer looked at him with sudden interest. "I had no straw to put in them, but they will last my life, and my old donkey's. We are happy there, Lotus and I."

"And the donkey? Is there pasture for him?"

"Not a blade, not a twig, young one. But he has learned to like papyrus." The Ancient gave his high-pitched chuckle, his one eye bright as enamel under the dark line of kohl painted on the upper lid. "Also, I buy him a handful of grain when I have an extra copper. He does not ask much." Affectionately he pulled the little beast's ear, then nodded toward a small street they were approaching. "I leave you here. Farewell, young and wise one. May I never see you hanging from the palace walls."

Cackling cheerfully, he turned off down the crooked lane, the old donkey plodding behind him. Ranofer watched until the shadow swallowed them, then walked on through the dusk-filled streets, in which an occasional torch bloomed now over doorway or gate.

He is happy, the boy thought. He eats, he sleeps in a house he made himself, he has coppers in his sash. Why could *I* not go in the early mornings to the marshes, cut papyrus and sell it to the sailmakers, then be Rekh's apprentice the rest of the day? Holy Mother Mut! Why not? I, too, could live on the edge of the desert, near my father's tomb. I could make bricks for a house. I could . . .

He turned a last corner and stopped, his excited daydreams fading. There was the familiar gate, the ugly street, reality.

I cannot do all that, he thought. I do not even have a donkey to carry the papyrus, and besides, there is Gebu. I must go on waiting.

Next morning there was a stranger in Ibni's place at the vats.

To Ranofer, it was as if the sun had come out at last after weeks of gloomy night. The sky was radiant, the air on his cheek miraculously caressing. Even the ovens seemed things of beauty, and every worker in the shop a skilled and witty fellow. He flew about his tasks, buoyant with triumph and overflowing with energy. Rekh watched him speed back and forth between shop and courtyard, and finally stopped him, smiling.

"You'll not last the day if you keep up this pace. What has got into you? Did you swallow a hive of bees?"

"Nay, Master, I—it is nothing." Ranofer did not know what to say.

"It is something, but I did not mean to pry. May the gods continue to smile on you, little one, for a change. Now. Run to Aba the potter's for me, and get the new crucible to replace that faulty one. Also buy five measures of natron on your way back. Tomorrow, perhaps, you may make me a few gold leaves for Lady Hatasu's bracelet."

Scarcely touching the ground in his rapture, Ranofer sped through the City of the Dead to Aba's shop and from there to the long, low shed in the market place where the dealers in natron and spices and incense sold their wares. He was leaving the market place, with his nostrils still full of rich fragrances, when he saw Ibni the Babylonian emerging from a wineshop just ahead of him. In a panic as sudden as it was unreasoned, Ranofer wheeled into an alley and crouched there, trembling, until the Babylonian was certain to be gone. Even then he dared not venture onto the big streets, but found his way back to the gold-house furtively, through the alleys, like one hiding from pursuers.

Why? Why? he kept asking himself angrily. I've nothing to fear from him. He cannot possibly know it was I who told Rekh. Indeed, it was *not* I who told Rekh. For all Ibni knows, no one told Rekh at all, he merely discovered it.

The rapture was gone from the day, nevertheless. Ibni was here and alive in the City of the Dead, whereas Ranofer had somehow been thinking of him as simply gone, like a puff of smoke. Gebu was still here and alive, too, very much so, and the aftermath of Ibni's dismissal was still to come. Ibni would certainly report to Gebu, if he had not already done so, and would Gebu ever believe Ranofer had nothing to do with it?

He dawdled on the way home, fighting off wave after wave of dread. When he reached the Street of the Crooked Dog he found the gate of Gebu's house open. Torchlight flickered within the courtyard, and there was a mumble of voices. Slowly, on feet that wanted badly to run the other way, Ranofer walked into the courtyard.

The voices belonged to Ibni and Gebu. They stood together in the middle of the paved space, and Gebu held a torch. He extended it and squinted through its light at Ranofer, but merely grunted without interest when he saw who it was, and turned back to Ibni.

"Nay, nay, you have served me well enough, but you're no use to me now, can you not see that? You must find some other master."

"Some other? But how will I live? You promised me."

"I promised you nothing. Come now, be off with you." Gebu started toward the gate, but Ibni clung to his arm and continued his panic-stricken whine.

"You did, aye, you did indeed, at the wineshop that night when we struck our bargain. You said—"

"I said nothing I remember. Be off." Gebu brushed him away with a careless gesture that nevertheless sent him sprawling, and strode on past Ranofer to the gate, where he looked this way and that along the street, holding his torch high.

"Ask the boy!" Ibni cried, apparently catching sight of Ranofer for the first time. "Here's the young one, ask him!" He scrambled to his feet and darted over to Ranofer with his most obsequious smile and the hateful hand-rubbing. "You'll help old Ibni, won't you? I'll wager you missed me today, and wondered where I was. Well, I've been turned off. I've been accused unfairly of someone else's evil doing. Can I help that? I'm the soul of honor, always have been. I trust people's promises. Tell your honored brother how he promised me a copper a day for life if I would serve him at the gold shop."

"I know nothing about it," Ranofer muttered. Brushing past the Babylonian in his turn, he walked quickly to the storeroom and went inside. There he stood in the darkness, clinging to the gritty edge of a shelf and breathing fast with joy. He could scarcely believe his luck. Obviously all was well at last, all was better than he had dared hope. Neither Ibni nor Gebu suspected him of any connection with the affair. Gebu was not in a rage. Incredibly, he did not even seem much interested. How could that be? After all the rages and beatings concerning those cursed wineskins. Still, thought Ranofer, the last time I brought the winekin he did not seem much interested either. He said to Wenamon, "It is of small importance now." Why just *then*? Nothing had changed that day that Ranofer could remember, except that Gebu's mood had suddenly altered, as it often did, and food had been more plentiful since.

He gave it up. What mattered was that Gebu was *not* interested. He was waiting for someone, no doubt Wenamon or that Nile-boat captain, and his mind was on something else. Ranofer prayed to Amon that it might stay there.

Groping along the shelf he found half a bread loaf and several onions. He ate them quickly while the voices went on outside, then dipped a mug of water and drank deep. A sudden roar of anger brought him to the doorway. Gebu had come to the end of his patience with Ibni's whining.

"Tie that tongue of yours in a basket and throw it in the Nile!" he bellowed. "You'll get nothing more from me. Get out and don't come back."

He gave the Babylonian a push that sent him careening out the gate into the arms of Wenamon, who was just coming in. Wenamon dropped his unexpected burden, side-stepped disdainfully, and entered the courtyard.

"Ah, here you are," Gebu grunted.

Ibni, picking himself up, was shrilling venomously. "Very well, very well. We'll see how you fare without me. You'll get no one else to do your bidding at Rekh the goldsmith's. That boy won't, no use to ask him."

Gebu closed the gate in his face. "Him and his paltry wineskins. There are far bigger birds in the air than Rekh the goldsmith. Eh, my friend?" He grinned at Wenamon in a slow, sly way that made Ranofer suddenly uneasy, much as he had enjoyed seeing the last of Ibni. Deciding abruptly that what he wished now was the obscurity of his corner, he started for the acacia tree. Gebu's voice stopped him.

"You, Ranofer! I'm going out. If any should ask for me, send them to Mutra's wineshop." Gebu turned away, then turned back. "About tomorrow. You're finished at Rekh's. Come to the stonecutting shop at first light in the morning. You're apprenticed to me now."

Again he turned to go, leaving Ranofer too stunned at first to move or even speak. Gebu was at the gate before he found his voice.

"Wait! Gebu, wait!"

"Well?" Gebu grunted, turning.

"I—I—please, what did you say just now?"

84

"I said come to the stonecutting shop at first light tomorrow. You will start your apprenticeship."

"But you cannot mean that! You cannot mean—"

"I mean what I say, as always," Gebu said, walking on again. Ranofer rushed after him and caught his sleeve.

"Do you mean I cannot go back to Rekh's? Not ever? Oh, please—"

"Hsttt! Leave off that yowling."

"But please! Oh, please do not make me leave goldworking! I do not want to be a stonecutter, I—"

"Silence. Get out of the way."

"But why are you doing this? Why? I have done nothing."

Gebu glanced at him impatiently. "Did you not hear the Babylonian? It is all over at the goldsmith's. I told you before, I must have some use of you."

"But I earn *deben* at Rekh's, and I bring them all home. Wait, listen to me, please! Let me go to the goldhouse tomorrow, only tomorrow! Rekh will expect me, he does not know—"

"I sent word to him an hour ago. Out of the way, now. Come, friend, we are late."

Pushing Ranofer aside, Gebu opened the gate and raised his torch for Wenamon to pass through.

"Nay, please, *please* let me go tomorrow! Only one more day! I was to make little golden leaves tomorrow."

The gate slammed, the torchlight was cut off by the wall. Ranofer dropped to his knees on the pavement and burst into sobs.

Later, when the moon had climbed high over the courtyard wall, Gebu came home again. Ranofer was waiting for him, huddled deep in the shadow of the acacia tree.

He had rehearsed many times every word he was going to say. Now the time had come. As Gebu bolted the gate behind him and started for the stairs, Ranofer came out of the shadows under the acacia tree and walked across the moonlit pavement toward him.

"Eh? Mother of Night! What is that?" Gebu gasped and fell back a few paces, then straightened himself in anger. "It is you, Worthless One! Curse you, what do you mean coming upon me like that? I thought you were a *kheft*."

"Gebu, I want to talk to you. Please listen."

"Well? Well? Make haste, I'm tired. I want my mat."

"I—it is about the apprenticeship." Ranofer stopped to swallow.

"You will begin it tomorrow, and that is all I have to say about the apprenticeship. Do not waste your breath arguing."

"Nay, I will not. I do not mean to argue. I mean to—to tell you of a plan I have. One that will please you," Ranofer added quickly.

Gebu grunted skeptically, but waited.

"You took me when my father went to the gods," began Ranofer carefully. "Out of the"—he swallowed, but forced it out—"out of the goodness of your heart. I, a gutter waif. If you had not offered me food and lodging I would be sleeping in the dust of the streets, and fighting the dogs for their leavings. Instead I live comfortably on your bread, and you found me work to my liking and did not apprentice me to a fishmonger or—or yourself, until now. I am a burden to you, a great burden. You have said so many times. Have you not, Gebu?" Ranofer cried, forgetting his speech for a moment in his emotion. "Is it not true, all I have said?"

86

"Go on," Gebu said.

Again Ranofer swallowed, a great gulp to give him courage, then poured out the rest in a torrent, for fear he would not get it out at all. "Therefore I wish to take away the burden of myself. I will leave you and not live on your bread, or sleep in your courtyard. Instead I will build myself a little house in the desert out of bricks that I shall make myself, and I will cut papyrus in the marsh and sell it to the sailmakers and buy my own bread and fish and you will not need to trouble about me ever again, any longer. And I can do this, all this, and never again be a burden to you, if only you will—you would—you will buy me a—a donkey, just one very small donkey to carry the papyrus to the sailmakers. It need not be a young donkey, just an old one. I can give you coppers for it when I earn them, and—"

He stopped because Gebu was laughing, at first softly in little bursts, then louder, then in great gales, first doubling over and then leaning far back with his chin tipped to the sky, until the courtyard rang with it and the neighbor across the wall flung back his lattice and began to curse at the noise. Still laughing, even staggering with the force of his laughter, Gebu moved on toward the stairway and up the steps to his room, leaving Ranofer standing silent in the moonlight.

When the door of the upstairs room had creaked shut on its leather hinges and the laughter had at last died away, Ranofer turned and walked slowly back to the acacia tree.

This plan had not succeeded. He had not really, in his heart, ever thought it would.

Chapter VI

THERE was nothing whatever to do but go to the stone-cutting shop next morning, and Ranofer went. Numbly he walked down familiar streets, past the papyrus marsh, past the beginning of the wharves. Then, with a longing glance ahead at the corner where he had always turned to go to Rekh's, he turned unwillingly, traitorously he felt, into a different street, walked past different shops and laboratories and warehouses, and stopped at last before the long, open shed that was Gebu's stonecutting shop.

He had been here only once or twice, and each time had left the place as soon as he could. The whole street rang with the harsh clamor that issued from it, the clatter of chisel on stone, hammer on chisel, granite shrieking against rough granite. It was as different from the music of the little gold hammers as anything could be. Under the low, palm-thatched roof he could see stone-dusted figures moving about among the great blocks and slabs of stone that stood here and there upon the cluttered dirt floor.

One of these figures would be Pai, the foreman, to

whom he must present himself. At this season Gebu was seldom in the shop. He and the greater part of his men were across the river, working on Pharaoh's new addition to the Great Temple, shaping and fitting stones as they were needed for the walls. Here in the shop only great sarcophagi were built, and blocks of stone roughhewn to size, ready for the sculptors. The sculptors themselves worked elsewhere, in their own workshops. No carving was done here, no huge image of the gods or Pharaoh emerged gradually, majestically, from some rough block. No lotus or twining marsh flower traced itself slowly upon an alabaster vase. No little ducks and vultures and baskets, all spelling words, appeared upon a slab under the skillful chisel of an artist. If Gebu had been a sculptor! Ranofer thought. Then, at least, I could have learned to make something beautiful, if not of gold, then of stone. It would have been something worth learning.

There was no use struggling. The gods and Gebu had decreed that he learn this instead: mere cutting and hacking to make the stone ready for others. He sighed and crossed the street to the shop.

Hesitating under the straggling fringe of palm fronds, he peered into the shop's interior, which seemed in deep gloom after the blaze of sun in the road. There were a dozen men moving here and there about their tasks, but no one took the slightest notice of him.

Near where he stood an old man squatted on his haunches beside a great slab of alabaster, examining and blowing at a small hollow in one corner of it. As Ranofer watched, he rose and hobbled to the next corner of the slab, sprinkled black sand from a box upon a chalk mark on the stone, set the bit of a hand drill on the spot, and began to bore another hollow. His face looked patient, worn and kindly, and Ranofer, hoping the man was Pai the foreman, approached him.

"I beg pardon, Master," he said hesitantly.

The old man went on drilling, slapping the stone weights around and around with one gnarled hand while holding the handle of the spindle with the other.

Ranofer raised his voice above the surrounding noises and touched the old man on the shoulder as he spoke. "I beg pardon, Master—"

At his touch the driller jumped and halted the circling stones, then looked around. He seemed surprised to see Ranofer.

"Eh? I thought you were the foreman, come to tell me I am doing it all wrong again. What do you want of me, little one?"

Obviously this could not be Pai.

"I am looking for the foreman," Ranofer said.

"Eh? You'll have to shout—this noise—"

"I am looking for the *foreman,* please," Ranofer shouted.

"Ah, the foreman. That would be Pai, young one. The skinny little man yonder—don't say I called him that!— in the far corner, beside the finishers. What do you want of him? I warn you, do not bother him with trifles, his temper is as short as my thumb."

The old man held up his right thumb, which Ranofer saw with a shock was hacked off at the first knuckle.

"Aye, the wedge slipped, when we were splitting a block of granite twenty years ago," said the old one with a sidewise grin. "And here"—he tucked the handle of the drill under his arm and held up the other hand—"the chisel went awry one time; and here a hammer crushed my finger tip instead of the sandstone. They are stonecutter's hands. Not pretty, nay, not pretty at all, but still fairly useful, praise be to the gods. What do you want of Pai, young one?"

"I am to report to him," Ranofer answered. He could not take his horrified gaze off the old man's mutilated hands. "I am the new apprentice."

"Aye, well, that's a necessary errand. Go and speak to him, but be sure you shout. He hates nothing so much as people who mumble."

"I will. Thank you—er—Master."

"Zahotep, that is my name. Only Zahotep, undercraftsman. Run along with you now. I must drill these sockets or Pai will have my tongue out for wagging so long."

Zahotep turned back to his drill and Ranofer started down the length of the shop, his bare feet cringing away from the gritty carpet of stone chips that covered the dirt floor.

Suppose my hands become like that, he was thinking. Why, I could never work with gold again. I could never handle the little tweezers, or solder a delicate joint, or shape the little gold leaves. I would be good for nothing but rough work, I could never learn skill in anything.

He circled a large block of some dark green stone, upon which two men knelt facing each other, scrubbing the surface with a block of sandstone. Their bodies worked rhythmically back and forth, and the sandstones produced a series of harsh, grating screeches that caused icy trickles to run down Ranofer's spine and set his teeth to aching. He dared not look at their hands.

Beyond him, in the farthest corner, three men worked around a great sarcophagus of pink granite, one stretching a red-chalked string across its side, the others chipping off the high spots where the string touched and the chalk rubbed off. A man stood surveying these works, his thin arms akimbo and his fists, one of which grasped an author-itative-looking stick, propped on his skinny hips. He was scarcely taller than Ranofer, but he looked as if he were made of twisted wire.

Swallowing, Ranofer moved reluctantly to his side and spoke up loudly. "I beg pardon, Master Foreman—"

"Aye? What? Who are you?" snapped Pai, turning his head and thrusting it toward Ranofer all in one rapid motion.

"I am Ranofer, the new apprentice. Gebu bade me find you and—"

"*Gebu?* You will call him Master, here, if you please. So you are the young brother."

"Half brother," Ranofer muttered rebelliously.

Pai either failed to hear or chose to ignore the correc-tion. He was looking with disdain at Ranofer's thin shoul-ders and arms. He seemed even to be counting his ribs.

"He sends me these creatures, then expects me to make something of them," he remarked to no one in particular. "Stonecutter! This one's more fit to become a ratcatcher or a twiner of flower wreaths. Well, come along, come along."

Burning with resentment and humiliation, Ranofer hur-ried after him toward the front of the shop. Pai moved with quick, jerky, impatient strides, swinging his stick, thrusting his head this way and that toward the workers he passed, like a long-necked bird of prey. He led Ranofer straight back to Zahotep and the drill, and pointed to the box of black sand near the alabaster slab.

"That is cutting sand," he shouted. "Put a little into the hole each time Zahotep raises the drill, that the bit may cut deeply. When the sockets are finished, I will set you another task."

He spun around and was off down the room with his jerky gait before Ranofer could do more than nod. Glancing at Zahotep inquiringly, Ranofer picked up the box of sand and squatted near the newly begun socket. Instantly the old man stopped the drill.

"Young one, stand up, or else squat yonder, at the other side, unless you wish your eyes put out. The sand flies and it will cut flesh as well as stone."

Ranofer recoiled so hastily that he stumbled and all but dropped the box.

"There! Now you've spilled some. Don't let Pai see it. Scrape it up with your fingers. Now put a pinch into the hole. This is not ordinary sand, you know, to be spilled and scattered. It is cutting sand. Harder than the hardest stone, it is. Aye, that's enough for the moment. Now stand back."

Zahotep set the drill twirling again, to the gritty, grating rasp of sand against stone, while Ranofer stood well aside, his teeth on edge, and looked disconsolately at the great inert slab which could cost a man his thumb, his skill or his eyesight as the price of his labor on it. What was being fashioned of it, anyway? The next time the drill stopped, he asked Zahotep.

"Why, this is the lid of the outer coffin of Pharaoh's fanbearer, young one. Do you see yonder where the finishers are working? That is the coffin itself. Aye, a grand one it will be, the finest pink granite, with this alabaster lid. I understand His High Lordship has ordered two inner coffins, also. One of acacia wood, finely joined, all painted and gilded, and the other, the innermost, of cedar wood, with his portrait in solid gold set into the lid. *Hai!* He will go to his tomb in style, that great one! Put in the sand, boy. A pinch only, that's enough."

His portrait in solid gold, Ranofer thought as he watched the old man's scarred hand slap the stone weights of the spindle around and around. How wonderful it would be to make such a thing. One would fashion it by raising, like a bowl, like a series of little bowls all joined together, and of strange shapes, one like the nose, one like the curve of the cheek, one like the chin. The mouth. What stakes would I use to shape a mouth in gold? Just the edge of Rekh's smallest one, perhaps, using the smallest of hammers.

The noises of the shop faded and Ranofer stood alone before a line of shaping stakes, moving from one to the other as he tapped out the full curve of a forehead, the clean line of a jaw, the subtle modeling of an upper lip, choosing one and then another little hammer from the rack before him. His mind had paused in puzzled frustration at the golden corner of an eye when Zahotep's touch on his shoulder brought him with a start out of his daydreaming.

"The sand, young one, the sand."

As Ranofer hastily knelt to the box, the old man darted a glance about the shop. "Eh, Pai was not looking that time, but beware of idleness and dreaming, young one. Never think he is not keeping his hawk eye on you. It is everywhere at once, that eye, and if it sees you idling, you'll soon find why he carries that stick."

"I will not dream any more, Zahotep."

Ranofer kept to his word, but it was difficult. His task

was so small, so monotonous, and so utterly lacking in interest that he found it almost impossible to keep even part of his mind on it. A pinch of sand, a long, dull wait, another pinch of sand. He spent what seemed an interminable time watching the hollows slowly form in the four corners of the coffin lid, his eyes glazed from staring at the whirling drill, his ears bombarded with the harsh noises of the shop.

"What are the hollows for?" he asked Zahotep at last, more to fight inattention than because he wanted to know.

"Why, they are the sockets for the pins to fit into," the old man said. He pointed down the shop to the coffin itself. "Do you see those bosses at the top edge of the coffin? One in each corner. When the lid is in place, they will fit just so into our sockets, young one, and make the lid fast. It would be too bad to have a lid slipping and sliding when they carry His High Lordship down into his tomb."

Privately Ranofer wished lid, coffin and Lordship in the tomb already, but he refrained from saying so. Wisely, it turned out, for as he dropped a last pinch of sand into the fourth socket and stood back, he found Pai at his elbow.

"Finished here, eh? Come along then. Zahotep has no more need of you. Hurry, hurry, don't lag behind, I'm a busy man. This way. There's a block of granite yonder ready for the smoothing and I want it out of here by tomorrow. *Nebre!*"

The last word was uttered in a roar so thunderous that Ranofer stopped in his tracks, wondering confusedly if it were some order he was supposed to understand and obey. Instantly Pai's stick was beating a tattoo about his ankles. With an irritable "Don't lag! Don't lag!" the foreman strode on again. Ranofer followed hastily. He realized now that the shout had been merely a summons to someone named Nebre, for a gangling figure was hurrying toward them from another part of the shop. Pai stopped beside a block of granite and pointed a bony finger at it just as the newcomer arrived. He was a boy, obviously another apprentice. He was a year or two older than Ranofer, and a full head taller, with a stolid, sullen face.

Pai gave them rectangular chunks of sandstone and a few barked-out orders. A moment later Ranofer found himself kneeling on the granite block face to face with Nebre, scrubbing back and forth with his sandstone as he had seen the two men doing earlier, and producing the same rasping shrieks from the granite surface.

Pai watched them a moment, mouth tight and eyes suspicious, but evidently he found nothing to criticize, for he turned suddenly and strode away. As soon as he was gone, Ranofer glanced at his companion and ventured a sideways smile.

"A horrid noise this makes," he said.

Nebre looked at him blankly and briefly. He said nothing. Ranofer's heart sank, but he tried once more.

"Have you been here long?"

Again Nebre raised blank, indifferent eyes. "Been here?" he repeated.

"As an apprentice. Have you worked long at the shop?"

Nebre stared a moment, still scrubbing the sandstone back and forth. "Aye," he said finally. His eyes went back to his work.

Ranofer gave up. The longer he knelt there, scrubbing away tediously with his glum companion, the more he desired to raise his chunk of sandstone and bring it down with a crack on Nebre's head. When he thought of Heqet he could scarcely keep the tears from his eyes.

During the next few days Ranofer learned many things about the stonecutter's trade. He learned that sandstoning was even more monotonous than sanding the drill, and far more fatiguing. He learned that roughdressing stone with chisel and hammer, to which he was introduced his third day, was the most fatiguing of all, and while it was slightly less boring it was much more dangerous than either of the other two tasks. He learned that when he grew tired he made mistakes, and when he made mistakes Pai pounced like the leopard of Upper Egypt, raining curses and blows indiscriminately upon his already aching back. He learned through fear to keep his mind every instant upon his work, not only because of Pai's wrath, but because of the painful scrapes and gouges inflicted on his hands by the slightest inattention. With the vision of Zahotep's mutilated hands floating always before his eyes like some evil prophecy, his shoulders and thin arms numb or afire from the unaccustomed labor, and his mind in a prison of monotony, he learned above all to hate the stonecutter's trade with a passion which matched, in intensity, his love for the goldsmith's.

Gebu came once each day to the shop, sometimes at midmorning, usually at the hour of noon when all work ceased for a time and a blessed silence descended on the shop. During this respite some of the men ate food they had brought from their homes. Others sprawled on the gritty floor to talk or snatch a few moments' sleep. Old Zahotep and the two finishers always walked to the wine-shop on the corner and drank their refreshment. Ranofer had no food to bring, no coppers to buy wine, no companion to talk to, and during his first few days he was too tired and sore to sleep or even rest. He merely sat exhausted on a block of stone and watched dully while Gebu conferred with Pai or strode about examining the progress of the work.

Sometimes Gebu went to a little storeroom at the rear of the shop and took out ragged rolls of papyrus or coarse linen, selected one, and growled orders to Pai as he showed it to him. Sometimes he brought a new one to add to the store. Often he took men with him when he left, and sent others back from the temple site to take their places, so there was a continual change of workmen in the shop and Ranofer gave up trying to remember them all.

Occasionally Wenamon came with Gebu and they would pore over some linen scroll together. When this happened Ranofer turned away and made himself as inconspicuous as possible, feeling the usual chill run up his spine at sight of the lank, stoop-shouldered figure, muffled from head to foot in a cloak that made him look like a molting vulture—Wenamon with his silent cat's feet and queerly bright eyes. However, neither Wenamon nor Gebu ever took the slightest notice of him. Even at home Gebu seemed to have all but forgotten his young half brother's existence. He kicked Ranofer awake each morning on his way out of the courtyard, tossed him a copper to buy bread or jerked his thumb toward the storeroom to indicate that there was food laid out. Each evening he appropriated the boy's scanty wages doled out by Pai at the close of every long day. The rest of the time, aside from a few furious cuffings to vent an ill humor, or mocking taunts to enhance a good one, he ignored Ranofer completely. Ranofer was glad enough to return the favor.

At least I am not stealing for him any more, he often told himself as he lay on his ragged mat at night, watching the moon float high and tangle itself in the branches of the acacia tree. Someday, please Amon, I will grow as big as he, and then I will free myself of him somehow and go back to goldworking. And then I will never, never, never look at another block of granite in my life.

Meanwhile he looked at them day after day. His muscles were slow to harden to the rough demands of this sort of labor, and as long as they were taxed beyond their strength each day, their soreness and throbbing disturbed his rest each night, and filled his sleep with fitful dreams.

One night it was not his own aching body but a certain sound that roused him in the night. Quickly he raised up on his elbow. Surely he had heard the thin squeak of the leather hinges on Gebu's bedroom door? Commonplace enough by day, in the depths of night the sound was strange and unnatural. He listened with beating heart, thinking that Gebu was coming to punish him for some error, and expecting every second to hear his step on the stair. He never heard the step. After a long silence he lay back, puzzled. Had he been mistaken? Or maybe, instead of coming out of his room, Gebu had just gone in. But why? From where? Surely it was later than he usually came home from the riverside wineshops. Indeed he had come home from there once already tonight, much earlier in the evening. If the hinges had squeaked just now, he must have been returning from a second trip. And this time, instead of slamming the gate and stumping noisily across the courtyard as usual, he had slipped as silently as his bulk would allow up the stairs and into his room. There had even been a furtive sound about the way the hinge

99

squeaked, as if he were cautiously easing it shut, as if he did not want even Ranofer to know he had been gone.

Queer, Ranofer thought as he lay down to sleep again, shivering. Queer and awful. During these hours *khefts* and mysteries possessed the world; everyone knew that. The *bas* of the dead fluttered out of their tombs and across the dark face of Egypt, revisiting the places they had known in life. The malevolent spirits of the unburied roamed at will seeking mischief they could do. The even more fearful beings like the Woman With Her Head On Backward snatched away any children whose mothers had not bound amulets about their wrists and said the night spell over them before they slept. Surely no errand was urgent enough to draw Gebu out into all that. Then what was the noise?

Something in his thoughts had stirred an elusive memory in Ranofer's mind. Finally he captured it. The night before that day he had brought home the last wineskin from the goldhouse he had heard this same tiny sound. Next morning, filled with his plan, he had believed it was the fluttering wings of his father's *ba* that had half-waked him. Had the *ba* come back again tonight, then? He tried to believe it, but it was difficult. Perhaps he had heard only the squeak of hinges that other night, too, and the *ba* had never come at all. Certainly he had not had much help from it. True, he had waked with the plan that next morning, and the plan had worked, but look at the disaster that had followed!

Still, he told himself hastily, Father could not have known *that* would happen. He tried to help me, he did help me. The rest was Gebu's fault, not his. No doubt he has come back to help me again. No doubt I shall wake in the morning with another plan.

Next morning, however, all was the same, no marvel had occurred, no plan or even hope had come.

A week or so later he was wakened by the same stealthy squeak. There was no mistaking the sound of the hinges this time. Ranofer sat straight up, the goose flesh rising on his arms and little trickles running down his spine. It was the very middle of the night, he could tell from the position of the moon. Yet he could hear furtive footsteps creeping down the stairs. He heard them cross the pavement, heard the faint rattle as the gate was opened, a tiny click as it closed. Incredulous, he let out his long-held breath. Not once but twice—three times, really, since he must now give up believing in the helpful *ba*—Gebu had gone out into that *kheft*-filled darkness at an hour when all men in their right minds stayed in bed. Where could he be going? And why, why?

Ranofer got no answer to his questions, but he did not cease to ask them whenever the nocturnal mystery was repeated, which it was at irregular intervals. He did not, of course, ask any questions of Gebu; he would sooner have thrown himself into a crocodile's jaws. After a time the hinge squeaked less frequently, then only rarely, or else, as his muscles hardened and his work grew correspondingly less exhausting, he slept more deeply and did not hear it. In either case, the matter receded to the back of his mind still unexplained. It was merely one more thing about Gebu that he could not understand.

Chapter VII

THE cool days of winter passed, and the face of Egypt changed in accordance with the rhythm of the Nile, that miraculous river which brought new life and wealth each year to the long valley it watered. Each fall it overflowed its banks and spread over the fields in a silver flood. Islands disappeared and men and animals walked about their business on a crisscross network of dykes. Each winter the waters withdrew, leaving behind a thick new layer of mud so black and fertile that two crops grew in Egypt while other lands eked out one. Slowly the river shrank as the grain sprouted, grew, and covered the black with emerald; continued to shrink under the ever more powerful sun as the emerald ripened into gold.

Now it was harvest time. Every available man went out into the fields to gather in the gold of grain and fodder. In the wake of the reapers' scythes the black land showed again through the stubble, no longer moist and rich but bone-hard, desiccated, and beginning to crack in all directions under the burning sun. Eventually the cracks would spread into treacherous gashes, sometimes ten or fifteen feet deep and wide enough to trap a man's leg. Temple building ceased in this season to free more men for the fields. The faces in the stonecutting shop changed accordingly. Only top craftsmen and young apprentices continued to work the stones. Gebu was in and out of the shop all day, usually remaining for several hours in either the morning or the afternoon, personally overseeing or working alongside his craftsmen.

The presence of the master, Ranofer discovered, sharpened Pai's already sharp eye and diminished his short temper to the vanishing point. To work under Pai these days was to feel yourself caught in a swarm of angry bees, all stinging, buzzing, and hurling themselves at you tirelessly. The only respite from the torment, which in Ranofer's resentful opinion caused more mistakes than it corrected, was during the midday break. In order to escape for a time from the sight of Pai as well as the sound of him, Ranofer began leaving the shop each day. He walked about the streets until the changing slope of his shadow on the heat-baked dirt underfoot told him he must return and begin again his interminable chipping at the rough red granite slab that would eventually become one side of the High Priest's outer coffin.

One midday, forty long and miserable days after his apprenticeship had begun, his feet turned of themselves toward the Street of the Goldsmiths, and carried him along the well-known way until he stood no more than a pebble's toss from Rekh's courtyard wall. He went no closer. Until now he had not dared to come this far. From the longing that rose inside him as he stood looking at the familiar, friendly gate, he knew it had been a mistake to come at all. Still he stood, and stared, and remem-

103

bered, until he felt the sun burning down on his bare feet and knew his shadow had crept behind him.

He turned quickly, hurried along the street, and almost collided with somebody who shot out of the Apprentices' Quarters at that moment. Ranofer found himself looking into Heqet's astonished face.

"Ranofer!" cried his friend, and the face split into a grin of delight.

"Greeting, Heqet," Ranofer said, but he backed off a step or two, suddenly overcome with self-consciousness. He had not meant to be caught hanging about Rekh's shop like a stray dog. The stone dust that powdered him seemed a badge of slavery, and the two bloodstained rags about fingers of his left hand proclaimed the unskilled depths to which he had fallen. No longer was he the budding craftsman who in spite of a menial position in the goldhouse could teach apprentices their tasks. Heqet would now be far ahead of him in knowledge and skill, and needed nothing he could offer. Ranofer hid his hands behind him and scuffed a toe in the dust, realizing unhappily that Heqet was doing the same; self-consciousness was catching.

"Well!" Heqet said with an effort at heartiness. "You're quite a stranger these days, as the caterpillar said to the butterfly."

Ranofer smiled in spite of himself, encountered Heqet's friendly, questioning eyes, and the self-consciousness diminished.

"Aye," he answered. "To myself as well as you. I do not know myself as apprentice to a stonecutter. I do not even wish to," he added, spitting contemptuously in the dust.

"You do not like it?"

"I hate it."

Heqet was silent. Ranofer did not blame him. There was nothing to say to such a statement.

"And you, Heqet?" he went on quickly. "Tell me how the work goes at Rekh's."

"It goes well. I have learned to draw wire and Sata is teaching me to solder."

This time Ranofer was silent. Sata's face floated before his eyes an instant. Even with the scowl that his memory reluctantly but justly added, it seemed a face as kindly as a father's compared to Pai's.

Pai's image suddenly blotted out the other, and Ranofer started guiltily. "The midday is over. I must run or I'll taste that foreman's stick."

"But wait, we've scarcely said a word to each other."

"I know. I wish it were different."

"Can you not come again?"

"Nay, I—" Ranofer glanced toward the goldhouse and turned away. "I cannot come here."

"Then somewhere else? At the day's end, perhaps? To-day! I'll meet you wherever you like."

"I can do *that*," said Ranofer, realizing for the first time that there was nothing to prevent it, that working in different shops, at different trades, did not mean he and Heqet must keep to different worlds. "I *will* do it. Where shall we meet? The ferry landing?"

"Aye, or better, the fish dock beyond. You'll surely come, now?"

"I'll come. Good-by till then."

With a wave Heqet made off toward the goldhouse, and Ranofer started at a run back to his red granite slab.

His feet were light with the thought of seeing Heqet again, seeing him often, perhaps every day. All afternoon he thought of nothing but the coming meeting, and when the day was over at last he was out of the shop and running toward the fish dock the instant his coppers were in his sash.

Heqet had farther to come. Ranofer stood for some moments among the great nets spread out to dry on the dock before he saw the familiar lithe figure, so much better fleshed than his own, squirming through the crowd about the ferry landing and running toward him.

"I was afraid you might change your mind," Heqet panted, joyfully clapping him on the shoulder. "Come, let us get away somewhere."

"The thicket by the river is cool and private," Ranofer suggested. As they started along the road he added, "Why did you think I would change your mind?"

"I don't know. You're an odd one sometimes." Heqet smiled sideways at him. Ranofer returned the smile uncomfortably, but could think of nothing to say.

They turned off the road presently into the lane between the flower fields, then followed the meandering path into the thicket. Foliage arched over their heads, casting a welcome shade made denser by the stands of tall reeds. Here there was still mud underfoot, cool and soothing after the hot baked clay of the roads.

"Ah! I can hear my toes telling each other what a fine fellow I am to bring them here!" Heqet said. "Look—that would make a fine place to sit." He pointed to a spot veiled from the path by only a thin fringe of swaying rushes. Something had crushed the grasses and weeds beyond down into a little nest. Heqet sloshed through the stretch of watery mud to it, then turned and bowed elaborately to Ranofer. "Come into my storeroom, as the pelican said to the fish."

Ranofer grinned and obeyed. It did look like a little cool, green room with walls of foliage, a door of sedge stalks, and a thick, springy carpet of matted undergrowth. There was just space enough for them to sit side by side and stretch their feet out.

"Now," Heqet said firmly. "Tell me about the stonework. Come, don't pull into your shell like a tortoise. It will do you good to say out loud how much you hate it. Curse if you like. There's no one to hear but me, and I don't mind."

Ranofer could not help laughing, and as he laughed he felt a knot untie somewhere inside him and realized he felt better already. It was impossible to stay in a shell with Heqet around, and it was impossible to feel altogether gloomy. He began to talk about the stonecutting shop. It was noisy, it was gritty, it was altogether horrid, the foreman was a living wasps' nest, the other apprentice a glum and stupid nobody with a chunk of granite where his head ought to be.

"That's better," Heqet said with satisfaction. "And what do you do? Shape blocks, or what?"

Ranofer told him, fairly spitting out his frustration, what he did, and how he must keep his mind on it, no matter how tired or bored he was.

"Otherwise this happens," he said, extending his bandaged fingers. "And worse, oh, much worse! The undercraftsman, Zahotep, his hands are a ruin. Heqet, if my hands became like his, I could never go back to goldworking."

107

He had dropped his voice with the horror he felt, and for once Heqet, too, was subdued, his eyes fixed on the bloodstained bandages.

"You mean to go back to goldworking someday, then, in spite of all?" he said.

"I do!" Ranofer flashed him a belligerent look. "You may think I cannot, but I will find a way somehow. I even know a way. I have a plan."

"You do? What is it?"

But Ranofer did not want to talk about the plan, about the donkey and the little house at the edge of the desert, and studying with Zau. It sounded too improbable, it was safer not told—not yet.

"No matter," he said. "Tell me instead about the gold-house. Is all the same there?"

"Nay, not without you."

Ranofer smiled one-sidedly. "No doubt Sata and Geryt and the others weep for me each morning before the gold is weighed. Aside from my absence, is all the same?"

"Others are absent also. Ibni, to whom good riddance. And the scribe—you remember Hotepek—left a week before harvesting began. His child has the falling sickness. Hotepek is taking her to Abydos to the priest of Ra there. Rekh fashioned a little amulet from the sweep for her, so the priests might say their spells over it. Meanwhile we have a new scribe."

"And you, you have learned to draw wire? And to solder?"

"I am learning, I think. As the hare said when he tried to fly," Heqet added wryly. "So far I have not succeeded in making anything stick to anything else. But no doubt next week, or perhaps next year . . ."

"Aye," Ranofer said. "My boxes fell apart too, at first. Don't lose hope. One day they will stick, and then you will have no more trouble."

"Your father taught you to solder?"

"Aye, but no doubt I have forgotten, it has been so long. And it will be longer before I can do it again. Curse Gebu and his granite!" The boys sat in silence a moment, then Ranofer added, "I would rather have Gebu for a master, though, than that friend of his."

"What friend is that?"

"Wenamon the mason. He comes often to the shop. He came today. He reminds me of a *kheft*."

"Wenamon," repeated Heqet, frowning. "Does he wear a long cloak, winter and summer?"

"Aye! That's the one."

"I have seen him often. He lives near the Apprentices' Quarters. He makes me shiver, but the man I sometimes see him with is worse. A great, heavy-shouldered fellow with a scowl and a face like stone—" Heqet broke off and turned to Ranofer with a sudden question in his eye.

"That is Gebu," Ranofer told him.

Heqet's expression changed. He looked at Ranofer as if he had never really seen him before, and there grew in his eyes a look of such troubled pity that Ranofer flushed and got quickly to his feet.

"It is late, the dark will be here soon."

"Wait." Heqet scrambled up, too, then hesitated as if he did not know how to say what he wanted to. "I was thinking," he said at last, "if we met often, in the evening or even at midday, I could tell you all I learn. I mean at the goldhouse. Unless it was something you'd learned already. That way you would have the knowledge. Then when you come back to Rekh's someday, you will lack only the practice."

Light broke and grew inside Ranofer; he felt as if the sun were coming up. "We *could* do that! You could learn from Sata and I could learn from you."

"Aye! Aye!" Heqet became very excited. "We'll do it every day. I will meet you here tomorrow. We could come at midday and eat our food here."

Ranofer, who never had food to eat anywhere at midday, saw more shame ahead and drew into his shell again. "Nay. That is, I do not know if I can get away."

"You got away today," Heqet reminded him.

"Aye, but—"

"Sata says I am to try beading in the morning. Have you learned that yet?"

"Nay, but—" Beading! The temptation was too strong. "All right, midday. I'll come."

I must get some food to bring, somehow, Ranofer thought as he hurried toward home. I will save part of what I have tonight, and part of the morning's. Perhaps Gebu will leave two loaves this time.

Gebu left the usual one, but there were three onions in a dish when Ranofer explored the dusky storeroom. Jubilant, he tucked one of them into his sash, along with half the loaf. When he had eaten the rest, however, and drunk deep from the water jar, he felt almost as empty as before. There was a small keg of salted fish in the storeroom; its enticing aroma always filled the place, but Gebu kept it sealed. Ranofer wandered over and inspected it, just in case, and found the usual fresh wad of clay covering the latch, with the imprint of Gebu's ring pressed into it. He wandered away again, out into the courtyard, fingering the half loaf in his sash. Tomorrow midday seemed far away and relatively unimportant compared to his present growling stomach.

I will eat just half of the half, he decided. And I will still save the onion.

But half the onion was gone, too, before he slept. In the morning he found a dish of stewed lentils on the store-room shelf. He looked at it in dismay; how could he tuck half of *this* into his sash? Scorning himself for his weakness of last night, he ate the lentils and started for the shop. A pinch of bread and half an onion. A fine midday meal to produce before Heqet's already pitying eyes.

I will dig a lotus root on my way to meet him, Ranofer thought, resolutely ignoring the fact that he had no knife to pare the root, and that the strong anise flavor of lotus root had always made him feel slightly nauseated.

The detour to find a stand of lotuses cost him several precious moments of his midday hour, and when he arrived at the little green room in the thicket, muddy root in hand, Heqet was there waiting. The latter looked up at him apologetically.

"After all, I did not learn beading this morning," he said. "I had to make charcoal instead. I am sorry. But I will learn it soon, and then I will tell you."

"No matter," Ranofer said, concealing his sharp disappointment. He sat down beside Heqet, eying the chunk of golden cheese, the two loaves, the salt fish and the figs spread out on his friend's lap. "I ate most of mine on the way here," he said carelessly, wondering why he had not thought of this excuse before. He took the bit of dry bread and the slightly wilted half of the onion from his sash, avoiding Heqet's eyes. When he had finished them—which he did in a humiliatingly short time—he surveyed the lotus root, wiping it on the mat of crushed grasses and wondering how he was going to cut it.

"I hate cheese," Heqet said suddenly. "I wish they would give us something else to eat with our bread at the Apprentices' Quarters. Now we never have lotus root, except boiled, and I like it better raw, don't you?"

"I don't like it at all," said Ranofer, startled into truthfulness. "Do you really hate cheese?"

"I do. Let's trade."

Ranofer held out the lotus root almost before the words were spoken. He had not tasted cheese since his father died. "I am sorry, I have no knife to cut the lotus," he confessed.

"I have. Would you like a piece of this fish, too? And a fig? I have more than I want."

Ranofer caught his breath. Such good fortune was almost impossible to believe. It *was* impossible to believe. In the act of reaching for the fish Heqet held out, he snatched his hand back.

"You don't have more than you want," he said angrily. "You don't hate cheese, either. You're lying."

Heqet eyed him a moment, then grinned uncertainly. "All right. But you were lying, too, when you said you ate most of your food on the way here. I could tell by the look of it you saved it from last night."

"And if I did?" Ranofer jumped to his feet, furious and shaking with humiliation. Heqet stood up too, an impatient scowl on his usually amiable face.

"I mean only that you have not enough food at your table. Is that so bad? Why must you get angry with me?

112

Come, I have plenty. Take half and let's forget the matter. It's stupid to quarrel."

"It's stupid to waste *pity* on your friends, who do not need it!" yelled Ranofer.

"Merciful Osiris," said a mild voice behind him. He whirled and saw the Ancient standing there, his hands parting the thin curtain of sedge stalks which hid their nest from the path. Beyond him was the placid, soft-eyed face of the donkey, Lotus.

"Will there be a fight soon?" the old man inquired. "Perhaps you would let me watch it. I enjoy a good fight on occasion."

"Nay, we are not going to fight," Ranofer muttered. "We are friends."

"Friends! Are you indeed?" The Ancient's straggly eyebrows climbed halfway up his forehead. "Now that's an odd thing. When I was a youth, friends laughed together and spoke in peaceable voices. Only enemies stood glaring and yelling, with their fists doubled. But then, times change." He shrugged and sighed so philosophically that Heqet burst out laughing, and even Ranofer smiled sheepishly.

"Come, old one," Heqet said. "You be our judge. This fellow here has more pride than Pharaoh. He considers himself too fine to accept a gift of something we both know he needs and wants."

"What gift?" asked the Ancient, pursing his lips judiciously.

"Food. Look at the flesh on his ribs, if you can find any. Yet he insists that I sit here like a pig in a trough rooting my way through cheese and fish and bread and figs while he eats a wilted onion. Is he a friend when he finds pleasure in ruining the taste of everything for me?"

Ranofer stared at him. "Is that the way it seems to you?"

"Aye." Heqet gave a defiant kick at the food scattered upon the matted ground. "If you will not take half this stuff, then I don't want the other half."

"I did not know I was ruining the taste," Ranofer said humbly.

The Ancient began to chuckle. "You need no judge, I see. But perhaps you will let me share your bower, which was my Lotus's before you came. I have food to eat, too."

"Come in." Ranofer stepped back as Heqet triumphantly began arranging the food in two piles. "This place was your donkey's?"

"Aye, how did you think such a nice little nest was made? It is his rolling place. I eat my bread and he takes his midday rest here. It is no matter. He can make another as easily as you can eat that cheese." Smiling slyly at Ranofer, the old man lowered himself to the ground and took a packet from his sash. "Now then, let us barter. In exchange for a fig or two I will share my nelumbo nuts, the best you ever ate."

"Done," Heqet said promptly, handing over a fig.

Ranofer liked nelumbo nuts, but figs were food for the gods, and to him rare as rain in Egypt. He hesitated just long enough for the Ancient to add quickly, "A fig or whatever else you care to barter."

"A loaf, perhaps?" Ranofer said self-consciously. He could not yet feel it was really his loaf to barter.

"Half a loaf, that's a fairer trade," the Ancient told him. He unwrapped his packet, in which were onions and a salt fish, and placed the fig and the half loaf beside them grave-ly. Then he produced from another fold of his voluminous sash one of the cone-shaped fruits of the nelumbo plant. There were fully twenty-five seeds studding the top of it, each as large as the end of his thumb. When they were cracked, and the almondlike, sweet white nuts inside freed from the bitter green leaf that separated their two lobes, they added the last touch to what seemed to Ranofer a feast suitable for Pharaoh himself and all his court. It was true, too, that Heqet appeared to enjoy his share the more for watching Ranofer eat. When he took out his knife and cut into the lotus root, he offered Ranofer a wedge of it.

"Nay," Ranofer said. "I was not lying. I really do not like those."

"And I really do, so I was not lying either, at least not about that," Heqet said blandly, offering the wedge to the Ancient instead.

"Eh, well, I'd be lying if I refused it," said the old man, taking it off the point of Heqet's knife. To Ranofer he added, "I'll show you where the nelumbos grow. There's a good stand of them just yonder, toward the river. You could have them every day if you wanted them. Who is it sets your table, young one, that you have only a wilted onion for your midday?"

"My half brother. Gebu, the stonecutter. I'm apprenticed to him."

"It is little food for such hard work."

"It is not always so little. This morning I had lentils. Besides, it is no matter. I will not be at such work long, if I can help it."

"Nay? Then what do you mean to do?"

"I mean to be a goldsmith, like my father."

"A goldsmith. *Ai!* That is a fine craft." The Ancient's sharp old eye lingered a moment on Ranofer's face before he added dubiously, "It is also a difficult craft, young one, I've heard tell."

Heqet dusted the crumbs from his fingers. "He tells you one half of it, Ancient, and not the other, like the dog who confesses he ate the bone, when the whole haunch is missing. Last winter he was more skilled than any apprentice at Rekh the goldsmith's, though he worked only as a porter. His father taught him more of goldworking than I'll know before another year has passed."

"But how is it, then, that you now work on the stones?" the Ancient asked.

"Because—" Ranofer broke off, exchanging a glance with Heqet, whose lips were tightly shut. "Because of a wineskin," Ranofer finished. "I do not care if *he* knows, Heqet. He will say nothing. Let us tell him."

They did so, while the reeds rustled stiffly in the sun-heated air, and the old donkey chewed patiently on the leaves a little distance away, where he had rolled himself out another nest. Before the meal was finished and the story ended there were three friends instead of two in the little green-walled chamber.

When they parted on the path a few moments later, Heqet said, "Let us meet again tomorrow. Will you come, Ancient?"

"Aye, unless I'm hired at the docks to haul cargo, or unless Lord Crocodile gets me first." The old man's shrill cackle sounded as he tugged his donkey to its feet. "Watched any hangings lately?" he added slyly to Ranofer.

"Nay."

"*Hai!* That's right. That's wise. Trouble enough in this

world without borrowing from others. Well, may Ra shine upon you, and Mother Mut smile."

The Ancient and his little beast trudged off through the papyrus, and the boys went back to their tasks, Ranofer strengthened by the unaccustomed food and companionship, and buoyant with the thought of more tomorrow.

Chapter VIII

ALL through the spring, while the heat swelled and the river shrank, Ranofer and Heqet met as often as they were able, at midday or in the evening after their day's work was done. Frequently the Ancient joined them, bringing nelumbo nuts and his cackling laugh, and his sly, wise teasing. One morning after a great many delays Heqet was finally instructed in beading, at the goldhouse. That evening he told Ranofer all about it.

"It is easy. You could do it any time you liked, if only you had the tools. Now, do you remember that charcoal block with the tiny round depressions in it? Rekh always keeps it next the big furnace, on that storage shelf."

"Aye, I remember it."

"Well, you simply melt scraps of metal in those little hollows. I used the sweep for it today. When the puddles turn the right color, you know, then you take the block from the fire and in a minute you turn the beads out. Then you boil them in pickle and wash them in water, and there they are, ready to be soldered to whatever you like. Rekh is using them for a bracelet now. He is making one for a judge's lady. Aye, and there's another way to make them, too. You make little rings by winding the wire about a straight, thin rod and then clipping each twist."

"Aye, links. I learned long ago to make links."

"Very well, then, you make links, and you pack some of them on a layer of finely broken charcoal in a clay box. Then you cover those with another layer of charcoal bits. Then you put in more links. You keep it up until the box is full, then you wire the lid on and heat it until box and wire are redder than the fire. When you shake the charcoal out, by Amon, it is surprising! The links have all turned to little round grains."

"The first way sounds quicker."

"Aye, but the second is more fun." Heqet grinned. "Said the rat as he walked straight past the cheese and robbed the trap. I will admit it's surer to use the charcoal block, where you can see the gold melt. I had to try twice before I got the box to the right shade of red. The first time I opened it I still had links, and Sata cuffed me all over the shop. I've no doubt *you* could do it, though, if you had the chance to try."

"Someday I will," Ranofer said, but he looked at his gritty hands, rough from a day's sandstoning, adorned with one of the ever-present bandages, and wondered dismally if the day would ever come.

He wondered more and more as the spring progressed and nothing changed in his life except that Gebu was sometimes in a good mood and sometimes in a bad. It was beginning to seem to him that he had only dreamed once of goldworking, of learning from his father, of working about Rekh's shop and making the little leaves, and that now he was awake once and for all, to a world of dreary stone. Heqet continued to describe every process he was

119

taught at the goldhouse, but the more interesting the processes, the more complicated they were, and the harder they were to describe. Besides, it was not long before Ranofer realized he could never increase his skill merely by listening to Heqet's earnest explanations. It was practice he required, not just information.

"I cannot learn these things," he told Heqet finally one day. "Not this way. It is useless. Could you shape a bowl if someone merely told you how to do it? Nay. Not until you held the hammer in your hand, and learned the sound it must make, and the way the stake must ring. Let us give it up, Heqet. It only makes me hate stonecutting more than I do already."

The Ancient, who was sitting beside them cracking nelumbo nuts, glanced up at him. "Why is it you hate stonework so, young one? It is a good trade."

"A good trade?" Ranofer exclaimed scornfully. "It is a clod's trade! It is a trade that spoils a man's hands and makes him a dullard and near breaks his back every day, and—"

He went on until he was out of breath, while the old man listened in silence, cracking his nuts and nodding patiently now and then.

"Aye, very well," the Ancient said when Ranofer had finished at last. "It is a clod's trade and you hate it. But it is a trade, young one. A man can earn his living by it, and not too poor a living either. Now I—" He paused, carefully removed the bitter leaf from the lobes of a nut with his knobby old hands, and handed the kernels to Heqet. "I never learned a trade at all." He lifted his one bright eye and looked directly at Ranofer. "My father was a cattle drover in Lower Egypt, and I helped him. We wandered

here and there, and when he died and went to the gods—
may his Three Thousand Years be full of joy—another
drover took his place, and I had to wander alone. I came
here at last and worked on the docks while I was young
enough and strong enough, but how I used to envy those
who knew a craft, and went each day to a shop, and took
home their coppers safe and sure each night, and went
again in the morning, instead of having to wonder who
would hire them today. *Hai!* Remember, young one, you
will be an old one too someday, though it is hard for you
to think so now. And it is not good to be an old one without a trade. If it is stonecutting instead of goldworking,
that is a pity. But learn it well anyway, while you have
the chance."

"But you—" Ranofer faltered. "I thought you—you have
the donkey, and the little house on the edge of the desert."

"Aye, I do not complain," the Ancient said, smiling. "But
I have not always had them. I know what I speak of, boy,
and though you may think me a dismal old crow, you'll
do well to heed my cawing."

No doubt he is right, Ranofer told himself as he walked
back to the shop. But he had no heart for trying to become a good stonecutter, or for taking notice of anything
in the shop beyond what he was forced to learn.

One day, a day of glaring, shimmering heat when one's
skin drew tight from dryness and even seemed likely to
crack into crazily spreading wounds as all the fields had
cracked, Heqet appeared at the thicket in a state of great
excitement.

"Ranofer!" he panted, flinging himself down upon the
matted rushes beside his friend. "Tomorrow Rekh is
sending me to the workshop of Zau the Master, to fetch a

stake. He did not say I must go alone. Do you want to go with me?"

"But I—but I cannot." Ranofer was stammering with the force of his wanting to go. "I will be all day at the stone shop."

"I am to go at the day's end, after work is done."

"Then I can! Unless Pai delays me with some stupid task. He must not. I will stay out of his sight and slip away when the first man lays down his tool. How did it happen? What sort of stake are you to fetch?"

"One of Zau's own design, which he uses in some way for the golden masks he makes to fit over the faces of the great ones when they go to their tombs. The stake has cracked and he is ordering a new one made. He has given Rekh leave to take the old one and have it copied for his own work."

"He is generous as well as great."

"Rekh is a kinsman of his brother's wife. You will meet me, then? Perhaps at the big tree by Aba the potter's. Then we will go on together. Zau's shop is near the palace."

"I know. Aye, I'll be there. My thanks, friend."

The next day dragged even more slowly than usual, with this prospect glittering at its end. Ranofer nicked his hand twice with a carelessly placed chisel as visions of the wonderful objects he would see in Zau's shop danced through his mind.

I will speak to Zau again, really speak to him, face to face, he kept thinking. He will ask me how I fare, and I will tell him everything, only little by little, as he asks. I must not pour it all out like some imbecile and make him think I ask for pity, Amon forbid it! I will answer his questions only, and be modest and proud like my father, but he will find it out, all about Gebu and the gold stealing and that I was taken from Rekh's and forced to work here among these cursed blocks of stone. And then he will frown and say that it is an evil thing, a slap in the faces of the gods, that the son of Thutra the goldsmith should be a stonecutter's apprentice. Aye, and he will remember that he once saw my little cups and arm bands, and that they showed skill, very unusual skill, and he will grow very stern at the thought of my hands being ruined and my days wasted, and he will go straight to Gebu and tell him he must release me, so that I can come and be his pupil.

Ranofer's thoughts slowed uneasily, then stopped. Daydreams had lost some of their old power; these days reality kept creeping in and ruining them with stony facts. He could not persuade himself, even in fancy, that Gebu would care a copper what Zau thought or said. Nor could he see himself speaking of the thieving. Nor could he see any way to become Zau's pupil, however warm the possible invitation, without a place to live and a way to earn his fee. The donkey. Zau would not present him with a donkey, any more than Gebu would.

Catching sight of Pai striding toward him with jaw outthrust and stick lifted, Ranofer bent hastily to his work.

No matter, he told himself. I shall see Zau again, and speak a little with him, and see things he has made. Perhaps I may even get to watch him work a little. It is enough, is it not? Yesterday brought no such gift from the gods, nor will tomorrow.

He was waiting at Aba the potter's late that afternoon when Heqet came running down the dusty street. They started at once for Zau's house, talking excitedly as they

threaded their way through the press of home-going The-
bans. The parched and wounded earth was rosy with the
sun's dying, and the Nile, shrunk to a red-brown trickle
in its season of death, looked exactly like what Ranofer
knew it was, the last feeble flowing of blood from the body
of the beloved, murdered god Osiris.

The nearer they drew to the palace, the thinner the
crowds became, and when they turned away from the
river into the Street of the Carpenters, they found the
street almost deserted, with the shops closed for the night.

"We must find a turning somewhere near here," Heqet
said. "Zau lives on the Street of Good Fortune."

"I know."

"You have been there before? With your father, perhaps?"

"Aye, but it was long ago. I remember little. I think it
has very high walls, with a purple vine tumbling over
them near the gate, and treetops showing behind. Nay, I
am not sure about the trees. But I know the design worked
into the grille of the gate. It is a straining vat and cloth, the
sign for 'gold.'"

Heqet turned large eyes upon him. "You can read? Like
a scribe?"

"Nay, I learned a little, when my father lived among
men. Look, here is a turning."

"Aye, it is the right one. Rekh said there would be a
wineshop on one side, and a tall palm opposite."

Their footsteps quickened as they left the rows of carpenters' shops and entered the other street. It was almost
another world. There were high walls on either side, with
the tops of palms and acacias showing above them. There

124

was no dust, much quiet, and a pervading fragrance of flowers and wealth. Here lived Pharaoh's favorites among the artisans. Farther along, beyond their comparatively modest houses, the street broadened and the grand villas of judges and officials rose on either side in the midst of large gardens and vineyards. At the extreme end of the street, like the dazzling tip on an arrow, the two boys could see a corner of the palace walls, stained pink by the sunset.

"Here it is," Heqet exclaimed, pointing. "High walls with a purple vine. But there are other purple vines," he added uncertainly.

They walked to the gate and found the gold sign worked in its grille.

"It is the one," Ranofer whispered.

"Then we open the gate and go in. That is what Rekh said."

Diffidently Ranofer raised the latch, opened the gate just wide enough for them both to squeeze through, and closed it carefully behind them. Immediately all the past miserable months fell away from him as he stood breathing the hot, well-remembered odor of molten gold and hearing the chiming of a little hammer. They had entered Zau's shop, not his dwelling, which must be beyond that inner courtyard wall. Across the clay-paved court was a row of stalls roofed with palm fronds. In the largest an old man knelt on a mat before a low workbench. Otherwise the shop was empty.

As Zau half turned, both boys bent their heads, each with one hand on the opposite shoulder in the gesture of respect.

"Who comes?" said a deep, even voice. "Straighten yourselves, so that I may see something besides the tops of your heads."

They obeyed hastily. "Greeting, Master of all Goldsmiths," Heqet said. "I come from Rekh. He has sent me to fetch the—"

"Aye, aye, the stake. I remember. Come here."

Heqet started across the court and Ranofer followed him dreamily, past small basket-shaped furnaces in which the fires were dying, past the balance scales and the washing vats. He was conscious of the gleam of gold here and there, the round shapes of crucibles, the smoothness of the clay floor under his bare feet, so different from the grit and stone dust of his present life. The familiar and well-loved details receded into the background, however, as they approached the austere old man leaning with one elbow on the workbench, a little copper hammer dangling from his long-fingered, supple, corded hand. Ranofer remembered the hand well and the broad, strong-boned face with its thinning eyebrows and full, carven mouth, but he had forgotten how austere Zau's manner was, and how difficult it had always been in the old days to summon courage to utter a few words in his presence, even when his father was beside him, even when Zau had asked some question of him first.

I need not have worried that I would pour out my troubles like an imbecile, Ranofer thought. I cannot even open my mouth. What made me think that I would dare to speak to this Great One? I, a nobody, a ragged stone-cutter's boy?

He stood tongue-tied, feeling his very existence an intrusion, while Zau directed Heqet to the farthest stall, and to the cupboard where he would find the stake. Then, when Heqet had bowed and hurried along the row of stalls on his errand, Zau glanced at Ranofer. For a moment that seemed as long as a day his eyes rested indifferently on Ranofer's face. Zau started to turn away, but hesitated; his scanty brows drew together in a puzzled expression.

"I know you, do I not?" he said.

Ranofer tried twice before he found his voice and discovered how to make it work. "Aye, Master. That is, you knew my father."

"Your father. *Ast!* It is the son of Thutra, my departed friend. May his Three Thousand Years be full of delight."

"If Amon wills," Ranofer murmured automatically.

"Aye, Thutra's boy. And your name is?"

"Ranofer, Master."

"Ranofer. I remember. How do you fare now, Ranofer? You are apprenticed at some goldhouse, I suppose."

"Nay, I—I am apprenticed to my half brother, Gebu the stonecutter."

"Stonecutter!" Zau's eyebrows lifted. "That is strange. I thought I remembered that you were interested in the smith's art. But then, I forget things nowadays." Indifferent again, he turned back to his work.

But I was, I am, I am! Ranofer wanted to cry out. He could not make a sound, confronted by Zau's back. Why did I say that? he thought furiously. It was all wrong, I should have explained first, then—

He forgot even his self-recrimination as his eye fell on the object lying on Zau's table. It was half finished, a wide gold collar formed of tiny chains strung with innumerable golden bees, each one delicately and imaginatively conceived, superbly wrought. Without knowing it he edged forward until he stood at the old man's shoulder, looking down at the wonder and breathing hard.

Zau, glancing up at him, followed his fascinated gaze. "An order from the palace," he remarked. "Sixty days hence, at the festival of the High Nile, Queen Tiy will wear about her beautiful neck Pharaoh's newest gift. Aye, it will be complete by then, if I keep working."

He picked up a tiny hammer and began to reshape a golden wing tip which seemed to the boy already perfect. Ranofer watched the long-fingered, agile old hands and clasped his own behind him. They felt harsh with stone dust, rough and clumsy.

"Oh, that I might learn to make such things!" he whispered.

The hammer paused, uplifted, as Zau shot him a keen glance over his shoulder. Then he went back to his hammering. "You will never learn to make them at a stone-cutting shop."

Ranofer gathered all his courage, resolved to right his mistake. "It is Gebu's will, not mine, that I am apprenticed there, Master. He took me from Rekh's goldhouse, where I had been working." Not learning, only working, he told himself fiercely. Get everything straight this time. "He took me from Rekh because I—because he—because I—" He stopped, swallowing hard. He could not believe it safe to mention the theft of gold and the name of the thief in the presence of any goldsmith. Even Zau might think he had stolen it himself.

"Because you lacked skill, perhaps?" Zau said.

"Nay, Master."

"Or aptitude?"

"Nay. I—"

"Or diligence? Goldworking is not for the lazy."

"Master, I would ask nothing better than to spend every moment of my life at it. It was nothing to do with me, I did not want to leave, I did not want to! But Gebu—"

Again Ranofer floundered and fell silent. Zau put down his hammer and turned. Placing both long, strong hands on his knees, he scrutinized Ranofer.

"There is something you do not tell me," he said finally.

"Aye, Master. There is something I dare not tell any-one." Except the Ancient, Ranofer thought. But *he* does not count.

Zau considered this for a moment. "Then why do you tell me anything at all?" he inquired.

"Because—because one day before my father died you looked at the little things I had made and said they showed skill. You said, 'Perhaps, when he is older ...'"

Zau regarded him thoughtfully for a while, then picked up his hammer again. Over the ring of its tappings he spoke composedly. "You wish to become my pupil?"

"I wish it! Who would not wish it? But I cannot pay the fee. Gebu takes the coppers I earn at stonecutting, and I have nothing else."

Cling, cling, cling, went the little hammer. "I do not take apprentices, Ranofer," Zau said.

"I know." Ranofer's voice was almost inaudible. "I ask for nothing, Master. I wished only to see you again, per-haps watch you work a little."

Why, indeed, had he spoken of all this to Zau, who could do nothing about it? No one could do anything about it. Ranofer felt a fool. He felt utterly miserable.

"I remember looking at your work," Zau said unexpect-edly. "My old friend Thutra took me one morning to a cupboard, and showed me a cup with a handle, and two arm bands. One of them was overambitious." He stopped work for an instant to level the hammer handle and a sharp glance over his shoulder at Ranofer. "You did not know enough to attempt that spiral pattern." His admonishing eye held Ranofer's a moment, then he resumed his work. "The other arm band was creditable, as was the cup. Aye, quite creditable."

"Thank you, Master." Ranofer was glowing with the praise, as joyful now as he had been miserable two minutes before.

Zau ceased his work on the wing tip, examined it intently, and seemed satisfied at last. He turned, with the collar still in his hand, and gave his full attention to Ranofer.

"Thutra was my friend for twenty years," he said. "I would be faithless if I looked the other way when his son has fallen upon evil days. Still—" Zau's ragged eyebrows lifted arrogantly. "Perhaps I *would* be faithless, if the cup and the arm band had been poor. I am interested in goldsmiths, not orphans."

"Of course, Master," Ranofer said humbly.

"However, the cup and the arm band were creditable. Promising. I wish to help you, Ranofer. You may come to me as a pupil and I will require no fee, but you must not speak of that to my other pupils."

For one moment Ranofer felt that he could soar straight into the air like any bird, but only for one moment. In the next, he plunged sickeningly to earth.

"Master, I am not free to be your pupil," he whispered. "I am apprenticed to Gebu."

"Dissolve your apprenticeship."

"I cannot."

"You speak with a flapping tongue," the old man said calmly. "When the reasons are sound, it is a simple process of law to part from one's master. Any scribe can write the papers."

Ranofer stood like a culprit, head hanging and face burning with humiliation. "Master, if I did that Gebu would kill me. Or sell me. Besides, one must eat. I have nothing except what he gives me."

After a moment Zau rose from his knees and carried the gold collar to a fire smoldering in a small hooded furnace. Coaxing a fresh blaze with a blowpipe, he found tongs and with them held a portion of the collar carefully to the blast, his corded, brown old back gleaming with the heat. The subject appeared to be closed. Everything in Ranofer fought frantically against its closing, so frantically that his racing mind found a solution.

"Master!" he exclaimed. He found himself standing by Zau's side without knowing he had moved. "Master, I work only in the day at the stonecutting shop. And at night Gebu is often gone from home, often and very late." Even in his eagerness the old question flashed through Ranofer's mind: *Where does he go?* He moistened his lips hastily and went on. "I could come at night and learn, if you would allow it."

Zau tossed the blowpipe aside and straightened. "That is impossible. Do you think I work without ceasing, like some god? I am an old man. I rest my weary bones at night."

"But Master—"

"Son of my old friend, it is clear that I can do nothing for you at the present. You must reshape your life into

131

some other form. When you have done this, come to me again, and I will teach you."

After a long and difficult moment, Ranofer managed to answer in a very low voice, "Thank you, Master. I understand. I will try *very* hard."

The old man nodded, not unkindly, and started toward one of the far stalls, carrying the collar. Ranofer walked slowly to the gate. There he found Heqet, whom he had completely forgotten, waiting with the stake beside him on the ground. Heqet's enormous eyes and attitude of respect indicated that he had heard everything Zau had said. In silence the two boys lifted the heavy stake and carried it between them out into the deserted street, in which the rosy light was graying into dusk. There was no need to speak, for each knew the other's thoughts. They said nothing until they had reached the Street of the Goldsmiths and were approaching the Apprentices' Quarters, with Rekh's shop in sight at the end of the street. Then Ranofer stopped, his eyes on the familiar gate ahead.

"You are to take the stake to the goldhouse?" he asked.

"Aye."

"Rekh will be there?"

"Aye, he said he would wait until I came." Heqet paused, then added, "I can carry it the rest of the way, Ranofer. You need not come."

Ranofer glanced at him gratefully and nodded, relieved that he did not have to explain. He had not seen Rekh nor set foot inside the shop since the day he had left it so abruptly months before, the same day Ibni had left abruptly too. Common sense told him that Rekh knew nothing of his connection with the affair, but he felt so certain that the odor of thievery must hang about his name at the goldhouse that he had no desire to test the point. If Rekh were to look at him with disdain and disappointment he knew he would shrivel with the shame. And if Rekh were unchanged? Kind and concerned with his welfare, as always? That would be worse, today of all days that would be far worse. Ranofer felt that if anyone were kind to him right now he would fly into a million pieces.

Heqet heaved the stake to his shoulder. "You will come to the papyrus marsh tomorrow at midday?"

"Aye. I'll come."

With no further talk the boys parted, Heqet to trudge up the dusky street toward the goldhouse, Ranofer to start the long walk home.

It was not until he reached the ferry docks—now rising high and queer-looking above the shrunken river, with the ferries moored far out in a basin of mud—that he began to realize, first, how tired he was, second, how late it had grown while he stood talking to Zau. If Gebu were home, waiting for him, growing more and more angry at having to wait . . . Ranofer's steps quickened in spite of his tired and aching body. I can rest later, he thought. The sooner I get home and hand over my coppers, the sooner—

He stopped short. He did not have his coppers. He had dashed out of the stonecutting shop this evening thinking of nothing but Zau, so afraid that Pai would detain him for some trivial task that he had not even waited for the daily ritual of wage paying, had not even thought of it until this moment.

How could I have forgotten? he thought, standing aghast in the middle of the darkening street. Still, why should he have remembered? He felt no interest at all in

133

his wages, since all he did was carry them home to Gebu. If I could *have* them once, he thought bitterly.

Never mind, he could not have them. Things were as they were, and right now they were very bad indeed. He could not stand here forever while night came on, yet he could scarcely conceive of going home to face Gebu empty-handed.

What will I tell him? Ranofer thought desperately, even while his feet took him hurrying homeward again. I cannot tell him I forgot. He will not believe it, and then he will beat me for lying. If he does believe it, he will beat me anyway, from fury. Aye, and he will want to know where I have been so long, what I have been doing and why I have been doing it. I cannot think of answers to all those questions. I will have to tell him nothing, or the truth.

When he reached the Street of the Crooked Dog he had not yet decided between these alternatives. Either was unthinkable. He stopped trying to decide, and in a sort of exhausted calm trotted the rest of the way down the gloom-filled street and into the familiar, barren courtyard. It was empty. Maybe there will be a miracle, Ranofer thought as he leaned, panting, against the gate. Maybe Gebu did not wait, this once. Maybe he forgot the coppers too, and went out somewhere and will stay a long, long time—until tomorrow—and will never know that I did not have them, or ask me questions, or find out that I went to Zau's.

The hinge of the door at the top of the stairs creaked loudly, the door banged back against the wall, and Gebu came violently down the stairs. There was to be no miracle that night.

Chapter IX

THE following morning Ranofer crept to the shop sore in every muscle, with the old, familiar strips of fire across his shoulders. As he had expected, Gebu had not believed the simple truth, that he had forgotten to collect his wages. The added truth which might have convinced him, the story of the visit to Zau, Ranofer had stubbornly withheld. He had paid a high price for his silence, but even a beating was preferable to turning his heart and hopes inside out for Gebu's scornful inspection, seeing them withered with ridicule and blown away like dust before his eyes. He had little enough hope left in him as it was, after the conversation with Zau.

Gebu came into the shop in the middle of the morning, snarled ill-naturedly at Pai and stalked about inspecting the work in a manner that caused every man to bend closer to his chisel or drill and all conversation to cease. Ranofer, scrubbing away with sandstone at a chunk of quartzite, dared not glance around when Gebu paused beside a half-finished stone coffin only a few feet away from him. His very skin shrank in an effort to put more distance between himself and his half brother, but he could not help being aware of the voices of Gebu and Pai, gradually raised in argument until they could be heard even over the clatter of the shop.

"You, Ranofer!" Pai roared suddenly.

Ranofer dropped his sandstone and looked around fearfully.

"That scroll on the lower shelf, the plan of the judge's tomb. Fetch it. Hurry."

Ranofer hurried, as much as the soreness of his legs allowed, to the storeroom at the far end of the shop. There were five scrolls on the lower shelf. With hands made clumsy by haste, he unrolled one after another. From being ordered often to bring some particular scroll to Pai, he had become superficially familiar with these drawings, which at first had looked like meaningless bird tracks to him. All tomb plans were similar in design, but he could now tell one from another by recognizing some detail. The judge's was the one with the narrowest entrance passage and only two rooms beside the burial chamber. It was the last he picked up. He snatched it and returned to Pai, who took it without a glance.

Ranofer was glad to be ignored; gladder still to be safely back at work when a moment later Gebu's voice rose in an angry bellow directed at Pai.

"You see, imbecile? The coffin is too wide. I told you. Perhaps you would care to chip away the sides of this passage on the day of the burial!"

"It is easy enough to alter the coffin," Pai answered sulkily.

"Then alter it, and hereafter heed what I say, or I will find a foreman who will."

Gebu stalked past Ranofer with nothing more than a glare, and Pai followed, thrusting the scroll at Ranofer as he went by. As Ranofer scrambled down from his stone to take the scroll back, he saw Pai at the pay box, counting out to Gebu the coppers from yesterday, and those for today as well.

He means to take no chances that I will forget tonight, Ranofer thought as he started for the storeroom. Cursed One! What does he care for my coppers, except to make sure *I* do not get them? If only I could keep them, I could hide them away and some day buy a donkey. But he does not even need them, especially these days when he swaggers about in fine headcloths and new-made sandals. He has *two* pairs of sandals now, one with buckles, like a judge's. Aye, and he eats fish often, and salted waterfowl. I can smell them in the storeroom at home. And he reeks always of wine or barley beer.

Ranofer's thoughts paused in surprise. He stood in the storeroom, the scroll forgotten in his hands, and considered these things. Until now he had paid them no attention. Certainly Gebu seemed to be increasingly well-to-do. The sandals, the headcloths of fine linen—several of them—yes, and for some time Gebu had reeked of expensive ointments as well as barley beer.

My coppers cannot have made all that difference, Ranofer reflected.

Perhaps the Fanbearer had paid a great sum for that red granite coffin with the alabaster lid. Or else Pharaoh must have rewarded the stonecutters handsomely indeed for the work on the temple. How else could the Cursed One have grown rich so suddenly, unless he—*unless he was stealing again.*

The instant the idea occurred to Ranofer he was sure it was the answer. A remark of Gebu's sprang into his mind: "... him and his paltry wineskins! There are far bigger birds in the air than Rekh the goldsmith." Obscure at the time they were spoken, the words were now as clear to Ranofer as the shape of the shelves in front of him. Gebu had found some other goldsmith to rob, and no doubt a better, safer way to do it. No wonder he had needed the Babylonian no longer, and scarcely taken notice of his dismissal! The new scheme must have been already in operation.

Ranofer thrust the scroll onto the shelf and hurried back to his work, filled again with the hope that he had thought almost quenched yesterday. This time, if he found Gebu out, he would make sure of his proof, he would find witnesses. Better, this time he had friends who might help, not only Heqet but the Ancient.

He could scarcely wait until midday. When it came at last he ran at full speed to the thicket, disregarding his soreness and passers-by alike. He ran so fast that he was the first to arrive in the little green room and had to wait, fuming with impatience and groaning a little in spite of himself at the flames he had stirred to life across his shoulders. Presently, however, Heqet and the Ancient arrived together, speaking in low tones as they came along the shaded little path, with the soft-eyed donkey plodding behind them. Ranofer suspected Heqet had been telling the old man about what had happened at Zau's, no doubt feeling he must explain beforehand Ranofer's probable gloom. They both looked surprised when Ranofer jumped to his feet and pulled them through the reeds into the little clearing, urging them to sit down quickly and listen.

"Gebu has been beating you again," Heqet said, with a sharp glance at his friend's shoulders.

"Aye, because I forgot my coppers yesterday. But I'm glad I did, because it made me think. Now listen to me."

The story poured out—Gebu's sandals, his headcloths, his ointments, his peculiar remark to Wenamon months before. Heqet and the Ancient mechanically performed the usual ritual of dividing what food there was, but their attention was riveted on Ranofer. Heqet grew so excited that by the time Ranofer paused for breath his snub-nosed face was transformed and he could scarcely sit still.

"You are right! I know you're right! Isn't it so, Ancient? How else could a man become so rich in a few months' time, unless Pharaoh had singled him out for favor? And *that* one is as likely to be singled out by Pharaoh as I am to lose my appetite overnight. Here, Ranofer, take one of these loaves and some grapes. Now, what shall we do about it?"

"I don't know," Ranofer answered, realizing for the first time that he had no idea of how to proceed. He glanced questioningly at the Ancient, who was old and must therefore know a great deal about everything, but he found the old man looking both thoughtful and dubious. The doubt was contagious. Ranofer turned away quickly and said in a louder tone than he intended, "But we can do something, that much is certain. We can find out more. I will watch Gebu, see where he goes."

He was talking at random, but Heqet pounced on the words. "Aye, that's it. Follow him as often as you can, see who he talks to, try to hear what they say. His companions, we must discover his companions. That skulking Wenamon is surely part of the scheme. Perhaps *I* could watch *him*, he lives but a step from the Apprentices' Quarters. We will become spies! Who else is Gebu's friend, or does he have any others?"

"There is a river captain. Of course I do not know if he has anything to do with this."

"Aha! A river captain!" Heqet was in transports. "Naturally there would be a river captain. Do you see? They must smuggle the gold out of the city in some way, perhaps to Abydos. They would not dare barter raw gold here for headcloths or sandals. Someone would soon ask how they came by it. Do you agree, Ancient?"

"Aye, that is doubtless the way they would do it," the old man said slowly, so slowly that Ranofer stole another anxious glance at him. Heqet was already talking again.

"The Ancient can spy on the river captain. What could be easier? He is here near the river all day, he goes each evening to the sailmaker's by the docks. An excellent idea! *Ast!* What a bright fellow I am, as the stone said when it looked into the copper mirror. What's this river captain's name?"

"Setma."

"Setma!" the Ancient echoed.

"Do you know him, Ancient?"

"Aye, I know him. I do not like his sort."

"Wenamon is worse," Ranofer said quickly.

"And Gebu worst of all," Heqet added.

Once more Ranofer searched the old man's face. "*Now* do you believe all this?" he ventured.

"I never said I did not believe you, young one."

"You have not said much of anything at all," Ranofer said uncertainly.

"Nay, I have not." The Ancient sighed and picked up Heqet's knife to slice a lotus root. "I fear for you two hotheads, mixing yourselves up with dangerous business. What if these men catch you spying on them? It would go hard with you."

"But we will be very careful!" Heqet exclaimed. "I mean to be a spy worthy of any noble's hire. Silent and invisible." He glanced challengingly at the Ancient. "Of course, Old One, if you are *afraid*—"

The Ancient's face relaxed into its usual good-natured creases. A slow grin turned into his high-pitched cackle. "May the gods love you, boy. Why should *I* be afraid? No one takes any notice of an old one-eyed nobody like me. I could tread on a man's heels for weeks before he'd suspect *me* of being dangerous."

"It is the same with us," Heqet argued eagerly. "Who takes notice of boys? Especially ragamuffins?"

"You are no ragamuffin, Heqet," Ranofer said with an admiring glance at his friend's new *shenti*, which was of firm-woven linen. His own was the flimsiest cotton, and tender in every fiber from long wear.

"I am no Lord High Fanbearer, either," retorted Heqet. "Though of course we both have our natural beauty, as the hippopotamus said to the rat." Heqet snatched up a bunch of grapes and held them across his throat like a necklace, meanwhile assuming an expression of such conceited hauteur that both Ranofer and the Ancient burst out laughing. He flung the grapes down and want on. "In any case, I am paid no more attention than a thousand other boys in Thebes, and neither are you, Ranofer. We need no magic to make us invisible so long as we do not actually stumble over anyone's feet. For my part, I am ready to be

141

Wenamon's shadow day and night, except when I am at the goldhouse, of course. And even there—" He stopped and his face lighted with a new idea.

"What is it?" Ranofer prodded him.

"Why, I have just realized something. I can do much more to help you. You know yourself, Ranofer, when gold is missing from any goldhouse in the city, the others learn of it. The smiths warn each other."

"Aye, that is true. Rekh sent Sata to his brother's shop, and others down the street."

"Exactly. Very well, then. I will keep my ears open. I will grow ears like that donkey yonder. If word comes of thievery in anyone's shop, I will know which one."

"Now *that* is a good plan," the Ancient said emphatically. "That will accomplish something, possibly."

Heqet, the irrepressible, glared at him an instant and then growled deep in his throat like some very small, fierce dog. "You do not think my spying plan of any value, then?" he demanded.

"Aye, of inestimable value," the old man cackled, shaking his head until his threadlike hair quavered. "Spy all you like, young one. You are probably right, no one will notice your antics. You might even find out something."

"And you will watch the river captain?"

"Aye, I'll watch him, though it will not be a pleasant sight, I assure you."

"Then you will watch Gebu," Heqet said to Ranofer.

"I will do my best. But I think he will notice if I try to follow him."

"Aye, that's a problem in your case, it's true."

"No matter, I will try it anyway," Ranofer said. "All he can do is beat me and send me home."

He hoped it was true. He did not really know what Gebu would do if he realized Ranofer was prying into his affairs, and he preferred not to think about it.

Something of the sort must have passed through Heqet's mind, for he said uneasily, "Take great care, though. Well, it is all arranged, then. We will meet here when we can, as always, and tell each other what we have learned. Agreed?"

"Agreed," Ranofer said solemnly.

"Agreed," the Ancient echoed, not solemnly at all. He was still chuckling now and then under his breath, and Ranofer suspected that he looked on the whole plan as a child's game. As they left the little green room to separate to their work, however, he beckoned Ranofer down the path in the direction of the shrunken river, and the familiar twinkle in his one eye had vanished.

"Come with me a moment, young one."

He left the path presently and pressed through the trackless growth of rushes and bushes, which he seemed to know as well as Ranofer knew the Street of the Crooked Dog. At a place where the undergrowth ended and the papyrus began—the water's edge in winter, now a stretch of mud—he stopped beside a spreading patch of some low, green plant. Stooping, he gathered a handful of the leaves and crushed them with a little mud in the palm of one hand. Then he turned Ranofer about and very gently smeared the mixture on his shoulders, where the fires still burned. Instantly they cooled; the relief was so great that tears sprang to Ranofer's eyes. He looked wonderingly at the old man, whose gentle touch seemed as great a magic as his salve. The Ancient smiled.

"I have not much wisdom, but I know a few things," he

remarked. "Now I want a promise from you about this spying, young one. Will you give it?"

"Aye."

"Do not follow this Gebu of yours after full night has fallen. Men can come and go in the darkness, and often no harm comes of it. But you are not yet a man and *khefts* fly away with children, even half-grown boys like you. Do not risk it. It would be better to spend your life as a stone-cutter."

"That is true, Ancient. I will not risk it."

"Well, then. Be off with you."

He is right, Ranofer reflected as he hurried back to the shop. I will tell Heqet, too. Heqet fears nothing. He might not even remember about the *khefts*.

A moment later, though, he realized that Heqet would do no dashing about after Wenamon at night, even if he should want to. The doors of the Apprentices' Quarters were locked and sealed at nightfall, and there were no exceptions to the rule. They would have few hours in the day for following and watching. Still, much could be done between the end of work and the coming of full dark, which was later now than in the winter seasons. And think what it might mean if they could discover something! Ranofer was determined to begin that very evening.

He went directly home at the day's end, with none of his usual reluctant dawdling. Gebu was there. Ranofer could hear him moving about in his room at the top of the stairs, but he did not come down. Why should he? thought Ranofer resentfully. He already has my coppers for today.

He found supper in the storeroom, drank from the water jar, and settled himself under the acacia tree, prepared to watch every motion Gebu made if he should come into sight.

He did not come into sight for what seemed an interminable length of time. Ranofer's eyelids were drooping and his head nodding when he heard the upper door suddenly open and footsteps come down the stairs. Every sense alert, he watched Gebu walk across the courtyard, open the gate, and go out. As soon as the gate closed, Ranofer scrambled to his feet, wincing as the abrupt movement reminded him of his soreness, and ran to the corner of the wall where cracks in the mud bricks and a straggling vine provided a precarious ladder for climbing to the top. Peering over anxiously into the street, he saw Gebu walking eastward in the direction of the river. Ranofer waited until he was a considerable distance down the street, then jumped from his perch, ran to the gate and let himself out cautiously. Staying close to the walls of houses and courtyards, he followed the distant bulky figure around a corner and into the thoroughfare, then along the thoroughfare to the beginning of the docks. There Gebu turned into one of the several doorways set into a solid line of palm-thatched buildings, and disappeared from sight.

Ranofer gazed blankly at the doorway, over which hung a leather wineskin. He was both relieved and disappointed. He knew what this place was. It was Mutra's wineshop. There was nothing very mysterious about Gebu's going there; he went there often. Still, he might be meeting someone. This might be the place where the thieving plots were laid.

It's certain I cannot follow him inside, Ranofer thought. I can watch the door, though. That is what Heqet would do. I will see who goes in to meet him.

Across the street, on the stone docks, was a row of over-turned fishing boats draped with nets spread out to dry. Ranofer selected one of the small punts made of bundles of papyrus reeds bound together, and crawled under it. Its sharp-pointed prow lifted it at an angle from the stone floor of the docks, and though its shelter concealed him he could still watch the doorway easily.

It was another long wait. Men came and went along the thoroughfare; several times one went into the wineshop and after an interval came out. Ranofer knew none of them. Wenamon did not come, nor did Setma, nor did anyone connected with any goldhouse, as far as he knew. The sunset light faded, the street grew dusky, and still Gebu did not appear. A fat-bellied man waddled out of the shop with a lighted torch, thrust it into a bracket be-side the door, and waddled back inside. Ranofer began to peer about uneasily, searching the deepening gloom among the boats for possible *khefts*.

At last, when he was thoroughly stiff from his cramped position and almost ready to retreat before the coming of night, the door of the wineshop opened. Gebu came out and turned immediately toward home.

I must get ahead of him, Ranofer thought. I must get there first, so he will not know I have been gone. But how will I do it? What if he is not going home? How can I tell unless I follow right behind him?

In a panic he crawled out from under the punt and raced silently down the street after Gebu, who walked stolidly ahead. When he turned at the end of the thor-oughfare Ranofer was sure he could be going nowhere but back to the Street of the Crooked Dog. Dodging into an alley, he ran as fast as he could until he was certain he was ahead of Gebu. Then he crossed back in the direction of home by another street, and emerged into the Street of the Crooked Dog to see Gebu still some distance away in the gloom. Ranofer flew across the street and into the courtyard, closing the gate as silently as possible behind him. An instant later he was safe on his mat under the acacia tree, breathless and panting but lying in an attitude of sleep. In a few moments Gebu came in the gate, banged it carelessly with no regard for noise, and climbed the stair to his room.

Ranofer relaxed and gradually regained his breath. He felt considerably flattened by the evening's events. If this was spying, it was anything but an exhilarating occupation. What good was there in crouching under a punt all evening, watching a wineshop door? Moreover, it was no less dangerous for being dull.

Still, I must keep on with it, he told himself as he settled more comfortably on his mat. This was only the *first* evening. Perhaps he will go someplace else tomorrow, or meet someone, or do something suspicious. Perhaps Wenamon and Setma have met tonight, and Heqet will have much to tell tomorrow.

He drifted off to sleep, anticipating.

Chapter X

THE following midday Ranofer was the first to reach the little green room in the thicket. Heqet appeared only a moment later.

"What news?" Ranofer asked breathlessly.

"A great deal!" Heqet flung himself down and began to divide his food as he talked. "I have discovered an *excellent* place to watch Wenamon's house. He lives near his shop, you know, in the Street of the Masons, which is only one street away from the Street of the Goldsmiths. Well, there is an alley behind the Apprentices' Quarters—"

"Greetings to you, fellow spies. Seen any hangings lately?" The Ancient's seamed face appeared through the fringe of reeds, and his one eye rolled from Ranofer to Heqet with an expression of exaggerated stealth.

"Greeting, Ancient. Come in, listen, Heqet has much to tell us. Go on, Heqet."

"Well, there is an alley behind the Apprentices' Quarters which runs directly behind Wenamon's house, too. I discovered this last evening as I was prowling about the place. And in this alley, just a short distance from Wenamon's rear wall, is a straggly old *dom* palm tree. And from the branches of this tree I can see directly over Wenamon's wall and into his courtyard. He has a wife with a voice like the hyena."

The Ancient cackled, and Ranofer leaned eagerly closer. "Well, go on. What did you see?"

"I saw Wenamon come home from his work, I saw his wife give him barley beer and set his food before him, nagging all the while. He had salted waterfowl and bread and onions for his meal. His wife ate what was left when he had finished."

"But did he go out after the meal?"

"Nay, he sat in the courtyard."

"Oh. Then, did someone come to see him?"

"Nay," Heqet confessed. "He did not do anything at all *last* evening. But I could see him perfectly, he was in my sight all the time. No doubt *this* evening something will happen. Then I will watch it all from my tree. It is an excellent thing to have discovered such a good place."

"Aye, aye, it is," Ranofer agreed, but he could not summon as much enthusiasm as Heqet seemed to expect. Boiled down, Heqet's story was the same as his own. Nothing whatever had happened.

"And you, Ancient?" Heqet said. "Did you find Setma last evening?"

"Aye, I found him. He was at the sailmaker's when my Lotus and I brought our papyrus. I kept my eye on him awhile. He went to a wineshop and bought his food and ate it. Then he walked across the mud to his vessel and went aboard. You can be sure he took no trip to Abydos or anywhere else. No vessel can move now until blessed Osiris rises and the Nile comes back to life. Possibly he entertained a few *khefts* or devils in his cabin later, but I

149

did not stay to see. My Lotus and I went home to our little house and rested our old bones."

Again, nothing.

Well? Ranofer asked himself angrily. What do you expect, after only one evening? Patience, stupid one. These things take time. Something will happen this evening, or perhaps tomorrow.

Nothing did, however. A week passed during which neither Gebu nor Wenamon did anything more suspicious than walk to some wineshop after the evening meal, or gamble at hounds-and-jackals with some crony in the privacy of their own courtyards. Setma's movements were even less interesting whenever the Ancient took time to spy on him. Ranofer found the whole thing very discouraging, but Heqet's interest never flagged; it seemed rather to increase.

"They are lying low," he told Ranofer one midday. "They are purposely avoiding one another. Wait and see. There is some deep reason behind it, and we'll find what it is, soon. Keep watch. Something is sure to happen any day now."

At last something did, several days after the river began to rise. Gebu went out one evening, with Ranofer doggedly behind him, and struck straight across the City of the Dead instead of turning toward Mutra's wineshop as usual. Ranofer grew more and more excited as he followed Gebu's twistings and turnings; more and more cautious, too, as he noticed that Gebu often looked behind him in a not-quite-convincingly casual manner. Surely something was afoot this time! Ranofer was certain of it when he realized they were nearing the Street of the Masons, and almost choked with excitement when he saw Gebu turn in at Wenamon's gate.

I must find the tree, he thought. Heqet will be there, and we can watch together. Perhaps we can even hear them plotting!

There was no way to pass from the Street of the Masons into the alley behind it except to pass through one of the houses, or else go far around by the next cross street. After considerable fuming hesitation as to whether he should leave his post, Ranofer decided to risk it. He ran for the far corner as hard as he could run, worrying all the way over the possibility that Gebu and Wenamon might walk out the front gate and be gone before he could find them. A glance back from the corner showed the long street still empty. He dashed on, around the corner and down the cross street, hurried into the alley and was triumphantly sprinting for the tree when just beyond it a door in the wall opened without warning and Gebu and Wenamon stepped out.

Ranofer stopped so abruptly that a little cloud of dust rose from his skidding feet and he almost lost his balance. They had not looked in his direction yet, but in no time at all they would. Frantically he groped at the wall beside him, clutched a latch and pushed. In an instant he was inside some stranger's courtyard. In another instant a dog was rushing toward him, giving tongue as he came. Ranofer turned in a panic to the wall again, seized a branch of some creeper and with the aid of a toehold in the roughness of the plaster pulled himself up a few inches above the dog's snapping jaws. They still looked frighteningly close; he took a better grip on the vine and loosed one foot to search for a wider crack. The moment he moved, the vine began to pull away from the wall. He froze. One more moment and he would fall straight on top of the dog, or else Gebu would open the gate and find him. In that minute some dark object sailed over his head and the dog's snarling changed to an offended yelp. Another object followed; this time Ranofer heard the *chunk* as it hit, and the dog howled and made off across the courtyard.

"Ranofer!" came an urgent whisper from somewhere above him. "Come out, quick. They've gone."

Ranofer dropped to the ground, staggered with relief and treacherously numbed toes, flung himself out the gate and closed it. As he leaned against it, panting, Heqet dropped from the branches of the *dom* palm and ran toward him.

"Hurry! They've gone that way. We can still follow and keep them in sight."

"How did you—what did you—do to that dog?" Ranofer gasped as Heqet pulled him relentlessly down the alley.

"I threw *dom* nuts at him. I could see everything that happened. I *knew* they were coming out that back gate and I thought they'd catch you for sure. Come, this way. There they are, ahead there. Lucky for you I could see into that courtyard where the dog was as well as I could see into Wenamon's. Where were you going so fast?"

"I was coming to join you." They had slowed down now and Ranofer's breath was beginning to return. "I followed Gebu to the Street of the Masons, saw him go in."

"Well, it's turned out well enough this time, as the ostrich said when he swallowed the melon. But there had better not be a next. That was too close for my peace of mind."

"Mine, too. Still, I'm glad I'm not hiding beside the front gate still, waiting for them to come out. Look, they're turning toward the shop."

"Gebu's shop?"

"Aye. It's just yonder. We'd best get out of sight a minute."

They ceased whispering and flattened themselves into a shadow. A little way down the dusk-filled street they could see Gebu and Wenamon pause at the door of the stone-cutting shop and, after a moment, go inside.

"Maybe Setma will come, now," Heqet whispered. "Maybe this is their meeting place."

Setma did not come, however. After a while a torch flared inside the shop and they could see it moving in a leisurely way here and there. It stayed some time in the scroll room, then flickered toward the place where Ranofer knew the judge's coffin stood.

"It is only some matter of business," Ranofer said, disappointed. "The judge's entrance passage is too narrow for his coffin, or the other way around. I heard Gebu speak of it once. That's all they're talking about now. This has nothing to do with gold stealing."

Heqet sighed. After lingering a few minutes longer, he said rather lamely, "Well, we have done all we can today, as one locust said to another. Perhaps tomorrow."

The two boys separated and went their ways. Again, nothing had happened.

The Nile rose freely in the next few weeks and, in spite of the relentless heat, the gloom of the god's death was gone from Egypt and the joy of his rebirth was in every man's speech and walk and brightened eye. Navigation began again on the river, and the pace of life quickened.

Except that he shared the deep relief of his fellow Egyptians at the river's rising, Ranofer's life did not change. For a time he and Heqet doggedly continued their spying and reporting to each other, and the Ancient joined in when he could. The old man could not come often to the little green room nowadays because he was cutting his papyrus in a distant part of the marsh and the sailmakers demanded bigger loads each day in this season of boat-building and refitting. Occasionally, though, his seamed old face would appear through the curtain of reeds, and with his cheerful cackle and his "Seen any hangings lately?" he would come in and share his food with them. He kept a faithful, if intermittent, eye on Setma, too; the riverman had begun regular trips up and down the Nile again. The Ancient always made them laugh with his mock-solemn reports, but he never found out anything. Probably, Ranofer reflected, because there was nothing to find out.

He himself was fast losing all faith in the spying. Never had Gebu behaved so innocently, never had a man seemed so devoted to his own courtyard and nagging wife as Wenamon. Occasionally the two met at Mutra's, or at the stonecutting shop to study the scrolls, and presumably to confer for long dull periods over building plans. Neither went anywhere near a goldhouse or appeared to be acquainted with so much as a goldsmith's apprentice. Gebu was not stealing anything, that was all. He was doing nothing whatever but live a stonecutter's routine life. No doubt Pharaoh *had* paid more than usual for the temple work. Whatever the explanation, the continuing signs of wealth were not due to stolen gold.

So Ranofer reasoned, and could find no fault in the

reasoning however much he wanted to, until one night when he was wakened again by the squeak of hinges. He lay still, listening to the stealthy pad of Gebu's feet on the stair and across the courtyard, feeling the usual tingling thrill down his spine as the gate latched softly and he knew Gebu was out in the dark street, moving among the nameless evils of the night on one of his unknown errands. What kind of errands could they be, that he would brave even demons and *khefts* to accomplish them? What could conceivably be that important, especially to Gebu? As far as Ranofer had ever been able to discover, nothing was important to Gebu, excepting gold.

Excepting gold!

Ranofer sat straight up on his mat and stared into the dark. Gold. Of course. Gebu was after gold. Why in the name of Amon had he not realized it before? *This* was when the thief was doing his thieving. Those squeaky hinges were the answer to everything, they explained the inexplicable, they wiped out the contradiction between Gebu's innocent daytime behavior and his mysteriously increasing wealth. It was no wonder, Ranofer thought disgustedly, that all his spying, and Heqet's and the Ancient's, had gained them nothing; everything was happening while they slept!

What exactly *was* happening, though? Who was Gebu robbing? Could he be climbing over courtyard walls, creeping into rich men's houses, prying into their storerooms and treasure chests in the dead of night? Ranofer could not picture it. As well picture a block of granite wafting like a feather, or a hippopotamus slithering like a cat. Rich men had guards about their courtyards, and light-dozing hounds, and servants who slept across the storeroom doors. Just one of Gebu's heavy footfalls—even at his stealthiest they were audible—and the whole household would be shouting the alarm.

Could he be stealing from some goldhouse, then? But there were guards at all goldhouses, too. The palace? Ridiculous, impossible.

Where, then? Ranofer asked himself, exasperated. Where does he go when he sneaks out like this? Where is he going this minute?

The question resounded in Ranofer's mind as if he had spoken it aloud. Slowly his eyes turned toward the gate, barely visible in the shadows of the wall.

If I followed him *now*, he thought, I could find out.

For an instant he did not move, only stared toward the gate while visions of *khefts* and horrors paraded before his eyes. Then he rose slowly to his feet and stole toward the gate. There he paused again, trembling, before he reached out for the latch. The gate swung open. Another dreadful pause and Ranofer stepped out into the street.

It looked utterly strange at this hour. The moon had set already, and the darkness was profound; not a torch flickered anywhere, not a gleam of lamplight shone from any house. Straight above were the stars, but their brilliance served only to emphasize the blackness of Egypt here below. What faint light they shed fell gloomily upon some roof corner or a waving strand of vine, transforming familiar daytime shapes to eerily unfamiliar phantoms. Gebu was not in sight.

I waited too long, Ranofer thought. He could be streets away by this time, and I don't know which way he went.

A voice inside him said, *Coward! You're simply making excuses.*

But I promised the Ancient I would never follow at night, Ranofer told the voice. I gave my word.

Coward. Here is your chance, at last, and you're afraid to take it. You're afraid!

Yes, I'm afraid, Ranofer thought desperately. But he could not endure the voice any longer. Tucking his head down as far as it would go between his hunched-up shoulders, he darted down the black street in the direction of the river. Whether it was the right direction or not he had no idea. Gebu might have gone the opposite way or followed one of a dozen crooked alleys across the city, toward Wenamon's house. Yes! Would he not have done that? Ranofer whirled and doubled back, casting a shrinking look over his shoulder as he did so. He saw nothing but blackness, heard nothing but the light staccato of his own frightened feet.

I must say a charm, he thought as he peered through the darkness for the darker rectangle which would be an alley's entrance, turning his eyes every instant to this side and that for fear some unknown thing would pounce upon him if he did not keep watch. "*Avaunt, ye dead man,*" he whispered hastily, "*who comes in the darkness, who enters stealthily, with nose behind, face turned backwards.*" The whisper changed to an uncontrollable chattering of teeth as Ranofer halted beside the narrow panel of blackness he was seeking. The alley was darker than the street, much darker and much more frightening, if that were possible. Gingerly he stepped into it. "*Avaunt, ye dead woman— who comes in the d-darkness—who enters stealthily, with— with nose behind, f-face turned backwards.*" The very words he was saying frightened him into a drenching sweat, they conjured up so clearly the horrors that might be creeping up behind him now, this minute, or lurking behind that object near the wall, whatever it was, or hovering just over his head with withered hands stretching out to seize him.

Ranofer whirled in a panic to stare behind him and above him, at the same time stumbling back away from the unknown object near the wall. At that instant three things happened. A blow behind his knees knocked his feet from under him and sent him sprawling; something soft and bodiless rushed past him even while sharp, claw-like fingers seized his shoulders in a dozen different places; and the night was rent by a wild and eerie screech.

Ranofer tried to scream but he could not, or else he screamed and could not hear it over the hideous reverberations of that other noise. He tore himself free of the clawing fingers, half-fell, half-threw himself out of the alley, and by the time the last shivering wail had died away was tugging at his own gate. One last agonized glance backward as he flung it open showed him a lean, gliding shape on the top of a wall, silhouetted against the stars. Then the gate slammed behind him.

He leaned against it, trembling all over and too weak to walk another step. After a while he went shakily to his mat and dropped upon it. It took him some time to quiet his breathing, longer to stop trembling, and longer still to remember some fleeting familiarity about that gliding shape he had seen. For a while his mind would not accept it. Then a cat called from somewhere down the street, a low and quavering, drawn-out wail. Ranofer's hair lifted in a cold tremor of recognition, which was followed by burning shame. Could it have been a cat, only a *cat*, from which he had fled as if it were a demon? No, impossible!

Remember the blow behind the knees, the bodiless something rushing past him, the clawing fingers. His shoulders still stung from the scratches; when he put his hand to them he could feel the little welts. He felt again, frowning. They felt remarkably like thorn scratches. And a cat, if he had stumbled back upon it and it had bounded away, might have hit him behind the knees as it escaped. Its fur, as it rushed past him, would have felt exactly like a bodiless Something touching him.

Aii, what a coward you are! Ranofer told himself disgustedly. You shied away from nothing, fell into a thornbush and frightened a cat as badly as it frightened you. Now you'll never find Gebu, he could be anywhere by this time.

Still, he could try. He went to the gate once more and opened it. The street was as black, as threatening, as enigmatic as before. There was no shape now upon that wall. Had it *really* been a cat? *Khefts* could take any shape they chose, any time they chose. Would a mere thornbush have felt *quite* so much like clutching fingers? Ranofer stared into the darkness, shivering.

Aye, perhaps it was a cat and a thornbush, he thought. And perhaps it was *not*. In any case, Gebu is gone.

He stepped back and closed the gate, making sure the latch caught securely. Just because there were cats in the world did not mean there were not *khefts*, also. One was as real as the other, and both were abroad at this hour. He did not care to encounter either again tonight.

Next time the hinges squeak, I will follow, Ranofer thought as he went back to his mat. The very next time.

There was no next time. For several nights he stayed awake as long as he could, but weariness always overtook him long before the hour at which the hinges might have squeaked. He changed his tactics and went to sleep early, hoping that by that hour he might be sleeping lightly enough to wake at any noise.

Neither plan produced results. He suspected there was no noise to hear. After all, he thought exasperatedly, I cannot *make* the hinges squeak, even if I stay awake all night. It is simply that Gebu is not going out. He had mentioned nothing of his nocturnal fiasco to Heqet or the Ancient, and now he was glad, very glad. It was enough to endure his own humiliating knowledge that if he had started after Gebu sooner, or pursued him faster, or been braver, all the mystery might have been unraveled now.

A fine spy I have turned out to be! Ranofer told himself. I am as great a bumbler as I am a coward. The Ancient was right. I would be better occupied in learning the stonecutter's trade as well as I can. It is at least a way to earn my bread when I am a man, and no doubt I shall never be a goldsmith.

Smothering the rage of protest that rose in him in spite of all reason, he set himself drearily to improving his skill at stonework, observing the methods of the craftsmen, trying to understand the running of the shop. When Pai sent him one morning to the scroll room and told him to set the shelves in order, he studied the drawings as he worked, noting the design for a further temple addition, comparing the plans for a royal shrine or two, and marking the variations in several tombs.

One of these latter drawings contained a detail he found in none of the others, either a truncated passage or a small room in a location which seemed either senseless or mistaken. He puzzled over it awhile, forcing himself to think of possible explanations in spite of his usual boredom and utter lack of interest in what its purpose might be. None of the explanations fit, and he threw the scroll aside impatiently.

A moment later he picked it up. He was a stonecutter's apprentice and, tedious though it might be, he had resolved to learn his trade. He carried the scroll into the shop and looked around for Pai. Instead he saw Gebu, just straightening from his inspection of the finisher's progress on a limestone slab.

"Well?" Gebu grunted. "What do you want? Why are you standing there?"

"I want to ask a question of Pai, about this scroll."

"Ask it then. Of me. I am the master here."

Wishing he had thrown the scroll in the Nile, Ranofer silently unrolled it and pointed to the little chamber.

"This room, I do not understand its purpose."

Instead of an answer he got a blow on the head that sent him sprawling on the gritty floor.

"Impudent mongrel!" Gebu flung the words at him like stones. "Why should you understand it? You'll do what you're told here, and nothing more, do you understand me?"

He leaned down, snatched the scroll from Ranofer's hand and thrust it into the folds of his sash. His face was contorted with rage; Ranofer had seldom seen him look more vicious. Dazed by the blow and the completely unexpected reaction he had provoked, Ranofer could only stare.

"Up with you!" Gebu snapped, digging the copper-sheathed toe of his sandal into the boy's ribs. "Back to work! And keep your questions to yourself hereafter."

He strode off across the shop and Ranofer escaped to the scroll room, consumed with resentment and bitterly resolved that he was through with trying to be of value in the shop. He finished the day in a silence as sullen as that of the other apprentice, Nebre, whose stony indifference to men and work alike he was beginning to understand very well indeed. In the late afternoon Wenamon came into the shop and glided in his chilling, catlike way toward the statue base Gebu was measuring. Watching the two from beneath sulkily lowered lids, Ranofer saw Gebu walk quickly to meet him and draw him aside. They conferred a moment, then the scroll was produced from Gebu's sash and transferred to Wenamon's.

Hateful thing, Ranofer thought as he stretched the red-chalked string across a block of granite. I hope it brings both of them bad luck. I hope the roof of that imbecile little room falls in on them while they are building it. I hope it is a stupid mistake they have made in their stupid drawings, and that the owner of the tomb will have them lashed, and refuse to pay, and discredit them in all the City of the Dead, and that Pharaoh hears of it and sends them far away into the desert to labor in the gold mines. *That* should please Gebu, greedy thief that he is.

Unfortunately, all the ill wishes he could invent were not powerful enough to rid him of Gebu's stubborn presence here in Thebes. Ranofer forced the scroll and his own anger to the back of his mind; it only made him hotter on an already oppressive day. That evening after work he met Heqet in the thicket and told him about it.

"I only asked a question," he finished sulkily. "And I get a cuff that makes my ears ring all day. He won't even let me learn *his* craft, much less the one I want."

"Perhaps there is something secret about that little room, something he did not want you to find out."

"Nay, how could there be? It was drawn there on the scroll, anyone could see it."

"But did you not say he gave the scroll to Wenamon, later?"

"Aye, but there is nothing unusual in that. I told you, they work together often. Let's not talk about it any more, I am sick of the subject."

The subject was not closed, however. Later that evening, much later, for he had even less desire than usual to go home and had dawdled about until almost nightfall, he opened the gate of the courtyard to find Gebu waiting for him, grim-jawed. Hoping it was only the coppers he wanted, Ranofer went directly to him and put them in his hand. He turned quickly toward the storeroom but Gebu spun him around.

"Now. I want an explanation of that question you asked today. I want no lies, either. Make haste, speak!"

"I only asked the purpose of that little room. What harm is there in that?"

One of Gebu's fists rose more swiftly than Ranofer could dodge, and struck him a glancing blow across the mouth which nevertheless felt as if it had loosened half his teeth.

"I know what you asked! I want to know why you asked it!"

"Because I was trying to learn your hateful trade!" Ranofer shouted. "I was trying to grow skillful, I was trying to understand how tombs are made and shrines are built! Never fear, I am finished with that now! I intend to do what I am told and not the smallest bit more!"

He fell silent, trembling with anger and with fright at his own temerity. One did not shout at Gebu without paying for it somehow, now or later. No matter, Ranofer thought. Let him beat me! It is worth it sometimes.

However, Gebu only stared at him fixedly, the one eye blinking. There was no possible way of telling what was going on behind the stony mask of his face. After several minutes that seemed a lifetime each, he turned away, walked to the gate and went out.

Ranofer's knees gave way from weariness and discouragement. He sat down where he was, on the rough stones of the pavement, and did not think at all for a while. After some time he became conscious of a trickle of something on his chin. He touched it gingerly and drew his hand away smeared with blood. His split lip was beginning to swell painfully. He got to his feet, walked to the storeroom and tugged open the door, feeling the saliva pour into his mouth as the fragrance of grain and salted fish came out to meet him. Stepping into the gloom, he felt his way from shelf to shelf, encountering the curve of bowls, the rough edge of a basket, the cool, sweating sides of the big water jar. Dipping a mug full, he splashed water freely on his lip and chin before he drank. There were a few crumbs in the basket and an onion in one of the bowls, but Gebu had left nothing else—on purpose, Ranofer was certain. The onion was small, but he ate it, thankful for part of Heqet's lunch at noon, then poured the crumbs carefully into his palm and licked it clean. Far from satisfying him, the sketchy meal only whetted his appetite; moreover, the onion had made his lip smart and burn. It was swelling rapidly and felt as big as a duck's egg.

More water eased his throbbing lip but not his hunger. He left the storeroom, banging the door behind him, and started for his sleeping mat under the tree. Halfway there an audacious thought stopped him. Slowly he turned toward the stairs. Gebu had frequently threatened to beat him insensible if he ever set foot in that upper room. On the other hand, Ranofer was in the mood to ignore all threats and defy Gebu if he could. Moreover, he was ready to wager his one *shenti* that there was food hidden away up there—and Gebu was gone.

Next instant he was creeping toward the stairs.

It was almost full dark, but the moon-god Thoth's heavenly barque, which revealed its high-prowed boat shape clearly these nights of its waning, was beginning to shed a gentle radiance over the littered pavement. Keeping well in the deep shadows next the wall, Ranofer hurried up the worn and slanting steps, his mind full of enticing images: honey cakes, a whole keg of dried fish, a handful of sweet, sticky dates. He reached the passage and moved to the closed door at its end. There he paused, breathing hard, his ears straining for any sound below. Then he tugged at the bolt. It resisted; he tugged harder, bracing his shoulder against the door. At last it gave way with a jolt and the door swung inward.

The thin squeal of the leather hinges made him shiver in spite of himself. He stepped into the room.

It was windowless, like all Egyptian dwellings; but just over the level of Ranofer's head the walls ended, and widely spaced wooden posts rose from them to support the ceiling several feet above. Through the space thus open to the fresh air of evening, moonlight poured in, dimly lighting Gebu's frayed sleeping mat and baked-clay headrest, a stool or two, a box in one corner and a battered wooden chest in another.

Ranofer tried the box first. He found nothing there but a kohl pot half full of the black eye paint, a copper mirror, a razor and a little jar of the ointment Gebu had been perfuming himself with lately. The chest looked no more promising; he fumbled hastily among sandals, headcloths, a couple of coarse white linen *shentis* four sizes larger than the one wrapped around his own narrow hips, and several of the new, fine-woven ones. There was something hard and curving in a corner, wrapped in a scrap of cotton rag. It might be a jug of honey. He tugged it out, jerked the cloth away impatiently and went numb all over with the shock of what he saw.

There in his hand lay a gold goblet more beautiful than the sun.

For a moment he stood perfectly still. Then he sank to his knees, for his legs had suddenly become too weak to support him. In a shaft of moonlight he examined his find more closely. It was pure gold, exquisitely fashioned in the shape of a lotus blossom. An inlaid band around its rim was of priceless silver, and so was its delicate stem. It was the work of some master who was Zau's equal or superior, and worth a prince's ranson.

Gebu had stolen it, that was certain. But where? From whom? There was not a goldhouse in the City of the Dead that produced such work as this. Only Zau could have made it, and Ranofer was growing more and more uncertain whether even Zau could have, or would have. There was something about it that was different from the work one saw nowadays; the manner of finishing the inside of the base, for instance. Perhaps it had been made long ago, handed down to some rich noble from his father.

Ranofer bent closer. Was that a bit of picture writing, etched into the golden curve of a petal? He twisted it to catch the light and saw a group of hieroglyphics enclosed in an oval line. The sign of royalty! Just so were the names of kings always written, with an oval line about them. Had that Accursed One stolen this from the palace itself? But how under heaven could anyone have done that?

Perhaps he could read the name, if the light was sufficient and if he had not forgotten too many of the little pictures he had learned at the scribe's school. Slowly, one by one, he spelled out the hieroglyphs: THUTMOSE-NEFER-KHEPERU.

Ranofer's hand grew slowly icy, while he knelt staring at the goblet as if it had turned to an adder in his grasp. He read the inscription again, and still again, but there was no mistake. This treasure bore the name of Thutmose the Conqueror, Pharaoh of Egypt *over a hundred years ago*.

Gebu had robbed a tomb. There was no other explanation.

Suddenly all Ranofer wanted was to get the goblet back into the chest and himself out of this evil room. Clumsy with fright and haste, he dropped the cotton rag three times before he was able to wrap it about the goblet as it had been before. He knew very well his life would not be worth a copper if Gebu came home at this moment.

He thrust the bundle deep into the chest and with shaking hands scattered the *shentis* and headcloths over it, shut the battered lid and sprang for the stairs. As he did so his bare feet grated on some gritty substance in the doorway. He stopped, peering down at scattered particles of dried clay on the moonlit floor. What was this? Some trap. He whirled to examine the bolt.

Only then did he see that it had been sealed with a lump of clay and marked with a clear imprint of Gebu's scarab ring, an imprint which was now half broken away by the door's having been opened. One glance and Gebu would know he had been in this room.

Chapter XI

I T was a sound on the street outside that finally roused Ranofer. He sprang into the dark passageway and flattened himself against the wall, listening to footsteps draw nearer, nearer, then pass and begin to recede down the street. Letting out his breath with a rush, he stumbled back to the door. Somehow he must mend that seal.

He knelt to examine it. It had broken in the middle when he forced open the bolt. A lump still clung to the bolt itself, and a smaller one to the socket on the doorframe. When the door was closed a jagged crack would show plainly between the two lumps. The clay that had filled it was now scattered in dry crumbs on the floor.

Standing in the passage, he closed the door gently, and in the process shut off every glimmer of the moonlight, which was all coming from Gebu's room. He could feel the crack but he could no more see it than he could see through the wall at his side. There was no help for it, he must have a light. He had no idea where Gebu kept his fire drill and tinder; they had not turned up in any box or chest in his room. It would take time to search for them, more time to kindle a torch, and time was what Ranofer

169

did not have. He must fetch a light. That meant venturing outside into the street and the *kheft*-haunted night.

This time there is a moon, at least, he thought. And it is not really so late or dark or silent as that other night. This time I shall be braver, I *have* to be. And there *has* to be a torch burning somewhere.

Quickly he opened the door again, gathered the scattered crumbs into a little pile with the aid of the moonlight. It was dim enough at best, and he had to feel anxiously into the shadows to be sure he had not missed some morsel of clay. Then he flew down the stairs and into the nearest of the storerooms. Again by touch, he located the oil pot, in which several torches soaked, head down. He snatched one and, shivering with dread, forced his reluctant feet across the courtyard and out the gate. A glance showed one torch burning in a wall bracket by a doorway far down the canyonlike street. He ran silently toward it, expecting each moment to hear the eerie flutter of a *kheft's* invisible wings, or feel its fleshless fingers on his throat. Once he glimpsed a moving shadow near an alleyway and sped faster, telling himself forcefully that it was a cat. Cat or *kheft*, by the time he reached the distant doorway he was weak with fright, but he thrust his torch into the flame, made himself wait while it caught well and, whispering what he could remember of the incantation against evil spirits, stumbled back the way he had come.

Safe once more inside the court, he leaned a moment, panting, against the wall. He had fetched the light, he had not been seen, the *khefts*—and cats—had stayed away. Now if only Gebu did not come back and catch him at this.

He hurried upstairs to the door and thrust the torch into the wall bracket beside it. Scooping the clay crumbs into his palm, he spat on them, softened and mixed them with a careful finger, then pressed them into the crack and smoothed the edges as well as he could. A sliver of palm fiber off the torch handle made a poor enough engraving tool, but it was all he had. With it he scratched in the missing bits of the scarab mark. It was done, but his heart sank as he saw how crude the patching looked. It would never pass Gebu's inspection.

I must run away, he thought. Gebu will kill me, I must go quickly.

But where? He had no place to go, and the night was thick with dangers.

Stumbling with fatigue and with the trembling weakness which follows fright, he went downstairs once more, extinguished the torch and replaced it in the oil jar, then flung himself on the familiar roughness of his mat. He would rest here just a moment. Then, *khefts* or no *khefts*, he must slip away through the streets and perhaps steal on board a Nile boat bound for Menfe or Abydos in the morning.

Perhaps an hour later, a sound in the darkness brought him bolt upright. Had he slept? He must get out of here, now, at once! He sprang to his feet, then froze at the sound of a muffled crash upstairs, followed by a stream of oaths. Gebu was home, he had seen the seal, it was too late!

He ran toward the gate, only to whirl and run back again as he heard the upstairs door crash back against the wall and Gebu's staggering footsteps sound in the passage. Gebu was very drunk; he stumbled and half fell down the stairs, cursing at the top of his voice. Ranofer shrank into the darkest corner of the courtyard, wishing he could disappear into the bricks of the wall. He heard an angry, sleepy voice from the next house. "Quiet, son of a pig! Can't a decent man rest?" Gebu roared some blurred profanity in answer. Ranofer, pressing still closer to the wall, watched the gleam of moonlight on Gebu's *shenti* as he wavered across the courtyard and into the storeroom. There was the familiar sound of a mug clinking against the water jar, then a tinkling crash of broken pottery. Gebu emerged and stood a moment, swaying. Then, miracle of miracles, he staggered to the stairs and climbed unsteadily up them. A moment later the door of the upper room banged shut.

Stunned at first, Ranofer gradually realized that he was safe. Gebu had not even noticed the seal, he had been too drunk.

The boy's breath escaped in a quivering sigh. He left his corner and went back gratefully to his mat, thanking all the gods of Egypt for the invention of barley beer. Weary, sore and still supperless, he fell at once into exhausted sleep.

He was roused at daybreak by the usual rude dig of Gebu's sandal in his ribs. "Up with you! Make haste to the shop. You can buy a loaf on the way." Gebu tossed a copper to the paving.

Ranofer groped for it and, rubbing his eyes with his knuckles, stumbled across the courtyard still half asleep. The cold water on his face helped wake him, and a careless touch on his hurt lip jogged his memory. Something important had happened. Suddenly he was wide awake, remembering everything—the seal, his fear, the golden goblet. Last night he had been too concerned with immediate problems to think about the goblet. Now it filled his mind.

He hurried down the Street of the Crooked Dog and into the dusty thoroughfare, which was stained pink with dawn and already dotted with the scurrying figures of men on their way to work. He knew he must eat; he was too foggy with hunger now to think what this discovery meant to him.

Near the Street of the Sailmakers he spied the baker's boy, Kai, emerging from his master's shop with a laden basket on his head. Kai turned at Ranofer's hail and lowered his basket.

"Yesterday's baking," he remarked laconically.

"No matter," Ranofer retorted. "I have yesterday's hunger."

He snatched one of the flat, round loaves and bit ravenously through the glazed crust, handing Kai his copper.

"You get two for a copper when they're yesterday's," Kai said. He handed over another loaf, started to raise the basket to his head again and hesitated. "Take three, nobody need know of it. You had best put Nile water on that broken lip of yours."

With a sympathetic glance Kai hurried off. Ranofer tucked the third loaf into his sash for midday and went on, more slowly now, toward the shop, eating as he walked.

It is the most important thing that ever happened, finding that goblet, he was thinking. I will be free now, and Gebu will hang head downward from the palace wall! It is right, it is just. He stole a treasure from the Precious Habitation of that great king. That is a terrible, evil thing to do. I will tell someone right away. I, Ranofer the son of Thutra, will make the crime known, and then the soldiers will come out of the palace and snatch Gebu, and he will be gone forever, he will never beat me any more and I will be free of him and free of the stone shop and everything will be like a wonderful dream. All Egypt will thank me. Pharaoh himself will thank me! He will summon me to his courtyard for the Shower of Gold, he will hang golden collars around my neck and order flowers strewn in front of me and tell Zau he must take me as his pupil. I will be rich and happy and eat roast waterfowl every day. I have only to tell this thing.

An old, familiar question broke in on his daydreams. *How* was he to tell of it? Take the goblet from the chest and show it to a soldier? But he would be accused of stealing it himself. Go to some noble, then, or seek an audience with a priest of Amon? Impossible. An insignificant stone-cutter's apprentice would get no farther than the first guard. Even if he managed to tell someone, there would be Gebu to deal with. Would anyone take an apprentice's word against his master's? No, it would be he, not Gebu, who would end up hanging from the palace wall. It was all the same as before, when he wanted to tell about the wineskins. The questions had no answers, the problem no solution.

Nevertheless he worried it as a dog worries a bone while he doled out cutting sand for old Zahotep's drill. Suddenly, at midmorning, the idea came like a flash of sunshine. Zau! Zau the goldsmith was known at the palace itself. The soldiers would trust his word. But would Zau trust Ranofer's word? Ranofer was not sure. Still, Zau might believe if he held the goblet in his hand. Surely he would believe then! The first step was to steal the goblet out of the chest. . . .

"The sand, boy! The sand!" Zahotep's voice crackled with impatience. "Do you think this drill is made to toy with like a lotus flower? If Pai sees me idle here . . ."

Ranofer hurried forward with the pinch of sand. Zahotep set the bit of the drill into the hole again, still grumbling. "If the master were here, I'll wager you'd need no reminding."

And where was the master? Ranofer thought as he stepped back. Gebu had not appeared this morning, though it had been his custom lately to come early to the shop and stay most of the day. He might show up at midday, but if he did not, the noon hour would be a perfect chance to slip away home and take the goblet.

Gebu did not show up at midday. After waiting a last nervous few minutes, Ranofer wandered casually from the shop and, once out of sight, ran like a hare. He shrank from the very thought of breaking another door seal and repeating the nerve-racking process of mending it, but there was no other way.

Breathless, he reached the courtyard gate and pressed his ear against it. All was still. Cautiously he stepped inside, padded across the empty court and listened again. Then he climbed the steps, silent as a wraith. Immediately he knew that Gebu was gone, for the door at the far end of the passage was bolted on the outside. But, wonder of wonders, it was not sealed! The gods were with him.

An instant later he was inside the room and searching frantically through the wooden chest. The goblet was gone.

Dazed by the collapse of all his hopes yet another time,

Ranofer started back to the shop. So certain had he been of finding the goblet waiting for him that even now he could almost feel it in his hands. Where had it gone? Maybe into some melting crucible, though it made him sick all through to imagine it; maybe into a bale of linen in the hold of some northbound Nile boat, probably Setma's, to be sold in some city downriver, or even in Crete or Phoenicia or Mycenae. In any case he would never see it again and soon Gebu would be wearing a fine new arm band and swaggering when he walked.

From habit, Ranofer's feet took him along the thoroughfare, past the lane that led between the flower fields toward the river; but his mind was so full of the goblet and his despair that when the Ancient suddenly appeared from the lane and hurried toward him, he had to stare a moment to realize who it was. Then he wanted only to escape. He could not tell anyone about the goblet, not yet, perhaps not ever.

"Oh! I—I cannot come to the thicket today," he stammered. "It grows late—I must go back to the shop—tell Heqet I will see him another time." He tried to edge around the Ancient, but the old man caught his arm.

"Heqet has come and gone, young one. I waited in hopes of a glimpse of you. I have something to report. Aye!" The Ancient chuckled as Ranofer's attention suddenly riveted on him. "I've been spying again, without really intending it, I confess, and this time I saw something. I did indeed."

"You saw something?" Ranofer repeated. The goblet? he thought. Could he have seen the goblet? Could he know where it is?

"I saw a quarrel, a bitter one."

Ranofer, who had opened his mouth to ask straight out about the goblet, closed it again abruptly. The Ancient nodded in a conspiratorial manner, winked his one eye, and chuckled again as he led Ranofer into the lane where his donkey was snuffling morosely along the baked roadside ditch in search of a blade of something green. "Come, I must keep an eye on Lotus while I tell you. It was Setma and that Gebu of yours who were quarreling. Only an hour ago, it was, on the edge of the papyrus marsh close by the fish docks. I was there cutting my day's load, no more than three cubits away from them, though they could not see me for the reeds. *Haii!* But they were angry! They all but came to blows, and I wished they had. That would have been a fine treat, now wouldn't it, young one?"

"But what did they say, Ancient? What was it they quarreled about?

"Gold, my boy. What else? When two rogues like that fall out, you may be sure it is over the price of some skulduggery one is to do for the other. I think that young scamp Heqet is right. Setma has been taking whatever Gebu steals and selling it for him in another city. But it's finished now."

"Finished? Ancient, what did you hear them *say?*"

"They whispered, young one. They hissed and spat and growled at each other, but all in whispers, angry as they were. I caught only a few words. One was 'never'—that was your stonecutter—another was 'dangerous' or 'danger.' It was Setma saying that. Then Gebu said, 'A third part, no more, *no more!*' There was more hissing and snarling, and a few fine names they called each other, but I heard nothing more of interest until Gebu swung away

177

and walked past the edge of the marsh so close to me I could have touched him. 'You're finished,' he was saying. 'There are other captains on the river.' I stood quiet as an image, and he went by me and away toward the docks. When I looked again Setma was gone too, and good riddance to them both."

"It seems quite clear what they were saying," Ranofer said finally.

"Aye, they've parted. That is certain. No doubt Setma raised his price and Gebu would have none of it."

So what of the goblet? Ranofer was thinking. What will he do with it? "Did—did Gebu—did they have anything with them?" he asked cautiously.

"Anything with them? Oh, gold, you mean. Nay, I think not, young one. I saw no pouch nor packet of any kind. Of course the reeds were in my way. Gebu carried something under his arm, but it looked to be a bundle of old clothes, nothing more."

"I see," Ranofer said, as well as he could for his heart jumping into his throat. A bundle of old clothes such as he had found in the chest last night? A bundle of old *shentis* with the golden goblet inside it?

He left the Ancient to his afternoon's reed cutting and hurried back to the shop. Gebu was not there. He had not been there during the midday, either, as Ranofer found out by casual questioning of Zahotep. He did not appear all day, though Ranofer watched for him constantly, his head buzzing with questions as he worked. At the day's end he hurried home, but Gebu was not there, either. A glance up the stairway showed the door at the top still closed but unsealed, exactly as it had been at noon.

What if he is gone for good? Ranofer thought as he walked slowly toward the storeroom. Nay, he could not be. He would not leave while he is growing rich, while there is so much stealing to be done. The whole Valley of the Tombs, with all the treasure in them.

He shivered and stepped into the storeroom. If only someone would catch Gebu! Suppose a soldier should see him sneaking into the Valley, or coming out of it with stolen gold, or should catch him walking about the streets right now, with that bundle under his arm. Suppose someone *had* caught him! It was not impossible, was it? It would explain his absence from the shop all day, his absence now. Suppose he was in Pharaoh's prison this minute, or being dragged before the judges, or ...

Happy possibilities were still racing each other through Ranofer's mind when he heard the gate crash open and Gebu's heavy footsteps start across the courtyard. Slowly Ranofer put down the water jug, feeling his whole spirit wilt and the old burdens settle down on him again. The footsteps had almost reached the stair when something occurred to him. Darting to the storeroom door, he peered out cautiously. Gebu was just turning to climb the stair but, in the instant before the angle of the stairway hid him, Ranofer glimpsed a bundle under his arm.

So he had brought the goblet home again, because of the quarrel with Setma, no doubt, because he had so far found no other riverman who would smuggle his treasure out of Thebes. It might be days before he found another, it might be weeks, and meanwhile the goblet would have to stay in that room upstairs, hidden in the chest.

The gods have given me another chance, Ranofer thought joyously. And *this* time I will not bungle things!

I will not wait for any days to pass. I will take the goblet tonight, as soon as he goes out.

Gebu came down the stairs again almost immediately, carrying a packet of bread loaves which he had evidently bought on his way home, for they smelled deliciously of new-baked crust. He paused when he saw Ranofer standing in the courtyard.

"You're early home, for a change," he growled.

"I have only just come," Ranofer said, hoping the lie would be believed. He did not care to set Gebu's suspicious mind working on any unusual behavior of his. He must remember hereafter to come and go exactly as always, at the same hours, in the same way.

Evidently Gebu did believe, for he merely grunted and walked on to the storeroom, jerking his head for Ranofer to follow. There he untied his packet, and leaving the loaves scattered on a shelf, broke the seal on the barrel of dried fish, extracted two and put them on an earthen plate. Ranofer, who had expected to be asked at once for his coppers, stood holding them in his hand and watching hungrily as Gebu resealed the barrel, put a couple of loaves on the plate and, taking it with him, started out of the storeroom.

"Don't you want my coppers?" Ranofer asked in surprise.

Gebu halted, turned with an oddly abstracted air and held out his hand for the coins. An instant later he turned back again, gave Ranofer one of the fish, went on to the next storeroom, emerging an instant later with an oil-soaked torch. Without another glance at Ranofer, who was standing astounded with a whole dried fish in his possession and the knowledge of three bread loaves un-

180

guarded on the shelf, he climbed the stairs and banged the door of his room behind him. In a moment Ranofer heard the whining scrape of his firedrill as he worked to kindle the torch.

Obviously Gebu had a great deal on his mind or he would never have forgotten the coppers or those other loaves or permitted his gutter-waif half brother to keep a whole fish for himself. Ranofer thought he could guess the causes of this strange preoccupation, and his guesses gave him considerable satisfaction. It could not be comfortable, having a stolen treasure in one's possession and no way to get rid of it. It could not be pleasant, either, to realize one had made an enemy of a rogue like Setma, and to wonder how soon and in what way that rogue might inform against one.

Ranofer thought about that a moment, hopefully, then decided he dared not count on Setma's malice to help his own cause. It might be a long time before Setma found a way to inform on Gebu without informing on himself as well, and during that time Gebu might have found another smuggler, and the goblet would be gone.

Nay, tonight is my chance, Ranofer told himself. Let him seal the door or not. As soon as he leaves for the wineshop I'll go up those stairs, then I'll take the goblet and run to Zau, even if it's midnight. I can wait.

Meanwhile, he had a feast to eat and plenty to save for morning, and the enjoyable knowledge that Gebu had a few burdens of his own for once.

Hours later he finally accepted the dismaying certainty that Gebu had not the slightest intention of leaving his room at all that night.

Very well, then, he told himself uneasily. I will come

here tomorrow, at midday. The goblet will still be in his room tomorrow, it must be! Let him hide it ever so well, I will find it somehow.

He woke the next morning just in time to see Gebu cross the courtyard and let himself out the gate, with the bundle of *shentis* under his arm.

Ranofer was up in a moment and after him, pausing only long enough to assure himself of a safe margin of distance between them. Gebu walked down the Street of the Crooked Dog toward the river, turned on a broad street leading southward, passed the fish docks and ferry landing, with Ranofer never losing sight of him a moment. Presently he turned again, at an all-too-familiar corner, and in another five minutes was walking straight into the stonecutting shop.

Ranofer stopped in a nearby doorway and stared after him, bewildered. Of all the moves Gebu might have made, this was the least to be expected. Why would Gebu take the goblet to his shop? How did he dare to? Where would he hide it? The whole idea seemed insane.

As soon as Ranofer felt reasonably safe in doing so, he walked quietly into the shop too, trying to appear as if he had merely come to work as on every other day. He did not risk so much as a glance in search of Gebu, but shortly after Pai had set him working at his first task, he saw Gebu emerging from the scroll room. His hands were empty, swinging by his sides. There was no sign of the bundle. He walked straight through the shop, spoke to Pai a moment at the entrance, then vanished into the street.

It was an hour before Pai needed a plan from the scroll room. The instant he bellowed the familiar order, Ranofer was flying across the gritty floor as fast as his feet would move. Once inside the little room, he looked frantically for some sign of the bundle, some place it could be hidden. There was nothing. In the dusky light that filtered through and under the roof thatch, the shelves looked the same as ever, several tiers of them lining three of the walls, and a cupboard beside the door on the fourth. Ranofer looked more closely at the cupboard. It was as dusty as everything else in the room, and its small doors were not sealed. Nothing could be in it except tools and cutting sand, as always. He looked to make sure, opening the doors gingerly with his fingernails so that he would leave no signs of his prying in the dust. Inside were tools and cutting sand, no more.

Still, Gebu had come into this room with the bundle, and come out without it.

"*Ranofer!*" came Pai's bellow from the shop.

Ranofer snatched the scroll he had been sent to fetch, and ran. He would look again, he would search whenever he got the chance. It must be there, it must, it must! he told himself, ready to burst into frustrated tears. But where? How could anyone hide it on those open shelves? It was not in the cupboard, it was too big to thrust into a scroll.

Later that day he searched again, prying hastily through piles of scrolls and hastily restacking them, staring defeated into that dusty, innocent cupboard. Gebu did not return to the shop that day; and when he came home at sunset he had no bundle with him. For all Ranofer could find of it, bundle and goblet alike had vanished into the air.

Chapter XII

FOR several days Ranofer did not go near the little green room in the thicket. He dared not tell Heqet anything about the goblet. Heqet would become wildly excited, he would make elaborate spying plans, there was no telling what he would do. Whatever he did, Ranofer feared he might overdo it; then the gods alone knew what trouble would descend upon them both.

On the other hand he did not see how he could sit and talk with Heqet and meet his eyes, unless he did tell him what had happened. I should trust him, Ranofer argued with himself. I trusted him before, about the wineskins, and think how he stood by me then. He knows how to keep his tongue from flapping. His father taught him, and he proved it was so.

The arguments had no effect. He could not tell anyone about that goblet. Not Heqet, not anyone. The only solution was to stay away from the thicket.

It did not occur to him that Heqet might finally come and find him; however, that was precisely what Heqet did. He was standing outside the shop one evening as Ranofer emerged to start for home.

"*Ast!* What are you doing here?" Ranofer stammered.

"Waiting for you, of course." Heqet's snub-nosed face had lighted with relief at sight of him. Now he stood gazing at him in such a puzzled, questioning way that Ranofer felt sweaty and hot with guilt.

"Where were you, all these days?" Heqet asked. "I feared that Gebu of yours had done one of those awful things he's always threatening. The Ancient and I, we didn't know what had happened."

"Nothing has happened," Ranofer mumbled, with a hasty glance over his shoulder. Gebu was only a few paces away, inside the shop. "Come, let's get away from here." As they started in the direction of the thicket he added, "I have been—very busy, that is all. Pai has kept me working until late, and—and sometimes at midday too, and—"

He swallowed and gave up trying to find an explanation that would sound reasonable. However, Heqet quickly began to chatter about Setma and the conversation the Ancient had overheard, and when that was exhausted he launched into a story about the Ancient's donkey, who had gone lame in one foot a few days before, and had required much rubbing with castor-bean oil and daubing with cool mud. Listening, Ranofer cautiously began to relax, and once they had reached the little green room in the thicket, had greeted the Ancient and examined Lotus's foot, which was well again now, and sat a while together in the old way, he decided that it was not, after all, impossible to be with Heqet and still keep silence about the goblet. Heqet was as full of talk as ever, and either failed to notice that Ranofer said little, or tactfully ignored the fact. As for the Ancient, though his one bright eye rested searchingly on Ranofer several times he asked no questions.

Only once did they approach the dangerous subject, so suddenly that Ranofer had a very bad moment indeed before he realized he was safe. Without warning, Heqet said, "Ranofer, I have had an idea. About this tomb affair."

"Tomb af-fair?" Ranofer stammered.

"The drawing. You remember. The little room you did not understand."

"Oh." Relief washed over Ranofer like cold water. He did remember now, about the scroll and Gebu's anger, though he had not thought of the incident since the day it occurred. The goblet had driven everything else from his mind.

"In my opinion," Heqet was saying in his craftiest manner, "they are going to use that room themselves, Gebu and Wenamon."

"Use it *themselves*?"

"Aye! For meeting in secret, and for hiding the gold they steal. Now that Setma will not take it away for them—"

The Ancient gave his high-pitched chortle of laughter. "*Ast!* young one, you should be a tale spinner in the market place. You'd soon be rich, with the coppers folk would pay to hear such fine, unlikely stories. Do you think even thieves are going to share a Departed One's dwelling with him? Of their own accord?"

"But the tomb is not occupied yet," Heqet argued. "It is not even finished, is it, Ranofer? They could make a separate entrance."

"The tomb is not even begun," Ranofer said more abruptly than he intended.

"Oh. Not even begun?"

Heqet sounded so disappointed that Ranofer was ashamed of his curtness. Anxious though he was to leave the subject of tombs, he went on. "They will not start work on it until floodtime, after the High Nile Festival. That is three weeks away yet. Then it will be months in building, with workmen in and out every day. They would not dare hide anything there."

"Nay, they would not," Heqet said sadly.

"It was a fine idea, anyway," the Ancient chuckled.

"Fine if it had worked, as the fish said when it tried to take a walk." Heqet grinned. "Never mind. I'll think of something else."

Ranofer wanted to tell him not to try, not to think or speak of tombs again. Instead, he changed the subject hastily. "Just think, three weeks, and it will be the Festival."

It was a good choice; all three began to talk of the greatest feast day of the year, when the waters of the great river would rise at last above their banks, and all the canals would be thrown open to receive the life-giving flood. There would be no work that day for anyone. All Egypt would make holiday in the streets, and the lowliest water carrier would feast at Pharaoh's expense and drink barley beer free. The prospect of honey cakes and dates, and all the dried fish he could eat, lifted even Ranofer's spirits. He agreed with enthusiasm to spend the feast day with his two friends, from dawn to dark, and thought no more of tombs or goblets until they parted on the thoroughfare.

On the way home, though, his troubles came back like *khefts* overtaking him on silent wings. The tomb drawing

187

clung in his mind, and so did Heqet's idea that there was some thieves' plan connected with that little room. Ranofer was sure it had nothing to do with a meeting place, or stealing gold from goldsmiths, or anything Heqet had imagined. But could it have something to do with robbing tombs? He did not see how. Not only was this tomb not finished, not even begun, but its owner, Pharaoh's Master of Storehouses, was still very much alive. There might be no burial, and thus no treasure in the tomb, for years. There could be no connection between that drawing and the goblet. Gebu had simply been short-tempered that day because he knew the goblet was hidden in his room and his guilt weighed heavy on him. And now it was hidden in the scroll room, where it weighed upon Ranofer. Search as he might, every time he had a chance, he had not found it yet.

Gebu must have *khefts* in league with him! Ranofer thought in despair. No mortal could hide a thing so well. Perhaps he has taken it away again after all, some time when I could not see. Perhaps late at night? But I have not heard the hinges for a long time now. Nay, it is still there, it must be. Then why can't I find it?

Day followed day; the river rose steadily toward its banks, growing broader, fuller, swifter. Ranofer's life remained a narrow routine of worry, occasional beatings, and work, varied only by the hour at midday or evening with his friends in the marsh. He was glad he no longer felt it necessary to avoid them, but it was still necessary to avoid telling them what he knew, and he often wished powerfully that this were not so, because it became more and more obvious that their meetings were not quite as successful as before. The thing he could not speak of hung over the little green room like an invisible presence, ruining, it seemed to Ranofer, everything he did speak of. Once, when the Ancient was not with them, Heqet brought the matter into the open.

"Ranofer, something troubles you. Something has happened. Why do you not tell me? Perhaps I could do something."

"Nay, there is nothing," Ranofer said as casually as he could.

"You mean nothing I could do?"

"I mean nothing has happened. Let us talk some more about the Festival."

"We *have* talked about it, only a few moments ago. Then I began telling you the new idea I had about that little room in the drawing, and you went back into your shell, and now suddenly you want to talk about the Festival again."

"Aye, I do. It is more pleasant, is it not? Than tombs, and rooms, and . . ." Ranofer's voice trailed off into a sulky mutter and he sat scowling at his toes and feeling miserable.

After a long, uncomfortable silence, Heqet said wryly, "Do I make myself unpleasant, as the viper said to the asp?"

Ranofer grinned in spite of himself, and in a moment they were laughing together, though still uncomfortably.

"I did not mean to be poisonous," Ranofer said.

"Nor I. I am sorry. It is only that you seem so different."

"Different?" Ranofer raised his eyes in alarm. Did the secret show so plainly?

"Perhaps not different . . ." Heqet studied him thoughtfully. "You seem more as you were when I first knew you at the goldhouse. When questions angered you, and you wanted only to be left alone."

"I do not want to be left alone," Ranofer said miserably. "Or perhaps I do. Just for a while. I cannot explain."

"No matter," Heqet said. After a moment he smiled. "Perhaps we had better talk about the Festival."

Everyone talked about it these days, made plans about it and thought of little else. Ranofer tried hard to do the same, but the goblet lurked always at the edge of his thoughts. More than ever he hated Gebu and his heavy fist, and the evil thing he had done. He hated most the feeling that the evil had spread like a plague to himself. With every day that passed the secret he knew weighed heavier and guiltier on his mind. A criminal walked free in the streets because Ranofer the son of Thutra was afraid to tell the crime. Still, in Amon's name, what would it do to get himself murdered or imprisoned by babbling such a tale without proof?

If I had taken the goblet when I had the chance! he thought. If I were sure it was in the scroll room now! I wish I knew what to do, and how to do it!

Then suddenly, on the day before the Festival, his wish came devastatingly true. At midday he went to the thicket to make final plans with his friends for the holiday. Heqet arrived late, full of news and bursting to tell it.

"Sit down quickly, Ranofer. Here, have this cheese. You'll never guess what has happened."

"What?" Ranofer asked warily. He had learned not to expect too much from Heqet's enthusiasms.

"Well, I have been spying again, only by chance this time, to be truthful. I was coming to meet you, just *now*, just a few moments ago, and I saw Wenamon ahead of me, so I thought I would follow him just for a while. He turned into the Street of the Potters—you know, at that corner where Abba's shop stands. Well, there is a big shed next to it, only a roof really, with poles to support it, where Abba dries his pots and jars."

"I know, I know. Go on." Something about this story was making Ranofer exceedingly uneasy. Surely Gebu would not hide treasure in pots and jars, but—

"Well, Gebu was waiting there. He was pretending to look at the pots, strolling about idly, you know, but really he was waiting. Wenamon made as if he would pass right by, then pretended to see Gebu—oh, quite by accident!—and stopped to greet him. Anyone watching, except *me*, of course," Heqet's eyes narrowed craftily, "would have thought they strolled into the shed merely to find shade while they exchanged a few civilities. Oh, it was cleverly done! But I was cleverer."

"What did they say? Could you hear them? Tell me quickly!"

Heqet would not be hurried. "I'm coming to that. I slipped into the shed too, and crept among the benches and tables where the pots are put to dry, and found a place quite close to them where I could hide behind a stack of new-made water jars. It took me some time, of course, because I dared not make *any* noise, so I did not hear the first of what they said."

"What *did* you hear? Please hurry!"

"I heard Gebu's voice first. He spoke very low, but it made a chill go up my spine, the way he spoke. He said, 'A curse on the Festival!' Fancy anyone cursing the High Nile Feast."

"Go *on*," Ranofer begged.

"I am. 'A curse on the Festival!' he said. 'The Nile can flood without us. Meet me at daybreak beside the broken tree. It is safe enough now.' "

Everything in Ranofer seemed to stop—heart, breath, thoughts. It was like the stonecutting shop at midday when the clatter suddenly died to silence all at once. Heqet must have been satisfied with the effect he had created, for his eyes glistened.

"Then Wenamon said, 'It would be safer a year hence.' And Gebu growled at him low, like a vicious dog. 'Or never! I've waited long enough,' he said. 'I made the plan. Now I want my reward, before I am too old to enjoy it. Do as I bid you!' "

I must get hold of myself, Ranofer thought. I must think of something very fast that will make Heqet forget all this. But what? What?

"And then?" he said in as calm a tone as he could manage.

"Then Wenamon said, 'And what of afterwards?' At first I did not know what he meant, but soon I did, for Gebu smiled in a *very* unpleasant way and said, 'I have attended to that, only an hour ago. Setma is not the only captain on the river, as I told him at the time.' "

So Gebu had found a new smuggler and the goblet would soon be gone, if it were not already.

"Go on," said Ranofer, swallowing.

"That is all. Gebu turned without another word and went off down the street, putting his feet down like chunks of stone. In a moment Wenamon left too."

Ranofer was silent, concentrating on keeping his expression casual while his mind spun furiously.

"Well?" Heqet said. "What do you think of it? I do not

know what broken tree they mean, but if they are meeting tomorrow, should we not spy on them again, and—"

"And miss the feasting?"

"We can feast later, when we have found out where they go. Surely you would not miss this chance."

"I do not think it is a chance," Ranofer said. Suddenly, out of sheer necessity, inspiration came. "Gebu is going to Abydos today. We cannot follow him there."

Heqet's face fell ludicrously. "To Abydos?"

"Aye. I heard him tell Pai so."

"Then why would he . . . Oh. I suppose the broken tree is *there*. No doubt Wenamon is going, too."

"Aye, very likely."

Ranofer nibbled on his cheese, attempting to seem thoughtful and even disappointed, looking anywhere but at Heqet. Heqet was silent for some minutes. "It does seem strange," he said at last in a puzzled voice, "that they would make their plans *here*, where they are known and might be overheard. Why not on the boat, going down the river?"

"Perhaps they are going on different boats."

Where do I find these explanations so fast? Ranofer thought, disgusted with himself. I am becoming as good a liar as that Babylonian.

"That is it, of course." Heqet sounded disgusted with himself too, for not seeing something so apparent. "Naturally they would not travel together, it might seem suspicious. Doubtless they will pretend not to know each other at all when they get to Abydos. *Ast!* I wish we had a friend who sails a Nile boat. I would give my new *shenti* to see what they do tomorrow. There's no doubt some goldsmith will be the poorer for it."

"Aye, I'm afraid you are right." Ranofer gave a sigh that Heqet need not know was one of relief instead of disappointment.

Heqet sighed too and got to his feet. "It's clear we can do nothing about it this time. I am sorry. It was *such* a good bit of spying. I will meet you tomorrow, as we planned. At least we have the Festival to console us."

With a grin he led the way out through the curtain of reeds, and Ranofer followed. He had not tasted a bite of the good cheese he had eaten, and the Festival had dwindled to nothing in his mind. He knew quite well that only one thing could lure Gebu from the prospect of free barley beer: the gold of the tombs. If he and that vulture who was his friend did not mean to join the merrymaking tomorrow, they were almost certainly going to the Valley of the Tombs of the Kings, in broad daylight this time, while all Thebes was occupied with feasting.

Profoundly disturbed, Ranofer scarcely knew what he did all afternoon at the shop. When work ended for the day he wandered through the scorching streets, blind and deaf to the spirit of holiday already sweeping the crowds around him. He had no desire to go home but no reason for going anyhere else. He found himself at last pushing through the rustling stiff reeds of the papyrus marsh, with the water lapping almost to his knees. The deep mud of the shallows was cool and soothing to his bare feet, but he could take no pleasure in it. Over and over in his mind appeared the image of the familiar mummy-shaped outline of the western hills, and the sheer red cliffs that hid the Valley of the Tombs of the Kings.

How could he feast tomorrow, knowing with every bit

of honey cake what was happening yonder? He would choke on the food.

"*Ai!* Look, my Lotus, we have a visitor," cried a familiar voice almost at his elbow. He spun around to see the Ancient and his donkey splashing through the tall reeds. The old man stopped and looked at him curiously. "What ails you, young one? Did you think I was a *kheft?*"

"Nay," Ranofer muttered, but his heart still pounded from the nervous start he had given. To cover it he waded a little farther, pushed aside the last fringe of papyrus, pretending to study the bright colored sails that dotted the river. The Ancient followed, talking cheerfully.

"It's a fine sight, isn't it, to see the river full to its brim again? Makes a man work with a will. I've a good load today, by the grace of Osiris. I'll wager the sailmakers will greet me with shouts of joy, and load me with coppers. Oh, aye, aye, certainly. May Set take their stingy hides! They'll give me as little as I'll take." The Ancient chuckled and loosed his donkey to drink. "But why worry, tomorrow everyone will have cakes and beer. Aye," he mused, "Great Osiris is ready to loose his flood over the land once more. Seen any hangings lately?"

For a moment the noisy sucking of the donkey was the only answer to the familiar joke. Then Ranofer said, "Nay." The word came out so choked that the old man turned to peer at him.

"What ails you, young one?" he asked again.

"Nothing." Ranofer's bare toes dug convulsively into the mud. "I—I was only thinking of those wicked ones we saw hanging there that day. Ancient, how was their crime found out?"

He could feel the old man still watching him, though he kept his own eyes on the sails.

"Why," the Ancient answered slowly, "they were followed."

"Followed to the Valley?" Startled out of his nervousness, Ranofer turned to stare at him.

"Aye, to the Valley, to the tomb itself. And into the tomb."

"Into the tomb! But—but who would dare—"

"One who loved his pharaoh and the gods of Egypt—he dared," the Ancient said simply. His one eye was shrewd and very thoughtful. "Why do you ask me, young one? What do you know of tomb thieves, save what I tell you?"

"Nothing! Nothing at all," Ranofer said quickly. "I am merely curious."

"Aye, curious. I know the ways of boys. They are like cats who thrust their noses into everything and oftentimes are sorry. You had best save your curiosity, young one, for safer subjects."

Ranofer swallowed and did not answer. The Ancient was still studying him as if trying to see straight through his eyes into his heart, and Ranofer was beginning to feel alarmingly transparent.

"Well, I—must take my leave," he stammered, edging away.

"We will meet tomorrow, at daybreak? The three of us?"

"Aye. Aye, of course."

"And you are—nothing ails you?"

"Nay!"

Ranofer turned and left abruptly, forgetting to mumble so much as a "Live forever" in his haste to get away.

Only after he was well beyond the thicket and emerging into the dusty lane did he call down Amon's protection on the old man, and on himself, who needed it far more; for when Gebu set out tomorrow for the Valley of the Tombs of the Kings, he knew he must follow.

Chapter XIII

THE stars still spangled the sky when Ranofer woke to the pad of Gebu's footsteps crossing the courtyard next morning. Memory swept over him, and with it a chilling knowledge of the thing in store for him today. He lay still, eyes tight shut against reality, but he could not shut out the whine of the storeroom door, the footsteps coming out again a little later, and finally the soft click of the gate.

Gebu was gone, and he must not get away this time. Ranofer rose from his mat and ran across the pavement and into the storeroom. A splash of water on his face, a thirsty swallow or two, and he was searching hastily for food. There was half a loaf and a couple of onions. Ranofer started on the bread as he left the room, trying not to picture the coming feasting in the streets of Thebes. The chances were slim that he would ever taste another honey cake.

He walked quickly across the courtyard, everything in him wanting to run the other way. At the gate he paused, his hand already on the latch, and suddenly leaned his head forward against the worn, familiar wood. He was shaking all over. I wish I were someone else! he thought. Heqet or the Ancient, or Kai the baker's boy, or even a cat or a dog! Then I would not know any secrets, I would be going out to feast today instead of to some dark and fearful tomb.

He was not someone else, though. He was Ranofer the son of Thutra, who loved his pharaoh and the gods of Egypt, and wanted to be free. He took a deep breath and opened the gate.

Gebu's *shenti* was only a faint glimmering in the dark street ahead, but Ranofer waited until it almost disappeared before he ventured out. Keeping the pale blur just in sight, he followed it through the winding, narrow alleyways of the City of the Dead and across the barren land beyond, while the sky above him turned faintly gray and the stars vanished one by one. By the time the high western cliffs were stained with the first pink of dawn, he was moving along directly below them, with the city, the flower fields, and the strip of desert all behind. Presently Gebu vanished into a cleft in the rock face, and when Ranofer arrived at the same spot a few moments later, he saw a winding pathway, strewn with boulders and hardly wider than a man's body, leading upward into the hills.

He moved up it nervously, not liking the sharp curves which prevented him from keeping Gebu in sight in order to assure a safe distance between them, not liking at all the walls that pressed in on either hand with no crevices in which a boy might hide.

He had passed the seventh curve and was still climbing when he heard a mutter of voices ahead. Gebu must have arrived at the meeting place and found Wenamon waiting.

Or had he encountered a guard? Ranofer crept closer, listening.

"...may regret this day, impatient one!" It was Wenamon's murmuring voice, that was certain. Gebu's lashed back at once.

"Fool! Who would follow us? Even the guards of the Valley will be feasting in Thebes."

There was another murmur, then Gebu snapped, "You are witless and a coward. Go look back down the path if you must."

Ranofer went numb. As a foostep crunched just around the curve ahead, he whirled and scrambled straight up the rocky wall, seizing at cracks, minute tufts of grass, whatever he could get hold of, and expecting every instant to feel a rough hand grasp his *shenti*. There was a narrow shelf formed by an outthrust boulder, just above the height of a man's head; Ranofer rolled himself onto it and lay as still as death. The next instant Wenamon's cloak-wrapped figure appeared around the bend.

The mason stopped, his bright, suspicious eyes darting every way but upward. He advanced soundlessly, passing so close under the shelf that Ranofer could have touched the black plaits of his hair. He padded down to the lower curve, peered around it and listened a long moment, while Ranofer lay rigid and sweating in plain sight above him. Then he turned, retraced his steps and vanished around the rocks ahead.

It was some time before Ranofer could gather strength to slide down to the path, and when he did, his legs were almost too weak to support him. Nevertheless he forced them to move in the direction Wenamon had taken. In view of the miracle just past, he could almost believe the gods were protecting him.

The next bend disclosed the "place of the broken tree," a wide spot in the canyonlike path, where a scrawny, strange-looking tree grew out of a cleft between boulders. Beyond, Gebu's hulking back and Wenamon's stooped, narrow one were just disappearing over a last rise. Ranofer could see now that the rise formed the summit of the western cliffs, up the furrowed and craggy face of which they had been climbing. To the east lay Thebes, spread on both sides of the swollen river like a many-figured carpet, stained in a hundred delicate colors by the morning light. Beyond the rise, to the west, the way opened out and the path descended into the Valley.

Ranofer paused a moment, looking back upon the spread-out city. As he watched, seven red and white pennants rose simultaneously on the palace walls, and he caught the faint, squealing notes of a trumpet. It was the signal for the Festival to begin. Soon the great procession would burst from the gates of the Temple of Amon far across the river. Later, at midday, Pharaoh would come from his palace to throw open the first canal with his own hand, and the streets of Thebes would be full of food-laden tables and joyful people and spilled barley beer. And he would not be there. Perhaps he would never be there again. Ranofer wanted nothing more, in that moment, than to be back in the Street of the Crooked Dog, or even in the stonecutting shop scrubbing at some block of granite with his sandstone, or chipping at a coffin lid. He bit his lip hard, turned abruptly away from the city that was his world and started down the stony path into a world inhabited only by the dead.

It stretched before him, a wasteland of glaring red hills rising from a giant's block pile of tumbled boulders—desolate, barren and ominously still. Nowhere was there a single sprig of green.

The sun had cleared the horizon now. By the time he reached the Valley floor it was beating fiercely upon his naked shoulders, reheating rocks and sands not yet cooled from yesterday, wrapping the whole Valley of the Tombs in shimmering, burning heat. Ranofer, threading his way among the scorching rocks, wondered in panic if he would ever be able to find his way out again. Every pile of boulders looked like every other; the cool, flooding Nile and the familiar streets of Thebes seemed as far away as stars. High above him in the brazen sky a lone falcon wheeled; far ahead the figures of Gebu and Wenamon were dwarfed by their surroundings to mere swatches of black and white. Two thieves, a falcon, and himself. Except for these not a living thing stirred in all this burning, silent world.

Other things stirred, though, wraithlike things, unseen, unheard, but present in their hordes even in this glaring daylight. The *bas* of the dead could roam by day as well as by night, if they so chose, and would they not often wing about this lonely city of their mansions, assuring themselves that all was safe and undisturbed? Surely a footstep, sounding faintly in their dwellings far below, would bring them fluttering in anger up their shafts into this hot, still air, set them searching this way and that for the intruder.

Licking his parched lips, Ranofer tiptoed nervously across the sands, wondering if even now he was treading over the hidden chambers of some long-dead pharaoh and rousing his outraged *ba*. He jumped as he heard the faint, seven-noted cry of the falcon and stood with pounding heart, watching it soar away toward the south. When he turned back, the two figures ahead of him had vanished without a trace.

In consternation he scanned the cluster of rocks where he had seen them only a moment before, then broke into a run. Even their dubious company was preferable to the death-haunted emptiness which surrounded him now.

Apprehensive and breathless, he arrived at the rock pile, stopped short, and sprang back behind it. Not three paces away on the other side of the rocks were the two he followed, working busily at something he had not time to make out. He stood flattened against a hot boulder, trying to control his jerky breathing. He could hear crunching and scraping, an occasional guttural curse. Then the noises stopped and all was still.

Moments later he dared peer out around the boulder. What he saw was an irregular black crevice in the rocks ahead, and a scattering of small stones around a large one which had evidently been rolled aside. Was this the entrance to the tomb, then? It looked barely large enough to admit a man's body, much less the huge coffin that must lie somewhere below. Ranofer crept out of hiding and stood peering fearfully into the crevice. It did not look like any tomb entrance he had ever seen or heard of. Casting a nervous glance over his shoulder at the desolate Valley, in which he was now utterly alone, he lay down flat on the hot sand and lowered his head into the dark, irregular hole. He could see nothing for a moment; then a dimly glimpsed surface made him stretch an arm down to explore it. It was a narrow projection. Perhaps a step?

Wriggling forward, he eased more of himself over the edge until he was hanging head-downward into the hole with the edge cutting his waist. His groping hand touched a second projection not quite an arm's length below the first. Another step. It was certainly an entrance of some sort. This flight of crude and uneven steps, hacked out of the rock and earth, led down the shaft. At the bottom a passage must tunnel away toward the tomb.

Ranofer wriggled backward again and got to his feet, threw another uneasy glance around him and turned back to the crevice. He could not make it out. Never could a huge coffin have been carried down that shaft. It must be a second entrance to the tomb, a secret one.

A secret one, of course! He stood transfixed by a flash of understanding. The whole of Gebu's plot was suddenly clear to him. He had heard tales of such tunnels, dug out during the construction of a tomb by scheming workers. They would hack through the wall of a tomb chamber secretly, and tunnel as far as time allowed toward the surface of the earth, adding the rock chips to the other debris from the excavation of the tomb. The hole in the chamber wall would then be plastered over like the other walls, so that no passage showed at all. A few years, or perhaps months, later, when the funerary visits of the surviving family became infrequent, they had only to dig a shaft down from the surface to meet their tunnel. When this was done they could enter the tomb at their leisure and cart away the gold, undetected by the guards at the real entrance, which might be a quarter of a league away and out of sight behind some rocky hillock.

Gebu was a stonecutter, Wenamon a mason. They had done this thing. It would be easy for them to arrange it.

Ranofer caught his breath as another realization struck him. The little room in the tomb drawing, the one for Pharoah's Master of Storehouses. It was no room at all. It was a passage like this, disguised so that the workmen could hack it out without knowing it was anything but another storage chamber. Small wonder Gebu had flown into a rage when he was asked about it! Ranofer went cold all over with fright as he saw himself calmly pointing to that very place on the drawing, recklessly asking the most dangerous of all questions. It was like crawling straight into a crocodile's jaws and only finding out later that you had done it.

Shaken as much by the past danger as by the present one, he huddled beside the crevice trying to gather his scattered wits. Poor Master of Storehouses, he thought distractedly. When the old man finally dies, he will not have long to rest.

A sudden queer noise made him swing around. What was it? He saw no one, nothing, only the same glaring, lifeless wasteland with its tumbled piles of boulders stretching all around him. His eyes went slowly to the rock pile near at hand, behind which he had hidden a few moments ago. Was Something Else hidden there now?

He edged closer to the crevice, still staring at the rock pile. Once more, even Gebu and Wenamon seemed companions fervently to be desired. At least they were human, they were alive.

But I do not want to go into a tomb! Ranofer thought desperately. I do not want to follow them clear into that dark and awful place. Surely it is enough that I know they are there. I can run now and give the alarm.

Run past that ominous rock pile? Through all that terrible, empty Valley again, alone? His flesh crawled, he shrank another step toward the crevice, and as he did so he heard the sound again, eerily distinct and close. It was the dry rustling of wings. A cold moisture chilled Ranofer's forehead, as if an icy hand had been laid there. At that moment a gust of wind swept across the sands, there was a loud clapping and beating, and from behind the rock pile a huge black form with outstretched wings rose cumbersomely, tilting and flapping directly toward him.

With a cry, Ranofer leaped for the crevice and slid feet-first into the dark.

At dawn Heqet and the Ancient had arrived at the fish dock, dressed in their best and eager for the day ahead. For a time they talked together happily, admiring each other's finery, teasing, laughing from sheer excitement, and glancing up the thoroughfare from time to time to see if Ranofer was in sight.

"What a lazy clod!" Heqet said finally. "Still on his mat, today of all days! Let's go rouse him."

"Do you know where he lives?" inquired the Ancient.

"Nay, I thought you might."

"Well, I do not. We'll have to wait."

They busied themselves watching more and more holidaymakers emerge from houses and side streets as the sky pinkened above. The sound of voices and laughter swelled, and the thoroughfare grew crowded as the inhabitants of the City of the Dead streamed into it and hurried toward the ferry landings. Still Ranofer did not come. Many other boys passed by, with their parents and their sisters and their aunts and cousins and grandfathers. Gilded palanquins and chariots, preceded by runners and followed by retinues of servants, began to appear from the direction of the noblemen's villas. Ferryboats and private barques were now putting out from every dock as fast as they could be loaded. Many had already reached the opposite bank, and others were strung across the river like a gala chain. The two friends waiting on the fish dock began to get restive. When the seven pennants rose high on the palace walls and the trumpet squealed its joyful signal, Heqet turned impatiently to the Ancient.

"Surely he will hear *that*," Heqet said. "Though he be sleeping like a rock, *that* sound will rouse him. He must come soon."

"Aye," the Ancient said in a somewhat dubious voice. "But I do not understand why he is not here already."

"Well, anyone can oversleep."

"On a festival day? An always-hungry boy?"

Heqet shrugged, but his face was puzzled as he peered down the crowded thoroughfare in the direction from which Ranofer must come.

Ten minutes later the crowds had noticeably diminished as they drained from the thoroughfare into the ferries and sailed across the river. Heqet and the Ancient were now frowning and uneasy.

"We will miss our ferry!" Heqet exclaimed. "They will all be gone soon. Did he not *say* he would meet us? I know he said it. We spoke of it a hundred times. Of course, I did not see him after midday yesterday."

"I did," said the Ancient.

"And did he not mention any change of plans?"

"Nay, he—" The Ancient's face altered suddenly. He turned and stared down the street as if staring alone would make Ranofer appear.

207

"What is wrong, Ancient?" Heqet asked anxiously.

"Perhaps nothing. Perhaps a great deal! Tell me, young one, did he seem disturbed, when you saw him at midday? Did he act a little strange, as if . . ."

"As if what?" Heqet prompted as the Ancient's voice trailed off.

"I do not know," the old man admitted. "I know only that when *I* saw him, at the day's end, I asked three times what ailed him. He was troubled about something, very troubled."

"It was that brother of his, no doubt," Heqet said. "He is always troubled about that brother and his thieving."

"Nay, he kept talking about tomb robbers. He—"

The Ancient broke off with his mouth still open. For a moment he and Heqet stared aghast at each other.

"Tomb robbers!" Heqet whispered. "Could he have found out Gebu is a tomb robber?"

"He had found out nothing at all, so far as I know," the Ancient said agitatedly. "He *told* me nothing, but then perhaps he would not."

"Surely he would have told you *that!* Still, he keeps his thoughts to himself, especially the bad ones, the ones that make him afraid. . . ." Heqet's voice trailed off too.

"Now what?"

"Yesterday, at midday, I was telling him something. I had overheard a conversation. I *thought* he was frightened. But then he spoke so calmly, told me it all meant nothing."

The Ancient seized his arm. "What conversation? What was it you overheard?"

Swiftly Heqet repeated the tale of his eavesdropping behind the potter's new-made jars, and what Ranofer had said of it later. When he mentioned the "place of the broken tree" the Ancient's one eye sharpened suddenly but he did not interrupt, though his face grew grimmer and paler as he listened.

"So you see," Heqet finished, "it could have nothing to do with Ranofer. Gebu is not even in Thebes today. No doubt those two Cursed Ones are meeting, but at that place of the tree, and if that is in Abydos—"

"It is not in Abydos," said the Ancient softly. "I know the place of the broken tree. It is an old, old landmark. And it is not in Abydos." His bony hand stretched out, a finger pointing toward the western cliffs. "It is there, near the summit, on the path to the Valley of the Tombs." As Heqet eyed him in frozen silence, he added, "That young one knew it too, or guessed it. He asked me how those thieves were caught, the ones we saw hanging from the palace wall one day. Aye, and I told him. I told him!"

"What did you tell him? How *were* they caught?"

"They were followed. Straight through the Valley and into the tomb. And I told him about it! I'll wager that's where he is this minute, trailing those villains across that place, with never a charm or an amulet to keep the *khefts* away."

"We must go after him," Heqet cried. "We can catch him, Ancient, bring him back."

The Ancient was already hobbling down the steps of the fish dock, his one eye fixed on the distant cliffs. "Aye, we'll catch him if we can. You're too young and I'm too old for such a venture, little one, but he's got nobody else."

"The guards?" puffed Heqet as they ran into the thoroughfare.

"Feasting yonder, across the river, with everyone else." The Ancient pointed bitterly toward midstream, where the last crowded ferryboat was bobbing toward the opposite bank. The thoroughfare was deserted. All the streets were deserted, and the shops and houses empty. It really did seem a City of the Dead now.

At its outskirts they were forced to slacken their pace; both were breathless, as much from anxiety as from their haste. The Ancient signaled for a halt, and they stood puffing, the eyes of both following the road across the desert. As soon as their breathing quieted the Ancient glanced at Heqet and nodded. Without a word they started toward the western cliffs.

Half an hour later they rounded a bend on the steep, narrow path and saw the strange, stunted tree thrusting out of the cleft in the boulders. Beside it the path broadened, and Heqet caught up to walk beside the Ancient. Together they topped the last rise and paused, gazing in silence out over the vast red wasteland that spread below. Heqet shivered slightly and moved toward the Ancient until their arms were touching.

"How can we find him, in that place?" he whispered. "Do you think we can find him, Ancient?"

"I don't know, young one. We must try."

"I thought—we might see him. But I see nothing. Nothing *alive*."

"One thing is alive," the old man said grimly. He pointed far across the boulder-strewn sands, where from a distant rock pile a great black vulture at that moment rose clumsily, tilting, flapping, and finally wheeling upward in a soaring glide. When it was high in the air, circling lazily against the blue, the two on the cliff path tore their eyes from it and started downward to the Valley floor.

Chapter XIV

Ranofer's plunge into the crevice sent him half falling, half jumping, from one to another of the crude, wide-spaced steps. After a moment he missed one altogether and simply tumbled, striking his knees and wildly waving arms on every rough projection he passed. He landed at the bottom feeling bruised, dazed, and as terrified of the inky blackness around him now as he was of the great winged thing from which he had fled. He got to his feet and stumbled about blindly, hands outstretched, until he located the opening of the passage he had guessed was there. It sloped gently downward as it led away into the unknown dark. As he hesitated, eyes stretched wide in a futile effort to see something, anything, a dim glow of light shone far ahead of him. Gebu and Wenamon must have kindled a torch; that glow was its faint reflection on some distant curve of the passage wall.

Ranofer fixed his gaze on it, licking his trembling lips. He could not stay here shivering and dreading, he must follow—or else climb back to the surface and be carried off to some unthinkable Land of Khefts by that great winged thing. He was still weighing bad against worse when the dim glow ahead faded and disappeared.

Setting his teeth hard, Ranofer started along the passage.

It sloped gently at first, then more steeply, leading ever deeper into the earth, growing blacker and still blacker until Ranofer was seized by the conviction that he was moving along a slim bridge over vast empty space, and repeatedly clutched in panic at the walls while his bare toe fearfully explored the step ahead. The floor was strewn with sharp fragments that hurt his feet. The air was hot and close, and so dry it seemed to shrivel his very flesh. It *was* shriveling, he was sure of it. Was it from the breath of that great black creature, still after him, or the deathly, withering wind of its wings? He moved faster, scrambling blindly forward, longing for another glimpse of that light. Once his head struck sharply against something hard and rough-edged, and he sank into a terrified heap, whispering prayers to the vengeful spirits and spells against them. He was too weak to run, too frightened to stay where he was. Stumbling to his feet, arms locked about his head, he bumped the same hard thing again and realized it was the ceiling of the passage, pressing so low that from here on he would have to crawl.

He crawled, his teeth chattering and his whole body shaking so uncontrollably that it felt as if it belonged to someone else. He had never felt so small, so alone, so outnumbered, as in this terrible black place haunted by Beings he could not see or hear or feel but only knew were there. Worse, every inch he moved forward took him nearer to an even more terrible place, the citadel of death itself, the dwelling of the outraged Departed One whose mere sentries these other creatures were. Now and then he caught sight of the torch glow ahead and flung himself recklessly toward it, though the faint, far-off gleam only intensified the blackness that enclosed him. Any living human—thieves and murderers included, Gebu included—would seem a friend and rescuer now.

After what seemed an eternity he realized that the blackness around him was no longer entirely black; it had turned to the lesser dark of night. Presently it became almost grayish, so that he could see faintly the hacked-out walls on either side. Obviously the torch had stopped moving, and he was drawing closer to the light.

There was a sudden sound of chipping, followed by the noise of falling plaster. Ranofer halted, his desire for Gebu's companionship abruptly vanishing. Even the fear of bodiless devils gave way before the sudden clear picture of this all-too-solid one up ahead. Gebu was still Gebu, human or not; and he was at this moment breaking through the plastered wall of a tomb. Ranofer waited until all sounds had ceased and the torch glow moved on before he cautiously crept ahead. Around a bend in the passage he was suddenly dazzled by a patch of golden light. He flung up his hand, blinking until his eyes grew accustomed to what seemed a brilliant glare, though it was only the torchlight, shining directly through an irregular hole in the wall. Even as his vision adjusted, the glare dimmed; the torch was being carried farther into the interior of the tomb. He could see now that, as he had expected, the opening ahead of him was jagged with broken plaster.

He eyed it fearfully, rubbing his cold hands against his thighs. For the first time he wondered who the man had been that now lay buried here. Some Great One, for the tomb was large. The torch had receded into what was apparently a second chamber, and the thieves' footsteps came echoing back to Ranofer eerily, as though in a vast space. His flesh crawled and the little hairs prickled on the back of his neck as he edged slowly toward the hole in the wall.

Shivering, he rose to his feet before it, peered fearfully in, and found himself staring into a pair of strange, glazed eyes not two paces from his own.

With a gasp he flung himself backward, eyes tight shut against the horror that was sure to strike him dead. At the same moment, a voice growled, "What was that?"

"Ancient," Heqet said in a weary voice. "Perhaps he is not even in this valley."

"Perhaps not," said the old man in a voice even wearier.

"Perhaps he followed Gebu somewhere on a boat, or to the stonecutting shop, or—" Heqet sighed and did not bother to finish.

"It is possible," said the Ancient.

They were leaning against a huge boulder near a heap of rubble that spoke silently of the entrance to a tomb somewhere nearby. They had investigated a dozen such rubble heaps, prowled and searched until they had located a few of the tomb entrances themselves, though all were well camouflaged behind rocks and piled-up sand. Not one had shown a sign of having been disturbed or even visited in years, and the few actual doors they had glimpsed after careful peering between the rocks had revealed the necropolis priest's seal unbroken upon the jamb.

They had located this near one too, and it too had disappointed and discouraged them. It was beginning to seem useless to keep up a search so futile, in a place so vast. They had wandered far north of the rock pile from which they had seen the vulture rise; no doubt there were just as many tombs to the south of it. There were tombs all over the Valley, dozens, perhaps hundreds of them.

"Surely we would have caught sight of him before now, if he is here," Heqet said. "Unless he has—" He turned to the Ancient with startled eyes. "Unless he has actually gone *into* a tomb."

"If he has done that, I fear it is too late for any help of ours," the Ancient said grimly.

"Do you think he *would* have, Ancient?"

"Nay, surely not," the old man muttered. He moved away from the boulder and glanced around him uneasily. "This Valley itself is bad enough, with a *kheft* watching from behind every rock, as like as not, to see what we are up to. I do not care overmuch for it myself."

"Nor I," Heqet agreed with feeling.

"And to enter a tomb, with those two for company, that would be worse by far. I cannot believe he would do it. Come, boy, let us go back to Thebes. Perhaps we will find him waiting."

Heqet nodded, but his nod carried no more conviction than did the Ancient's voice. They started drearily back the way they had come, through the sand and glaring rocks, each one radiant with heat.

Heqet stumbled and put both hands up to shade his eyes a little from the blinding light. "Ancient," he said in a small and dismal voice, "how do we know that brother of his has not done something to him? Maybe hours ago? Maybe even last night?"

"We do not know," said the Ancient. He too shaded his one eye for a moment to locate the distant cleft in the hill that marked the path back to Thebes. Then he lowered his head and hobbled on.

There was a silence that seemed as long as time itself to Ranofer, who lay in a tight ball, dizzy with fright, on the floor of the passage. Then he heard Gebu's voice in the second room, sounding unconcerned as ever.

"It was nothing, son of the jackal, son of a pig! You're afraid of your own shadow."

"I tell you I heard a sound," the voice of Wenamon insisted.

"There is no one here but us and the dead. Make haste with those boxes, now."

Slowly, uncertainly, Ranofer rose to his knees, then stood. No one here? But what was that face he had seen? Trembling, he peered again through the opening, and met the same pair of eyes. This time, though he shrank back involuntarily, he realized that they did not move, did not live. They were the inlaid glass eyes of a life-sized wooden statue, and he saw now that they had been partially smashed, as if from the blow of a dagger hilt. Gebu and Wenamon had wanted no gaze upon them as they went about their evil work, especially the gaze of this watchful *ushabti* placed here as servant and guardian of the dead.

Nervously Ranofer examined the figure more closely, and his fear of its vengeance changed to an unexpected pity. It was the statue of a slim and lovely servant girl, wearing a painted white dress and a painted gilt necklace, steadying a box on one shoulder and carrying a painted wooden duck by its feet in her other hand. Her expression was one of serenity and joy, and the sculptor who carved her had been a master. Now her clear, wide eyes were cloudy and blinded by the blow that had splintered them; her beauty was marred and her usefulness as a watchful guardian ended. It was like seeing some innocent, happy creature lying murdered, victim of Gebu's callous greed.

Ranofer's gaze turned from her to move in wonder about the rest of the chamber, which was dimly illumined by the glow of the torch from the next room. As he looked a strange emotion took possession of him. Beyond and around the graceful statue were articles of household furniture, arranged as in a beautiful home. There were armchairs and beds of carved wood decorated with gold, there were alabaster honey jars, painted boxes resting on delicately wrought ivory legs. There was a wicker trunk ventilated by little slatted openings, through which the fragrance of the perfumed garments within escaped into the room. There were winecups arranged on shelves, there were scent jars and jeweled collars and arm bands. Everywhere was the gleam of gold.

It was not the gold, however, that held Ranofer's gaze and drew him slowly through the jagged entrance to stand, silent and awed, within the Precious Habitation. It was the garlands of flowers, only a little withered, as if placed here in love and grief only yesterday, and the sight of a worn oaken staff leaning against the wall, of two pairs of sandals, a new and an old, of favorite joints of meat placed neatly in boxes as if for a journey. Whatever he had expected, it was not this intimate look of home, of a well-loved room to which its owner might at any moment return. Whatever horrors haunted the passage, they were not here, in this quiet sanctuary.

Who was the owner? Ranofer's eyes searched farther,

and halted in surprise. There were two owners. Slowly, soundlessly, he crossed the chamber to the pair of silver-inlaid coffins, on the lids of which were sculptured in gold the figures of their occupants, a man and a woman. They lay as if sleeping, side by side, their folded hands eloquent of the same defenseless trust that had caused them to order a sweet-faced servant girl as their only guardian. As Ranofer looked into their quiet golden faces the stealthy sounds of plundering in the next room became horrible to him. For the first time he fully understood this crime.

He straightened, all his fear gone and in its place hot fury. Those merciless and wicked ones!—to break into this sacred place and steal the treasures meant to comfort this old couple through their Three Thousand Years! Whether rich gold or worn-out sandals, these things belonged to them, no living human had a right to set foot in this chamber, not even the son of Thutra, who meant no harm. Almost, he could hear the helpless fluttering of these Old Ones' frightened *bas*. So strong was the sensation that he dropped to his knees in profound apology for his own intrusion. As he did so he saw something else, a stack of wine jars just beyond one of the coffins. They were capped with linen and sealed with clay, and pressed into the clay was a mark as well known to Ranofer as it was to everyone else in Egypt. It was the personal seal of the great noble, Huaa, only two years dead, the beloved father of Queen Tiy.

Shocked to his very toes, Ranofer scrambled up and retreated a few respectful steps, involuntarily stretching out his hands toward the coffins in the gesture of homage. Here lay Huaa and his cherished wife Tuaa, the parents of the queen of Egypt. And here he stood, an insignificant nobody, daring to gaze into their faces! He was acutely, desperately embarrassed; he felt like a dusty urchin trespassing in a palace, which he was. Worse, at any moment those thieves would be in here to wreck and pillage, to tear the gold trim from chairs and chests, to snatch the jewel boxes, to break open the beautiful coffins and even strip the wrappings from the royal mummies themselves in search of golden amulets. It must not happen. These Old Ones should have someone grand and fierce to protect them.

They have only me, Ranofer thought. I must do something—anything—go fetch help—

He turned and started swiftly toward the entrance hole, too swiftly, for his elbow grazed a little inlaid table and tilted the alabaster vase upon it. He clutched at it wildly but it fell, shattering on the stone floor with a crash that echoed like the very sound of doom.

The small noises in the chamber beyond ceased instantly. Ranofer breathed a prayer to Osiris and flung himself behind the coffins, which was all he had time to do before the torch and Gebu's murderous face appeared in the doorway.

"*Ast!*" came Wenamon's hiss. "I told you we were not alone!"

"We will be soon," Gebu answered in tones that turned Ranofer cold. He could see their two shadows on the wall, black and clear-cut: Gebu's bulky one, Wenamon's, thin and vulture-shaped, behind it. The shadows moved, rippled in deadly silence along the wall, leaped crazily to the rough ceiling and down again as the two began methodically to search the room. The dancing black shapes advanced relentlessly toward the coffins, looming huge as giants as they came nearer. Ranofer's hand groped out blindly and closed on a small heavy object that felt like a jewel box. At that instant Gebu's rage-distorted face was thrust over the coffin.

Ranofer lunged to his feet and hurled the box with all his strength.

There was a glittering shower of gems as the box struck Gebu full in the eyes, jarring the torch from his hand. He gave a hoarse cry and staggered backward into Wena-mon, who began to scream and curse as he fought the flame that was licking upwards into his cloak. In that one instant of confusion Ranofer saw his chance. He seized the nearest wine jar and aimed it straight at the blaze. There was a splattering crash and the torch hissed out, plunging the chamber into darkness. With the reek of wine and scorched cloth rising strong about him, Ranofer leaped for the far wall, feeling frantically along it for the entrance hole. Behind him the dark was hideous with yells and curses, with the sounds of splintering wood and jewelry crushed under foot as the two thieves plunged this way and that over the wine-slippery floor in search of him.

Where, in the name of all the gods, was the hole?

His fingers met a jagged bit of plaster and, beside it, empty space. In an instant he was through the hole and stumbling along the black passage, bent double under its crowding roof, banging and bumping into its roughhewn walls, but running, flying away from the death behind him. The sounds of rage faded as he ran, grew fainter with every bend, then suddenly grew louder. The thieves had found the wall opening, too, and were after him, in the passage. He scrambled around a curve, almost fell, dashed on again and brought up with a stunning impact against solid wall. Walls on three sides of him? Was he trapped? He wasted precious moments seeking a way around the obstruction; then his hand touched a rough shelf of stone. A step! He had reached the bottom of the entrance shaft much sooner than he had expected, for his headlong flight back had consumed far less time than his first cautious, crawling journey.

He clawed at the wall, found step after narrow step and hoisted his trembling body up them one by one. As he put his weight on the last one it crumbled under him. In a panic he flung both arms over the top of the shaft and for a terrible moment hung there, then wriggling, straining, pushing, he was over the top and through the crevice in the rocks.

The sunlight hit him like a blow. Half blind and shaking all over, he could think only of that last crumbled step and what it could mean to him. The thieves might climb past by jumping and then wriggling as he had done, but they could not get out if the top of the shaft were solidly blocked. They would have nothing to stand on to shove away the stones. He could hear stumbling, rapid footsteps approaching the bottom of the shaft, and Gebu's enraged voice bellowing his name; but already he was grabbing up rocks as fast as he could move, his eyes squinted tight against the glare of day. He hurled a few into the shaft and felt a fierce joy at the roar of pain below, and the thud of someone falling. Quickly he wedged some larger stones into the crevice, then began to shove and strain at the biggest, a boulder three times the size of his head, which had originally blocked the entrance.

It would not budge. He put his shoulder to it, dug his

toes into the hot sands, and shoved with all his strength. It stirred a little, tilted. He heard more scrambling sounds below and gave one last desperate thrust. The boulder tipped and rolled across the opening.

For a moment he could do nothing but lean upon the boulder and gasp for breath. There was still space behind it, but he could push it no closer. Amon willing, it would delay them a little while, but that was all.

He turned and started running across the red waste-land of the Valley in the direction of the Nile. After the closeness of the tomb the hot, free wind of the desert poured over him like the breath of life itself, but he could take no joy in it. If only the stone had rolled closer, there would be time to plan, to act in safety; but there was no time, there was nothing but more and more danger. Gebu was strong as Set himself. Sooner or later the stone would be tilting, moving, rolling free.

Chapter XV

Heqet and the Ancient had reached the path that led up to the cliffs. Tired, sweaty and weighted with fear for their friend, they paused a moment to rest, then started with dragging feet up the stony trail. At the first bend, where the path crooked about on itself and led behind a jagged outcrop of rock, Heqet stopped again, to look out across the empty red expanse which had defeated them. One hopeless glance, and he turned to follow the old man. Then suddenly he turned back, squinted, shaded his eyes with cupped hands. An instant later he let out a yell of excitement.

"Ancient, Ancient, Ancient—look yonder!" As the old man whirled and hurried back to him Heqet grabbed his arm and pointed. "There, beyond that line of rocks that looks like a crocodile. Isn't it someone running? Isn't it?"

"It is!" said the Ancient.

They stood motionless, peering toward the distant figure, which vanished behind boulders, reappeared briefly in clear stretches of sand, only to be hidden from them again. Presently, however, it was close enough for them to be certain it was a boy, and not a man.

"It's Ranofer, it must be!" Heqet cried. He turned and plunged recklessly down the path, with the Ancient behind him. A moment later he was running across the sands toward the place he had last seen the figure, shouting Ranofer's name and waving his arms like banners. At the second shout the figure emerged from behind an outcrop, stared, then almost flew the remaining distance between them.

"Heqet! Heqet!" Ranofer reached his friend and fell upon him. "How did you get here? What are you doing in this place? Oh, Ancient!"

As the old man came hobbling up, Ranofer flung his arms around him and burst into tears.

"Aii, young one." The Ancient groaned and hugged him hard. "We guessed you had come here. We've been searching and searching."

"But where were you hiding?" Heqet broke in. "What have you been doing? Look at you, all dirt and scratches."

"I've been in the tomb, after those Cursed Ones! They're still there, I've trapped them, but I doubt it will hold them long, I could not push the boulder tight enough. Oh, Ancient, it is the tomb of the queen's father and mother, Honored Huaa and Tuaa."

"You trapped the thieves, you say?" The Ancient pushed him away and seized his shoulders. "Trapped them where? Speak quickly!"

As coherently as he could Ranofer panted out his story. "Do you see? The two of them dug that passage long ago, they've been biding their time, stealing from Rekh and breaking into other tombs, too. Aye, I found a goblet that

224

proves it. It's in the scroll room at the shop this minute, but I can't find it. I can't find it *anywhere*."

"Never mind the goblet, where is this stone? I'll wager Heqet and I together can make it move."

"Aye, and we'll guard the place, while you fetch help." Heqet's eyes were shining. He looked as if he had never been tired in his life. "Make haste, show us!"

"It is yonder." Ranofer pointed, then scrambled to the top of a massive boulder and beckoned Heqet up beside him. "You can see it from here. Look, that pile of rocks with the slanted flat one balanced on top. Do you see it?"

"Ancient, it is the place where that vulture flew up."

"Vulture?" Ranofer gazed at him, wide-eyed, then with an expression so peculiar that Heqet frowned and caught his arm.

"What ails you? Take care, Ranofer, don't fall!"

"I won't. Vulture! Well, no matter. I am glad he flew. Otherwise I never would have known. . . . Come, hurry. Did you note the way well? There is a crevice behind that rock pile, with stones before it."

"We'll find it," Heqet said as they jumped to the ground. "Won't we, Ancient? You can depend on us."

"Farewell, then, but be careful. Those two devils, they have knives, I think. Nay, I will come with you."

"What use would that be? Go, go! Fetch help!"

Heqet gave him a shove and turned away. Reluctantly Ranofer started toward the hill, then whirled back, stricken. "Aye, but where shall I go to fetch it? Oh, Mother of Amon, everybody will be across the river watching the procession, and no one would listen anyway. It is the same as before!"

The others frowned, then came back to him. "They must

listen!" the Ancient said. "Tell them you have been into the tomb."

"Tell who? And how can I get them to believe me? They will think I am spinning tales."

"You brought nothing from the tomb, no proof?"

"Nay, nothing, nothing!"

"The goblet!" Heqet said. "If you showed the goblet—"

"I told you, I cannot find it. Perhaps it is not even there! Oh, if Zau were at his house today, or Rekh."

"Nay, Rekh is not, that I know. But Zau might be," Heqet exclaimed. "He is an old man, Ranofer, he might not have gone across the river."

"I will try. It is all I can do. Farewell, Osiris guard you!"

"And you!" the Ancient's voice came floating after him as he sped away.

I should not leave them here with those two devils, Ranofer thought as he forced his tired legs over the sands and up into the hill trail. A glance back, at the first bend in the path, showed him their small figures hurrying along in the distance, straight for the rock pile. What if Gebu had pushed that stone away already? What if they had to face him and that *kheft* of a Wenamon as they crawled out of the shaft? They would never survive it, not an old man and a boy inexperienced at dodging blows.

Oh, I must go back, go back, cried one part of Ranofer. But the rest of him said, Nay, go on!

On he went, trying to forget the danger in which he had placed his dearest and only friends. Pain tore at his side and his lungs felt as if they would burst by the time he reached the summit of the hill. He hurried past the place of the broken tree, past the shelf that had saved his life, and down the narrow, winding cleft up which he had crept so fearfully an hour or so ago. It seemed more like a year ago; he himself felt a different person from the boy who had started out this morning. That boy had been an infant, a know-nothing, a frightened fool, thinking he had real troubles. He had not even known what troubles were.

Reflecting bitterly on that ignorant morning self, Ranofer emerged at last into the open sands at the foot of the cliffs. He stopped, leaned against the rocks and gulped for breath. There before him lay Egypt, green and familiar, with the Nile glinting beyond the houses of the City of the Dead.

Zau will not be home, he thought with hopeless certainty. He will be feasting with all the others. If there were a boat at the docks . . . but even if I found one, and some paddles inside it, and got across the river somehow . . . *Ai!* Foolishness! I could not paddle a boat across the Nile now, not all alone, it is too high and swift. And even if I could, how would I find Zau in the crowds? All Thebes is over there, and all half drunk by now, I'll wager. I will go to his house, I must try that at least.

He set out across the strip of desert, running until the pain in his side returned, walking until it went away, then running again. At the outskirts of the City of the Dead he turned southward on the first street to the area of villas and gardens near the palace, then eastward toward the river until he recognized the Street of Good Fortune curving off to his right. A few minutes later he was trying Zau's gate, rattling it frantically when it resisted him, and finally pounding and pounding on it.

He gave up at last, let his hands drop heavily to his sides

and stood with tears in his eyes gazing at the gold sign worked into the grill and the purple vine spilling over it.

He turned away and started aimlessly along the empty street. All he had accomplished was to place his friends in mortal danger, then run away and leave them. There was no one even to hear his tale, much less listen and believe. All these houses were as empty as the street, the whole city was deserted. His gaze traveled sadly over the blank, deaf walls, the closed gates and indifferent trees, and reached the palace looming far ahead at the street's end. There it suddenly riveted. The palace! *It* was not deserted. Not until midday, at the height of the Festival, would the royal procession embark for Thebes and the Temple of Amon.

Even as he broke into a trot he knew it was hopeless, worse than hopeless. How could he get into the palace? The guards would never let him pass, he would never be allowed to tell what he knew. He would die at the gates or else later, when Gebu escaped and found him.

He did not turn back. His mind filled again with the memory of a quiet chamber deep under the earth, now wrecked and looted, with its helpless occupants still in danger of destruction. Renewed fury drove away the last shreds of his caution. He ran down the empty street, forbidding himself to think of anything but covering the distance he had to cover. At last he arrived, breathless, at the palace wall and glared at it. So I am to die, he thought furiously. So be it, I will die now, at once, and not wait for Gebu's help. But first I will yell out some of it, some of it!

Discarding all thought of approaching the main gates, he ran in the opposite direction along the wall until he

228

found a tall palm growing near it. After a moment's inspection he leaped to its rough trunk and crawled up it like a cat, swayed precariously outward on a thick frond and dropped to the top of the wall. Beneath him, inside the wall, he saw a courtyard edged with sheds and stables. There were three chariots glittering with gold, and a dozen grooms who were bedecking horses with plumes and flowers for the coming procession. None of them looked up.

Crouching, Ranofer crept along the top of the wall to the next courtyard. This one was lined with the stalls of the palace weavers and basketmakers and potters and bakers, but there was no one in sight. After a moment's intent listening, Ranofer could hear no movement from inside the workshops. This was the place to enter. Swallowing, he hesitated, then dropped to the palm-thatched roof of one of the stalls and from there to the pavement.

His heart was thundering so that he felt sure someone would hear it. With a quick glance around he started across the open space toward a gate in the opposite wall, which seemed likely to bring him closer to the palace itself. Suddenly a voice bellowed out behind him.

"*Hai!* Halt, there! Who is that? Stop, I say!"

Without waiting to look around, Ranofer sprinted for the gate and tugged it open. Next instant he had burst into an open-air kitchen, full of ovens and fresh-plucked fowl and the fragrance of new bread, and swarming with cooks and kitchen slaves. With a dismayed gasp he plunged straight through them, ignoring their startled cries and outstretched hands, while the voice behind him bellowed, "Catch him! Catch him!"

A dozen yelling cooks were after him by the time he had clambered up a vine on the nearest wall of the courtyard, flung his feet over and landed, running, in the kitchen garden on the other side. As his pursuers burst through a gate behind him he fled up a red graveled path between rows of onions and beans, into a grape arbor and presently out the other end. He was panting, stumbling, and by now utterly confused. The angry cries seemed to come from everywhere, and he had lost all sense of direction. He could see no other wall to climb, no way out, no place to hide, and he did not know which way the palace was, which way the street he had come from. He found himself confronted suddenly by a thick hedge and swerved away from it, only to see a burly gardener emerge into the path ahead and run straight toward him. Whirling, Ranofer plunged into the hedge. It was dense and tough; by the time he had managed to wriggle through it, his flesh was scratched and torn and his *shenti* in rags. Exhausted, he tumbled onto the velvet grass on the other side and tried to scramble up. At once he was pinned hand and foot.

"Now then, you river scum!" panted a voice beside him.

The gardener and a shaggy-headed slave were holding him fast, glaring down at him. Beyond them he caught a glimpse of lawns and shade trees, a pool blue with lotus blossoms, a pavilion set among flower beds—and a group of people staring in his direction. One of them, a soldier with a drawn sword, had started toward him. He struggled helplessly, tried to speak but could only gulp for breath.

"Great Bast's whiskers! It's only a boy!" the slave said disgustedly. "Say something, you! What are you doing in the royal grounds?"

"The tomb!" Ranofer croaked. "I must warn Queen Tiy—"

A heavy hand slammed across his face. "Insolent!" the gardener roared. "Who are you to speak the name of the Sun's Daughter?"

"I must warn her, I tell you! I saw them—I followed—"

"Hathor's mercy, he's mad!" the slave exclaimed, backing away a little, though without loosening his grip on Ranofer's arm, and making a gesture to ward off the Evil Eye.

"I'm not, I'm not!" Ranofer struggled frantically, his eyes on the drawn sword of the approaching soldier and his mind full of that desecrated underground chamber. "May Set destroy you!" he screamed at his captors. "The queen herself will, unless you listen to me! The tomb is plundered—"

"Silence!" The soldier arrived, brandishing his curved sword at all three of them. "Out of here, riffraff! How dare you set foot in the queen's own pleasure garden?"

"We followed this urchin," cried the slave, ducking away from the sword. "It is a mad boy who came over the wall and through the courtyards babbling of tombs and the queen."

"Silence! Return to your duties. *You* stay." The soldier yanked Ranofer to one side and waved the others out of sight into the kitchen garden. "Now, then! I'll deal with you."

He made a swift, expert movement and Ranofer found himself stumbling along a path with one arm twisted behind him. It did not hurt until he tried to break away, then pain like fire shot from wrist to shoulder. He rapidly decided not to struggle.

"Please, captain—honored general—" he began.

"Silence."

The fire shot up his arm again. There was nothing to do but keep still and go where he was taken, which was, he realized, to the pool and the group of people gathered near it, who were watching his approach. At a respectful distance from them the soldier halted and murmured in quite a new voice, "A thousand pardons, Excellency! I will remove this blemish from your sight with all haste. It is but a mad boy who ..."

During the brief, apologetic narrative Ranofer managed to twist into a position where he could study these new people. Foremost among them was a tall, cold-faced man with a massive gold chain about his neck. Behind him clustered a few scandalized palace servants, a gardener to whom the Excellency had evidently been issuing instructions, and a strange little man no more than four feet high, wearing a silver headcloth and two enormous rings of silver dragging at his ear lobes.

Ranofer forced his eyes away from this astonishing little personage and back to the tall man, who he guessed must be the palace overseer. "Excellency, listen to me, I pray you!" he begged, cutting through the soldier's mumblings. "There are robbers this very minute in the sacred tomb of the—"

He broke off with a cry as the soldier gave a sharp jerk to his arm, snapping, "Hold your tongue, scum!"

"Very well, Captain. Remove him," the overseer said indifferently.

The Great One turned away, and Ranofer sagged with discouragement in the soldier's grasp. "In the name of Amon," he pled. "In the name of the queen—" But already he was being marched relentlessly across the grass toward a wooden gate and oblivion.

Then a curious, piping voice behind him called, "Captain! Wait!" and the dwarf in the silver headcloth came pattering up on his stubby legs. "Free his arms, I want to look at him," the little man ordered in a tone fully as haughty as the overseer's.

Loosed at once, Ranofer straightened dazedly, rubbing his numbed arm and staring at his deliverer. Could this strange little man be someone of importance? "Live forever, Master," the boy faltered.

The dwarf thrust forward his head with a movement that set the huge earrings bobbing. "Who are you, Mad One?" he demanded.

"Master, I am Ranofer the son of Thutra the goldsmith, and indeed, I am not mad! I—"

"Silence! Do you know who I am?"

"Nay, Master."

"Tell him, Captain."

"His Excellency is Qa-nefer of Abydos, favorite pet of Her Sublime Majesty the Daughter of the Sun, the Divine Consort Tiy, may she live forever!" the soldier rattled off stiffly. Ranofer glanced at him and saw that his face had turned purple with rage. Obviously he did not like taking orders from a person half his size. Just as obviously Qa-nefer, whose name meant "Tall and Beautiful," enjoyed giving them enormously. He smiled like a cat with a particularly tasty mouse, strutted up and down a time or two to make his earrings sway gaudily, then waved an arrogant and much-bejeweled hand.

"Dismissed, Captain," he piped. "I will take charge of the prisoner."

"But Your Excellency!" the soldier roared.

"Dismissed!" the dwarf roared back at him.

The soldier turned on his heel and stalked through the wooden gate. Instantly Qa-nefer seized Ranofer's wrist. "Now, speak. Quickly. What is this babble of tombs and thieves?"

Dizzy with sudden hope, the boy sank to his knees. "Master," he stammered. "I—I—I—" He forced himself to be coherent. "There are robbers in the tomb of the Royal Parents! I saw them enter! I followed and they had smashed the eyes of the guardian statue, and they were stealing the gold from the two Old Ones who lay there so quiet."

"Fool!" The dwarf gave his wrist a yank. "You did not see these things! You babble!"

"I swear it, I swear it!" Desperately Ranofer poured out the story, how he had knocked over the vase and they had searched for him, how he had flung the box and then the wine jar, and escaped and rolled a stone over the crevice. "But Master, I could not push it tight and they will come out of there. I left two friends to guard the place but one is an old man and the other only a boy like me, and I do not know if they can keep the stone in place. Perhaps those Cursed Ones have killed them by now—"

Another yank at his wrist cut off the rest. "What Cursed Ones? Who are these robbers? Come, are you not making the whole tale up? You do not know their names, I'll wager my earrings."

"I do! They are Wenamon the mason, and Gebu the stonecutter! I know them well. Too well," added Ranofer bitterly. "Gebu is my half brother. I live in his house, and eat his bread."

The dwarf's expression underwent a change. He examined Ranofer's face minutely for a moment, then turned and started along the graveled path, pulling Ranofer after him with surprising strength.

"We will see, we will see," he muttered as he flung open a gate. "If you are lying to me—"

"I am not lying, Master!"

Joy rushed through Ranofer. He wanted to thank this strange little man, to heap praises upon him, but Qa-nefer was pattering along so fast he had scarcely breath enough to keep up. They hurried through a flowery arbor, down another walk and up a flight of stairs that climbed the side of a huge building.

The palace! Ranofer thought. I am going into the palace of Pharaoh—I!

The door at the top of the stair opened into a vast hallway down which the dwarf pulled him without slackening his rapid, half-trotting walk. Ranofer caught confused glimpses of shining walls and pavements painted in glowing colors. Then suddenly he was dragged through a doorway and given a final shove.

"Stay here!" the dwarf hissed fiercely, and vanished into the hall.

Chapter XVI

BEWILDERED and suddenly uneasy, Ranofer stared about him at a room luxurious beyond his wildest imaginings. On its polished floor was a rug of many colors. Chairs made of fragrant cedarwood adorned with gold stood here and there; their cushions were fine linen stuffed with down, light as bubbles and incredibly soft to the touch. In one corner there was a folding stool with a leopard pelt thrown over it; it was made of ebony inlaid with ivory, and its legs were carved into the shape of a leopard's clawed feet. On a low table in the center of the room stood a flower-twined wine jar and a goblet bluer than the sky; beside them a basket was heaped with fruit and honey cakes.

Ranofer's empty stomach growled dismally; saliva flooded his mouth and he swallowed, turning away from the food. Where had the dwarf gone? Had his haste meant nothing but disbelief, after all? Perhaps he had decided Ranofer was lying, had been frightened at his own interference with the overseer's orders, and had simply abandoned the project, leaving Ranofer to be discovered by the next servant to step into this room, whereupon the alarm would be raised again and the chase start all over.

Aghast at this new danger, Ranofer was still trying to decide whether to flee or hide when he heard hurrying footsteps in the hall. An instant later Qa-nefer appeared in the doorway.

"Come, Rash One," the little man said grimly. "We are going to see the queen. And may the gods of Egypt help you and me if you are lying."

He pulled a dazed and awe-struck Ranofer out into the hall and down it a few paces to a broad, square archway through which they passed into another chamber. A soldier, but not Ranofer's enemy the captain, stood erect beside a doorway in the far wall. Ignoring him completely, the dwarf opened the door and pushed Ranofer through a small anteroom with a shining floor and linen-hung walls, which was occupied by two more sentries. One of these stepped forward and opened double doors, through which Ranofer and Qa-nefer stepped into a spacious room radiant with light and thronged with people.

After the first instant, Ranofer saw none of them except one, a woman. She was small and slender, with wide, carven cheekbones, eyebrows like black wings, and a full, downward-curving mouth. She stood tense and still in the very center of the room, and on her forehead reared the golden cobra of Egypt.

Ranofer's knees gave under him; he knelt and touched his head to the floor. As he did so he heard the queen's voice, abrupt and husky, with a peculiar timbre, like a young boy's.

"Is *this* the one, Qa-nefer?"

"Aye, Your Radiance."

"I thought you meant a big boy. This is only a child!"

"Nevertheless, Your Majesty—"

"Hush. Tell him to rise."

"Rise!" hissed the dwarf, nudging Ranofer with his toe. Almost paralyzed with awe, Ranofer managed to obey. The queen studied him a moment.

"What is your name?" she asked.

"Ranofer the son of Thutra, Majesty," he whispered.

"Come here, Ranofer."

Again he obeyed, on quaking legs. The queen seized him by the shoulders, peering into his face.

"You told my dwarf there are thieves in the tomb of my parents. Why do you say this thing?"

"It is true, Your Majesty. They are there!"

"How do you know, then?"

"I followed them, Majesty! I saw them! They have dug a secret entrance—"

"So you say," the queen said softly. She was searching his face with a fierce intensity, and her fingers had tightened on his shoulders.

The gruff voice of a noble behind her spoke. "Your Majesty, I beg you, calm yourself. It is extremely unlikely that this boy was anywhere near the Precious Habitation. Boys are given to inventing wild tales with themselves as heroes. It is really too difficult to believe—"

"I know all that." The queen straightened and loosed Ranofer's shoulders without taking her eyes off his agitated face. "Still, it is not impossible. I must be sure he is lying, if he is."

"Oh, please, I am not," Ranofer broke in. "I know—"

"Silence!" the dwarf hissed from somewhere behind him. "Wait till you are questioned."

"Nay, let him speak." The queen obliterated the dwarf with a gesture and nodded to Ranofer. "Go on."

"I know the men," Ranofer finished in a humbler tone. "I *know* them. One is my half brother, the other his friend. They have been stealing before this. I found a golden goblet in my brother's clothes chest. It bore the name of Thutmose the Conqueror."

He stopped as a strange sound swept the room, as if everyone in it had drawn a sharp breath at once. The queen's eyes had widened; she leaned forward and grasped his shoulders again.

"Where is the goblet now?" she demanded. As Ranofer hesitated, aghast at the trap he had made for himself, she gave him a sudden little shake. "Where is it? Speak!"

"It is—in my brother's stonecutting shop—in the scroll room—but it is hidden. I do not know where he has put it, I cannot find it! That is why I had to wait, and follow.... Oh please, believe me! Send someone to the Valley, they will see it is true, let them test everything I have said."

"Hush, let me think." The focus of the queen's eyes changed; she looked into space a moment, then abruptly back at Ranofer. Her fingers dug fiercely into his shoulders, but her strange, boyish voice was quieter than before. "Ranofer the son of Thutra, I will test your memory instead. I am going to ask you a question. If your tale is true you will be able to answer it. Do you understand?"

"Aye, Your Majesty," Ranofer breathed.

"Very well. *What was the object leaning against the north wall of my parents' burial chamber?*"

Ranofer's brain whirled helplessly. The north wall? North? He had lost all sense of direction in that crooked black passage. He groped for some starting point, some

239

means of getting his bearings. The crevice. Was the eastern hill at his back or to one side of him when he plunged down that hole? He had no notion. The rock pile? His attention had all been on Gebu—and later, on that vulture; he had not given a thought to north or south.

All around him he could feel the skeptical glances, hear the unbelieving silence, as a roomful of Great Ones—nobles, courtiers, the Daughter of the Sun herself—waited for proof of his tale. And he could not give it, he had failed. He would be dragged off to the darkest prison in Egypt, and the good little dwarf along with him.

Suddenly something burst open in his memory, and his mind cleared. The coffins! he thought. How can I be so stupid? Do not all coffins point west, toward the Land of the Gods? Stay, now, get it straight! If the coffins faced west, then the north wall would be . . .

He raised his eyes to the probing, fierce ones of the queen. "Majesty," he whispered, "it was your father's oaken staff."

There was an instant of profound stillness. Then the queen's hands slid from his shoulders and flew up to cover her face.

"He speaks truth!" she cried. "Fetch soldiers, send them to the Valley! Make haste, make haste!"

There was a swirl of movement in the room; voices rose in excitement, the gruff-voiced noble strode swiftly to the door, jerked it open and went out, followed by several others. A graceful young man wheeled and began giving orders to three servants who stood along the rear wall. When they had bowed and hurried through a different doorway, he turned back to the queen. She had sunk into a chair someone had placed for her, bowing her head in her hands; several exquisitely clad ladies were already bending over her, as well as an old man with a rich gold collar around his neck.

Everyone seemed to have forgotten Ranofer. He had forgotten himself. He was standing exactly where the queen had left him, watching with wide eyes the hasty goings and comings of these Great Ones, which he himself had set in motion. He might have remained where he was for hours had he not felt a touch on his arm and turned to find Qa-nefer at his side.

"Come. It is not fitting for us to be here now."

The dwarf jerked his head toward the antechamber, and Ranofer went with him hastily, turning hot with embarassment at his own presence, a blemish of rags and dirt and unsightly scratches, in this beautiful, shining room. They had almost reached the door when a peremptory voice stopped them.

"Wait, Qa-nefer!"

They looked around to see the graceful young man coming toward them.

"Go to Her Majesty," he told the dwarf. "She has a command for you." As Qa-nefer pattered away on his short legs, the young man turned to Ranofer. His manner was impassive and assured, his bearing a noble's; but his eyes were warm and intent. "I am Count Zobek, chief cupbearer to the queen," he said. "Come with me, I wish to ask you a question."

He led Ranofer into the antechamber, and across it to a bench standing by one of the linen-hung walls. There he motioned Ranofer to take a seat, and after a glance toward the door of the outer passage, through which people were still rushing in and out, he sat down beside him.

"Now. Tell me all you know about this goblet," he said.

"It was gold," Ranofer began timidly. He was very awed by this splendid young man. "With a silver rim and stem. It had the name of the Conqueror inscribed on the bowl. I saw it."

"You are sure? You can read?"

"Only a little, Excellency. But I am sure. I will write the pictures for you, if you wish me to, then you can summon a scribe."

"Nay, you have proved yourself truthful. If you are sure, I believe you." Count Zobek glanced again toward the passage; he seemed to be impatiently awaiting someone. "And you found this treasure in your brother's clothes chest? Why did you not take it then?"

Ranofer explained, and under the count's close questioning described how he had returned next day to find it gone, later following Gebu to the shop only to lose track of the bundle of *shentis* entirely.

"So you believe it is still there, hidden somewhere in the shop?"

"I do. In the scroll room. But I have looked and looked for it. There are only shelves and a cupboard. I do not know where he could have put it, Excellency."

"Perhaps we can find out," the count said softly. This time when he glanced toward the passage, he beckoned quickly to two men who had just come in. Ranofer recognized one of the servants the count had sent on some errand earlier, the huskier one, a man with thick shoulders and a heavy neck. The other was a burly fellow in a helmet who carried a chariot whip dangling from one hand.

"These men," the count said to Ranofer, "are of my

242

household retinue. I want you to tell them exactly how to find your brother's stonecutting shop."

Ranofer's heart beat fast with joy. The beautiful goblet was to be rescued, it would never be melted or smuggled away downriver in some smelly ship's hold, or sold in the market places of Crete or Mycenae to ignorant barbarians, *if* it were still there, wherever Gebu had put it.

"You must go to the Street of the Stonecutters," he told the men, stammering a little with eagerness. "Walk west from the wide road that runs beside the Nile, and after a time you will pass a wineshop with a wooden pig's head hung before it. The stonecutting shop is only a little way farther, on the opposite side. You will know it by a great chunk of black granite standing beside the door. Aye, and the thatch on the left side is loose, it flaps in the wind. But the door will be latched and sealed."

"That need not trouble us, little one," remarked Count Zobek. "And the scroll room? Where is that?"

"At the rear of the shop."

The count rose and faced his men. "There is a roll of old linen in the scroll room, with a goblet inside. I want it found. Tear the room apart brick by brick if necessary. Pay close attention to a cupboard against one wall. You had best pry it loose first of all, it may have a false back. Go now. Make haste, but do not return without that goblet."

The men bowed and left, almost running. Ranofer did not see them go; he was gazing up at the count's calm face.

"What is it, boy? Why do you look so?"

"A false back to the cupboard. *Aii*, it is just like Gebu! Why did I never think of it before!"

The count looked at him a moment, then smiled. "Perhaps because you have never had a fortune to hide," he said. "Or a greater one to gain." His smile twisted slightly, in a way Ranofer did not quite understand, and he turned away, motioning for Ranofer to wait where he was. At that moment Qa-nefer appeared in the door of the queen's room and approached them, strutting.

"You have finished with this boy, Excellency?"

"I have, Qa-nefer."

"Then come with me, Ranofer." The dwarf smiled and puffed out his cheeks importantly. "I have orders concerning you."

Some hours later Ranofer stood on a balcony of the palace, watching the sun sink and the long day draw to a close. The flooded Nile was once more dotted with ferryboats bringing the weary merrymakers back to their homes in the City of the Dead. Ranofer no longer envied them their day of feasting. He himself had feasted on roasted waterfowl and honey cakes. He had rested on down-filled cushions in a beautiful room, he had had his scratched legs bandaged by the finest surgeon in Egypt. Now, freshly bathed, reeking with scented oils and dressed in a *shenti* of fine linen and a snowy headcloth, he waited, as he had been told to do, for a summons from the queen.

The sky was flaming when the door of the room behind him opened and Qa-nefer beckoned him imperiously. The little man wore golden earrings this evening, even larger than the silver ones, and he was swaggering with pride.

"The thieves were captured," he announced. "In the shaft, below the crevice, just where you said they would be. The gold and jewels they carried were brought back to the Precious Habitation, and all has been set in order. It

244

was a great thing we did for Egypt this day, Reckless One —you and I, Qa-nefer of Abydos—for if I had not listened to your tale, all would have come to nothing. Is it not so?"

"It is so, Master. Oh, I thank you for listening! Her Majesty will thank you."

"Her Majesty has already thanked me," the dwarf said with a broad grin, gesturing toward the enormous earrings. "Now she wishes to thank you. Come."

Ranofer followed him through the shining halls, wondering what Heqet would say if he could see him now. Heqet! The Ancient! He caught Qa-nefer's arm.

"My friends, Qa-nefer, those I left to guard the tomb! Are they safe? They were not harmed by those Cursed Ones?"

Qa-nefer looked at him blankly. "I do not know. *I* did not go to the Valley. I saw no friends."

"Oh, please! Will you ask Her Majesty? Will you speak to her for me? She will listen to you."

"In the queen's presence, one speaks when one is addressed," said Qa-nefer in a chilly tone. "Come along, don't stand there. The court is waiting."

"But the goblet? Did Count Zobek find the—"

"Make haste, I said!"

Ranofer made haste, but he was still bursting with questions when he entered the shining room and the presence of the queen.

She bade him rise from his knees at once and come near her. The old man in the gold collar stood at her right elbow; Count Zobek now stood at her left. She was smiling radiantly. Around her throat was the necklace of golden bees Ranofer had seen Zau making, and beside her on a

245

low, carved table stood the golden goblet. Its beauty seemed to light the room.

Ranofer's breath escaped in a long-drawn, joyful sigh as he raised a face more radiant than hers.

"It is found. It is safe," he whispered.

"It is found and safe, thanks to His Excellency, my new High Chamberlain." The queen glanced at Count Zobek, who bowed serenely. "It will be returned to the Precious Habitation of my ancestor at daybreak tomorrow."

"And my friends? They are—" Ranofer faltered. He had not been addressed. He spoke anyhow. "Your Majesty, are *they* safe too?"

The queen seemed puzzled. "Your friends?"

"Aye, a boy and on old man. They came in search of me and I left them to guard the shaft. Oh, please, were they harmed? I—"

He broke off as the queen turned to speak to the old noble on her right. He turned away, too, and spoke to someone else, who crossed the room swiftly and opened the door to the antechamber. After a moment this last personage returned and hurried back to the old noble, who listened to an instant's murmuring and turned back to the queen.

"Your Majesty, the captain of the guard reports that he saw a boy and an old man at the tomb, both sitting on the stone that blocked the shaft. They climbed down when they saw the soldiers coming. He did not see them after that. He assumes they returned to Thebes."

The noble bowed low; the personage bowed lower, and retired to his place. The queen smiled at Ranofer. "Your friends are safe," she said. "When you leave the palace you shall take a gift to them. Tell me, are your wounds more comfortable?"

"Aye, Your Majesty!" Heqet was safe, they were both all right. He would see them soon.

"And did my servants feed you well?"

"Oh, aye, Your Majesty!" No doubt they were waiting for him somewhere now, the two of them. Heqet would be dancing with excitement. Suddenly Ranofer could scarcely wait to go to them.

"Then all my wishes have been carried out," the queen was saying. "Excepting one." She paused and leaned forward; her tone changed a little. "Ranofer the son of Thutra, all is well in the tomb of my beloved parents because of you and your courage. I wish to reward you. Tell me, what do you crave most in all the world? You have only to ask for it."

Ranofer lifted wide, incredulous eyes. He could ask for anything? *Anything?* Visions of golden collars and vast palaces flashed through his mind, and then out again. He knew what he wanted.

"Your Majesty," he said tremulously, "could I have a donkey?"

The queen's eyebrows rose in astonishment. "A *donkey?*" she repeated.

"Aye, Majesty. If I had a donkey, I could cut papyrus stalks in the marshes and the donkey would carry them to the sailmaker's for me, and the sailmaker would give me coppers to buy bread, and I could make myself a little house on the edge of the desert and then I could be a pupil of Zau the goldsmith and then *I* would become a master goldsmith and grow rich and famous and someday perhaps make necklaces for Your Majesty, and—"

He stopped, hot with confusion because all the elegant courtiers in the room were laughing. It was not scornful laughter, though, he realized an instant later. It was the laughter of surprise and pleasure. As for the queen, she was not laughing at all; her long eyes glistened as if they had tears in them. She beckoned to the stately old man who stood near her.

"Lord Merya," she said softly. "Give this boy the finest donkey in all Egypt. And tell Zau the goldsmith that the first necklace made by the hands of his new pupil must belong to no one but Queen Tiy."

Half an hour later Ranofer walked through the City of the Dead in his new, soft leather sandals—with buckles—blissfully unaware of the crowds that jostled and passed him in the fading crimson light. In his sash nestled two fine finger rings set with greenstone amulets, one for Heqet, one for the Ancient, both inscribed with the name of the queen. In his hand were six of the finest goldsmith's hammers, each of a different shape and use. And at his side walked a veritable pharaoh of a donkey—long-eared, strong, beautiful, and in the prime of life. His head still rang with the music of the queen's praises, and his heart swelled with the knowledge that he could go tomorrow to Zau the Master and say, "I have done as you told me. I have reshaped my life into another form."

He rounded a corner into the thoroughfare and saw ahead of him two familiar figures leaning side by side against the fish docks. At sight of him Heqet gave a shout and flung up one hand, and the Ancient started hobbling toward him as fast as he could come. Ranofer gripped his donkey's rope and began to run.